HEARTWARMING

The Parent Trap

Lee McKenzie

HARLEQUIN® HEARTWARMING™

Recycling programs for this product may not exist in your area.

ISBN-13: 978-0-373-36697-2

The Parent Trap

This edition published by arrangement with Harlequin Books S.A.

For questions and comments about the quality of this book, please contact us at CustomerService@Harlequin.com.

HARLEQUIN®
www.Harlequin.com

Printed in U.S.A.

"I'd say they've turned into a pair of matchmakers."

"I think you're right," Sarah replied.

"It's not the worst idea." It was definitely better than trolling for a fake wife online.

"It's a terrible idea! We hardly know each other. You really don't know me at all if you believe I would go into court and lie to a judge."

"I was thinking more along the lines of it being the truth," Jonathan said.

"Oh, please. We just met a few weeks ago. You can't honestly expect me to believe that you think you're..."

In love with her? He knew he was, and it was stab-a-knife-in-his-heart apparent that the feeling wasn't mutual.

"And what sort of example would this set for our daughters? We'd be telling them that if they want something badly enough, it's okay to do whatever it takes to get it."

If she believed that about him, then she didn't know him very well, either. "We should go back," he said.

They made the brisk walk home in stony silence.

Dear Reader,

Ah, the teen years. Even if you haven't raised a teenager, I'm sure you remember being one. While writing *The Parent Trap*, I loved having the opportunity to revisit both. And in case the title brings an old movie to mind, I want you to know that this is not that story!

This "parent trap" involves a single mom and a single dad who happen to live next door to each other and who are each living with the pleasures and pitfalls of raising teenage girls. Throw in a cat, a dog and a collection of other critters, and there's never a dull moment.

Instead of a story about a family reuniting, this one's about two families uniting to overcome the challenges life brings and to share the laughter and the joy that comes with falling in love.

I love hearing from readers and am always happy to send out bookmarks and recipe cards, so please feel free to contact me through my website at www.leemckenzie.com.

Happy reading!

Lee

LEE McKENZIE

knew she wanted to be a writer from the time she was ten years old and read *Anne of Green Gables* and *Little Women.* A writer just like Anne and Jo. In the intervening years, she has written everything from advertising copy to an honors thesis in paleontology, but becoming a four-time Golden Heart finalist and a Harlequin author are among her proudest accomplishments. Lee and her artist/teacher husband live on an island along Canada's west coast, and she loves to spend time with two of her best friends—her grown-up children.

For Michaela, with love

CHAPTER ONE

SPYING ON THE new neighbor was not a good use of her time, but Sarah Stewart had spent most of the morning peeking past the curtain in her office window anyway. At the sound of footsteps pounding up the front porch, she let the curtain fall and hastily took a seat at her desk, giving the mouse a jiggle and bringing a spreadsheet to life.

The screen door banged shut. "Mom? You still home?"

"I'm upstairs, Casey." Upstairs and appalled at the still-empty columns in her file.

Her daughter thundered up the stairs and burst into her office, eyes bright and blond ponytail swinging. Sarah accepted a hug, holding her sweet girl's slender, too-tall-for-her-age frame until she squirmed out of the embrace. Her hair was scented with equal parts animal shelter and summer sunshine.

"They gave me six dogs to walk today. Can you believe it? Six!" Casey's level of excitement would rival any lottery winner.

"That's wonderful, hon. Everyone at the animal shelter must be very impressed with you." *As they should be,* Sarah thought with a mother's pride. Casey was a great kid, and she was one incredibly lucky mom. "Did they give you any trouble?"

"The people at the shelter?"

Sarah laughed. "No, silly. The dogs."

"Not a bit. Remember I told you about Petey? The little shih tzu-Maltese cross? It's so cute to see him walking with the bigger dogs." Casey perched on the corner of Sarah's desk, one foot swinging. "Petey's little legs are going like a mile a minute but he totally keeps up with them, then when we get back to the shelter he has a drink of water, curls up in his kennel and goes right to sleep."

"I'm sure he's adorable."

"Yeah. He is."

Sarah recognized the wistful tone, having heard it many times, but Casey didn't need to be reminded that they simply couldn't have a dog. Letting her volunteer as a dog walker at the Serenity Bay animal shelter had seemed like a good idea. Now Sarah wondered if that had been a mistake because being around all those dogs only made Casey want one even more. Between school starting next week, homework, soccer practice and all the other activities Casey took on, plus all the hours Sarah spent at the store to keep her business running smoothly and profitably, a dog would be left home alone for hours at a stretch. That wouldn't be fair to a dog, and it got Sarah off the hook.

Besides, Casey had an ever-expanding menagerie in her bedroom, which at last count included two mice in a cage, a lizard in a terrarium, a half dozen fish in a small aquarium and a praying mantis in an enormous glass jar. Not exactly warm and fuzzy, except for the mice, but they didn't need to be walked and groomed and taught to stay off the furniture.

"Oh, I almost forgot," Casey said. "There's a moving van next door."

"Yes, I heard them pull up." Sarah hoped she appeared nonchalant as she squinted at the numbers on her monitor.

Midmorning, a man and his daughter had pulled their charcoal-gray SUV into the shared driveway that separated Sarah's house from theirs. Since then she'd lurked at the window of her second-floor home office, distracted by the clang and thump of a furniture dolly as two men clad in navy blue overalls rolled furniture and stacks of boxes down the ramp and onto the front porch of the house, which had sat silent and empty for the past month and a half.

Not that she would ever admit her mild neuroses to another living soul, but she had worried about this day ever since the empty-nesters who had lived there retired, set out to fulfill their lifelong dream of traveling the world and found a tenant willing to sign a one-year lease on their home. Bill and Marjorie hadn't just been good neighbors; they were good friends. Six years ago they'd been there for her and her daughter after her husband died in a car accident and she had struggled to fit the jagged pieces of her life back together.

If Sarah could, she would push the pause button on her current life and keep everything exactly as it was—happy, stable, secure—because if she disliked anything more than change, it was not knowing what that change had in store for her.

The small West Coast community of Serenity Bay had only one real estate company, and Sarah knew the two agents who ran it, so getting a little background information about her new neighbor had been easy. Jonathan Marshall was the new physical education teacher at the high school, a single dad with a teenage daughter. But that didn't tell her who he really was, nor did it explain why he was a single parent, why his daughter lived with him and not her mother, why they had moved to Serenity Bay.

What she did know, from having surreptitiously watched from her office window, was that Jonathan Marshall's blue jeans and white T-shirt portrayed a man in the kind of shape his profession would demand. Tall, well built, well proportioned, of course, but he also had an easy rhythm when he walked, a genuine smile for the people around him and a charming way of stabbing both hands through his hair while he made a decision. She was sure it was unconscious on his part, and she wished it wasn't so completely endearing.

His daughter appeared to be about the same age as Casey, but while Casey was equal parts tomboy and bookworm, that girl could have stepped off the page of a teen fashion magazine. Sarah could spot a designer label from a mile way, and that dad would have easily paid two hundred dollars for his daughter's skinny jeans. Then there was the bag slung over the girl's shoulder. There was a chance it was a knockoff, but Sarah would wager a week's worth of sales that it was the real deal. On a teacher's salary? That didn't compute.

Then they disappeared into the house, the man carrying a small pet carrier, the sullen-looking girl straggling behind, empty-handed.

"Have you met them yet?" Casey asked. "Did you take them the cookies we baked last night?"

"No, I thought we'd go over together." Last night the cookies had seemed the neighborly thing to do. Pillsbury refrigerated cookie dough was one of her specialties, after all. Today the cookies seemed to hint that she was angling for a way to meet Serenity Bay's newest and most eligible bachelor. Would he think she was being neighborly or out to snare him?

Oh, for heaven's sake, they're just cookies. Who cares what he thinks?

Casey slid Sarah's iPad out of its case and turned it on. "You said he's a new teacher at SBH, right?"

"That's right."

"What's his name?"

"Oh, um, Jonathan Marshall. I think. Why?"

Her daughter tapped on the screen. "Marshall. One *L* or two?"

"Probably two. What are you doing?"

"Searching for him online."

"Casey! You shouldn't do that. It's like an invasion of privacy."

"If it's on the internet, Mom, it's not private."

"That's true, but it still seems kind of stalkerish."

"Yep, but everybody does it." Her daughter grinned widely, angling the device so Sarah could see the screen. "Does this look like him?"

"Oh. Yes, it does." And she didn't have to ask the identity of the woman next to him in the photograph. The stunning brunette was Georgette Ogilvie, who last year left her job as news anchor at Vancouver's top-rated TV station, divorced her husband, and was already remarried and living in Europe. So… Jonathan Marshall was the ex-husband.

"He used to be married to that lady from the TV." Casey swiped the screen. "And they have a daughter named Kate."

Sarah stood and glanced out the window in time to see him on the driveway below, opening the back of his SUV and hauling out two potted plants. Thinking that a man who kept houseplants must have something going for him was silly, but she thought it just the same. And he was a teacher, after all, and a parent. Probably a good parent, since he seemed to have custody of his daughter.

"Says here that he used to teach at a high

school in West Vancouver and…oh, he coaches soccer. Cool. I wonder if he'll coach my team."

"I don't know, and you can't very well ask him."

"Why not?"

"Because he'll wonder how you found out he's a coach."

Casey flashed another grin. "Good point. I'll have to be more subtle."

The thought of her daughter being anything other than direct had Sarah smiling as she turned back to her desk, organized the invoices and bank statements that still hadn't been entered into her accounting program, and tucked them into her briefcase. She would have to take them to the store and hope to carve some time out of a busy afternoon to process them. Otherwise she'd have to put in an extra hour or two tonight.

"I'll run downstairs and see what we have for lunch, then I have to get to the shop. Juliet's on her own this morning and she'll need a break. What would you like?"

"What've we got?"

Not much. "Grilled cheese sandwiches?"

Casey shook her head. "Nuh-uh. I threw out the bread at breakfast." She scrunched her nose. "Moldy."

Gross. “Then I guess that leaves us with a can of chicken noodle soup and crackers. I’ll grab a few groceries on my way home.” For the millionth time, she wondered how every area of her life was so well organized and yet her culinary skills were nonexistent.

“It’s pizza and movie night. One pepperoni and one ham and pineapple.” Casey shoved the iPad back into its sleeve and peeled off her sweatshirt. “I need to have a shower. I’m covered with doggy slobber and kitty litter. They were shorthanded this morning so I helped clean out the kennels after I brought the dogs back.”

“Pizza it is.” *She really is a good kid,* Sarah thought, making a mental note of the request while thinking she should also bring home something a little more nutritious. As long as she didn’t have to cook it.

“Speaking of cats…”

“Actually, we were talking about pizza.”

This time her daughter’s grin had a mischievous innocence to it. “Nice try, Mom. Cats make good pets and they don’t need nearly as much attention as a dog.”

“Casey,” she warned. Even the thought of having a cat in the house made her eyelids itch. “Don’t even think about it.”

“All right, then. We’ll have to settle for

Petey." Casey tossed the final sassy suggestion over her shoulder as she dashed out of the room, leaving Sarah no opportunity to respond.

Every day Sarah counted her blessings that she had a daughter who worked hard at school and she was beyond grateful that at fourteen, her girl was still more interested in animals than she was in boys. All good qualities, but Sarah couldn't relent on adding a dog to their already-hectic household. Her daughter had a way of wearing her down, but not this time. While she was the first to acknowledge that Casey's hard work and enthusiasm deserved recognition, giving in to her desire to have a dog was not the way to go.

She double-checked the contents of her briefcase, zipped it shut and carried it downstairs just as the moving van pulled away from the house next door. From inside the screen door she watched until it disappeared around the corner, and then the street was quiet again.

Lunch, she reminded herself. She would heat the soup in the microwave and have a quick meal with Casey, then they would deliver the cookies and welcome their new neighbors to Serenity Bay before she left for work. Until then, she wouldn't let herself think about the man next door who was both single and singularly good-looking. If there was no room in her life for man's best friend, there was definitely no room for a man.

"DAD? HAVE YOU seen the box that has my shoes in it?"

Jonathan Marshall studied his fourteen-year-old fashionista as she clattered down the stairs of their new home. Then he shifted his attention to the piles of packing boxes piled willy-nilly in the foyer, living room and beyond. Stacked in their former home in West Vancouver, they had represented a fresh start. Now those same boxes were the source of some serious second thoughts.

Was this the right decision? Was leaving the city and moving to the small coastal town of Serenity Bay the best thing for him? For Kate? She sure didn't think so. She hadn't wanted to leave her friends, the city, their home or her school, and in that order, although he suspected their condo's close proximity to the mall was what she'd really miss. He understood that, all of it. He only asked that she keep an open mind, all the while realizing that was a tall order. If there was one thing a high school teacher knew above all else, it was that teenagers rarely had open minds. And why would they? They already knew at least as much as the average adult and definitely more than their parents.

Kate tore open a box and turned up her nose at the contents. “Kitchen stuff.”

“Good to know. How about you keep opening boxes and I’ll put them where they belong?”

“Seriously?”

“This’ll go a lot faster if we work together.”

Kate exhaled a long, dramatic sigh. “I guess, but I need my shoes.”

Knowing it would be futile to remind her that she was already wearing a perfectly good pair of shoes, Jon carried the box of pots and pans into the kitchen and set it on the counter. Kate had ripped opened two more boxes by the time he returned.

“Another one for the kitchen and this one—” She touched the box with the toe of her pink sneaker. “Bathroom. We should have labeled these.”

“There was no time,” he said, depositing the box of towels at the bottom of the stairs. “Did you write anything on your boxes?”

“Never thought of it. I’ll remember that for next time.”

Next time? Best let that drop, he decided as he returned to the kitchen with the second box. He had signed a one-year lease on this place and until that was up he was in no hurry to move again, so there was no point in giving her a chance to say she wanted to move back to the city. He had already accepted the position as PE teacher at Serenity Bay High School, and he had every intention of giving this fresh start his best shot.

Besides, this was a great house with its front facing onto a quiet cul-de-sac. Jubilation Court—which really was their new address—had lived up to its name from the moment he'd gazed out the kitchen window. He stared out the window now and surveyed the cedar-plank deck and, between the two towering firs growing at the bottom of the slope that was his backyard, the sweeping curve of Serenity Bay and the Salish Sea beyond.

Okay, maybe *jubilant* wasn't exactly right, but in spite of his daughter's resentment he sensed he could feel settled here, content even. Emotions that had evaded him since his ex-wife had dropped her bombshell. With a shake of his head, he chased the memories away. *Fresh start, remember?* The old baggage had been left behind. Right? Right. That's what he told the kids on his soccer team. We can't dwell on the past, we can only analyse it and improve our game. If they could believe it, so could he.

Kate, suddenly quiet, was sitting on the floor and gazing intently at framed family photographs when he once again returned to the living room.

"Are you going to put these on the mantel?" There was no missing the hint of accusation in her voice. "Or did you plan to leave them in the box and hope I didn't find them?"

With her long dark hair and engaging blue eyes, she was every bit as stunning as her media-darling mother, and that scared him more than he liked to admit. It also hurt, more than a little, that she thought he would try to erase her mother from her life. He was a bigger man than that, or at least he wanted to be.

"I had no intention of hiding that box of photographs. Tell you what, why don't you unpack as many as you want and put them on the mantel right now?"

Kate rolled her eyes as only a teenager could. "Maybe later. I'm looking for my shoes, remember?"

How could he forget? And what had become of the little girl who used to hang on every word he said? Huh. Who was he kidding? Long before her fourteenth birthday last month, his little girl had been morphing into a beautiful young woman with a personal sense of style and a mind of her own. He watched her shift boxes, tear flaps open, peer inside and purposefully move on to the next.

Never get between a woman and her wardrobe, he reminded himself. If he'd learned nothing else about women during his marriage to Georgette, he'd learned that.

"All right!" Kate's gleeful exclamation indicated the all-important shoes had been found. Before she picked the box up, she returned to the photographs. "Can I have this one of Mom for my room?"

"Of course." It was important that she maintain a connection with the mother who'd moved halfway across the world, he knew that, but he worried that daily phone calls wouldn't be enough.

She set her mother's photograph in the box and closed the flaps. "Did you give her the phone number here?"

"I did. Emailed it yesterday along with the address and our new cell phone numbers."

"Good." She picked up the coveted carton of footwear and made her way upstairs, leaving the unasked question hanging in the air. When would Georgette call? She had initially promised to call every day but that was impractical, given her hectic travel schedule, but she did her best. She always called on Saturday, though, and he knew Georgette wouldn't let Kate down. He hoped. She seldom did, and she had to understand what an important day this was for their daughter. If she didn't call by dinnertime, he would send a text message reminder. If that was too late for her, well, that was too bad.

He went back to opening boxes and moving them to the rooms where they belonged. As he did, his thoughts drifted, searching for the exact moment his marriage had run off the rails. The reality was that there hadn't been *a* moment. He and Georgette had spent most of their marriage slowly growing apart. He'd gradually become accustomed to being the very-much-on-the-sidelines husband of Vancouver's most talked-about news anchor, and she had eventually stopped trying to turn her "I'd rather be at the gym" husband into a tuxedo-wearing socialite. Even after they knew it was over, they'd both spent several agonizing months coming to grips with it and helping Kate adjust to their new reality.

The real end had come in the form of a European businessman named Xavier who had swept Georgette off her feet and onto his Paris-bound private jet. She had agreed to Jon's having full custody of their daughter and generous child support in exchange for summer visits. The first visit should have happened at the end of the last school year. It hadn't. Then Kate was supposed to join her mother for a week in Rome, but that had fallen through. Instead Georgette had promised to be in Vancouver several weeks ago, and that, too, had fallen through at the last minute. Now it was going to be Thanksgiving. He knew Georgette loved their daughter and wanted to make her a priority. He just wasn't sure Kate knew that.

The doorbell rang as he was contemplating, for something like the millionth time, the overwhelming difference between being a divorced guy with shared custody and a single dad with total responsibility for a rebellious teenager.

Jason Oliver, the real estate agent who'd rented the house to him, had said he would drop by sometime today. Given that Jon didn't know anyone else in Serenity Bay, it had to be him. Grateful for the distraction from demoralizing self-doubt and disorganized packing boxes, he wound his way through the clutter and opened the front door to a beautiful woman with a paper plate of cookies in her hands and a teenage girl by her side.

"Hi," she said. "I'm Sarah Stewart. My

daughter, Casey, and I live next door and we wanted to welcome you and your daughter to the neighborhood, to Serenity Bay."

Jon's heart sank, and not in an entirely good way. The real estate agent had mentioned that a widow lived next door. *This* was the widow? This expensively dressed and stunningly beautiful woman whose poise and self-control reminded him of Georgette.

"These are for you." Sarah held out the plate.

"Thanks. I'm Jonathan Marshall. Jon."

"We baked them," the girl said. She looked to be about Kate's age, but the similarity ended there. This girl's blond hair was pulled back in a casual ponytail, and Kate wouldn't be caught dead in faded jeans, high-top runners, and a red-and-white T-shirt with the letters *L-O-V-E* across the front. The *O* was a soccer ball.

He accepted the offering, backed away from the door, and called upstairs. "Kate? Come down and say hi to our neighbors."

"Be there in a minute."

He gave them what probably looked like an awkward smile. It sure felt awkward. "My daughter's minutes tend to be a little on the long side. Would you like to come in?"

"Oh, well, okay." Sarah cautiously stepped

inside and glanced around. "I have to work this afternoon and you have your hands full here so we won't stay, but we would like to meet your daughter."

"Of course." There was an awkward pause. She had beautiful gray-green eyes, and he wished he hadn't noticed. "So…where do you work?"

"I own a clothing boutique downtown."

He'd checked out the town before putting an offer on this house. Serenity Bay's shopping district on Shoreline Boulevard consisted of three or four blocks of high-end shops, art galleries, bistros and coffeehouses, which hardly qualified as "downtown." Her occupation explained the elegant outfit, though, and justified his wariness. Over the years his ex-wife had become more and more fixated on appearances, until finally his appearance in her life was no longer important.

Sarah's daughter was a different matter. "You're a soccer fan?" he asked, referring to her T-shirt.

The girl and her mother shared a knowing look and a quick grin, which was both puzzling and just a bit odd.

"I love soccer! I play on the girls' team at school."

"You do? Then I'll be your coach."

"Cool," Casey said. "Me and the other girls on the team were wondering—"

Kate's descent down the staircase ended the conversation. "Princess is hiding under my bed. I've been trying to get her to come out."

She'd swapped the pink sneakers for black sandals that had three straps buckled around her ankles and open toes that showed off the black-and-white-striped pedicure she'd insisted she needed before being dragged away from civilization.

"Princess is our cat," he said for no particular reason. "Kate, this is Sarah and her daughter, Casey. They live next door."

"Hi."

The two teens eyed each other self-consciously.

"Kate's going into ninth grade," he said to break the ice.

"Me, too." Casey sounded a lot more eager than Kate looked. "I can show you around if you'd like, introduce you to some of my friends. I've lived here forever so I know everybody."

Jon held his breath.

"Oh. Sure, that'd be great."

To his relief, his daughter's tone was considerably sweeter than it had been earlier.

Was it genuine? Only time would tell, but at least for now she was being polite.

"It's lovely to meet you both, but I'm afraid we have to go." Sarah stepped out onto the porch and her daughter followed. "You're welcome to drop by my store sometime," she said, turning back to speak to Kate. "It's called To the Nines. A shipment of jeans and tees came in yesterday, perfect for back to school. If you're interested, that is."

"Really? Thanks. I'll check it out for sure." Kate's voice held more enthusiasm than he'd heard in weeks.

Jon indulged in an inward sigh as his daughter retreated upstairs and he watched his new neighbors cross their adjoining driveways. Sarah Stewart's makeup and blond hair were flawless. Her beige linen jacket and skirt were the kind of classic that came with a hefty price tag. He hadn't counted on having another woman in their lives who put way too much emphasis on appearances. Not that the woman next door was *in* their lives, and to be fair, he reminded himself, there were subtle differences. Georgette had never baked cookies, not even the kind sliced from a roll of store-bought cookie dough. His ex-wife's stilettos had been her personal trademark, but Sarah Stewart's simple off-white leather flats looked as though they might actually be comfortable.

And he had to admit that a fashion plate of a woman who was raising a soccer-playing tomboy daughter kind of intrigued him on some level. Yes, her appearance and her occupation represented things he didn't much care for, but were those sensible shoes an indication that she had more substance than he gave her credit for? Time would tell.

CHAPTER TWO

SARAH'S PHONE LIT UP as she was writing up her final sale of the day. A discreet glance showed a text from her daughter, which she would read after she locked up. She'd had a productive afternoon, and that was a good thing since she'd frittered away most of the morning. She was ready for some mother-daughter time, but her customer didn't need to know that.

"Thank you, Mrs. Bentley." Sarah folded a brightly patterned silk scarf in pale pink tissue paper, admiring as she always did the delicate fabric as it slid between her fingers. She sealed the paper with a To the Nines label and slipped it into the shopping bag with the blouse and jacket her customer had purchased. "I'll have our seamstress shorten the skirt as soon as she comes in next week and call you when it's ready."

"Thank you, dear. I want to wear this to my grandson's christening in Vancouver next Sunday."

"You'll be the most elegant grandmother in town." Eleanor Bentley had a husband with deep pockets, a hairdresser who kept the gray away and a wardrobe most women would die for. "How is the new baby?" she asked.

"Oh, he's the cutest little fellow. I know everyone says that about their grandchildren, but he really is," the woman said, beaming as she opened her black patent Louis Vuitton clutch and produced a photograph.

"He's adorable." He really was. Sarah made a point of getting to know her customers on a personal level, and Eleanor Bentley was one of her most devoted. Sarah would agree to pretty much anything to make sure she was also a satisfied customer. "He looks like his grandfather."

The woman's smile widened. "He does, doesn't he? The Bentley men are a handsome bunch."

Sarah had learned that Eleanor, while tiny in stature, had raised four sons who all had their father's height and good looks. The youngest had recently passed the bar and was now practicing law with his three older brothers, as their father had before retiring with his wife to Serenity Bay.

In some ways, the elder Bentleys' marriage reminded her of her parents', minus the bank account, of course. Her mom and dad still lived in Ucluelet, where Sarah had grown up, in a house full of books and cats where her mother gardened and cooked organic food and her father tinkered with various inventions and engineering projects. No designer duds for them and no sign of retirement, either. They were good people and she loved them dearly—so did Casey—but there had been times growing up that she would have given anything to have a conventional family.

"Speaking of handsome…" Eleanor said. "I understand the new high school teacher moved in next door to you. Have you met him yet?"

Sarah's face went warm as she stepped around the counter and handed the shopping bag to the Bentley family's matriarch. "Just briefly."

Handsome hardly did the man justice, but that was no reason for her to be blushing like a schoolgirl.

"I'll see you next week, Mrs. Bentley. If you bring the jacket back with you, and shoes you'll be wearing with this outfit, you can try everything on while the seamstress is here and she can make any little last-minute adjustments."

"What a good idea. Thank you, dear."

After Eleanor left the store, Sarah flipped the dead bolt in place and returned to the sales counter as her assistant Juliet came out of the back stockroom that doubled as Sarah's office.

"The back door's locked and I shut down the computer," Juliet said. "And I unpacked the dresses that came in this afternoon. They're on hangers and I've gone over them with the steamer, but they may still need a little touch-up on Monday morning."

"Thank you so much. Before you leave, could you put this skirt in the alterations cupboard while I close up?" Sarah checked her watch, then remembered Casey's text message. She read it while she tidied up the sales counter and slid some paperwork into her briefcase.

Got the last Twilight movie. Luv ya! PS: 1 ham n pineapple, 1 pepperoni!

Sarah smiled at the reminder as she replied to her daughter's message.

Leaving now. See you in a half hour.

Today had been busier than usual, but thanks to Juliet's help with the hordes of back-to-school shoppers, Sarah's financial records were up to date and ready to go to the accountant, and she'd entered the new merchandise into the inventory database. Now she could go home, change into comfortable clothes, and settle in for movie-and-pizza night with Casey.

They'd started the tradition right after Sarah opened the store, when Casey was only seven years old, and she was grateful that her daughter was still enthusiastic about it. Yes, she'd raised a great kid, but outside of school, Casey still spent more time with her menagerie of animals or her nose in a book than with kids her own age. Would that change after she started high school? Would her daughter want to spend Saturday evenings with friends? Maybe even a boyfriend, perish the thought.

Sarah often reflected on her own childhood and teen years spent as an avid bookworm and a committed wallflower. She'd missed out on a lot and she wanted more for Casey, she really did, but for now these precious Saturday nights were theirs, and Sarah intended to cherish each and every minute of them.

JON PULLED INTO the parking lot next to Paolo's Primo Pizzeria. He doubted a "primo" pizza could be found in an out-of-the-way place like Serenity Bay, but as the saying went, beggars couldn't be choosers. If it were just him, he would have settled for whatever he could find in the boxes in the kitchen, and then power through till he had everything unpacked. Kate was "starving," though, and the only thing harder to handle than a hormonal teenager was a hungry hormonal teenager. Besides, they could both use a break, and one night of cardboard pizza wouldn't kill them.

Inside, the warm air scented with freshly baked crust, spicy tomato sauce and melted cheese almost had him buying the primo promise. Two of the half dozen booths were occupied, one by a family of four and the other by a pair of teenagers, maybe sixteen or seventeen, who were obviously on a date, judging by the way they were nestled together on the same side of the table.

"Be right with you," a dark-haired woman said, clearing plates and napkins from a recently vacated table, her Italian accent in perfect keeping with the ambient aromas.

"No hurry." He scanned the menu options on the wall behind the take-out counter. One large should be plenty for the two of them if they would do different toppings on each half. Kate, who three months ago had announced she was vegetarian, wanted a Neapolitan pizza because everything else was gross. He was debating over pancetta or prosciutto for his half of the pie when he was greeted by a soft female voice.

"Jonathan? Hi." His new neighbor smiled up at him.

"Oh, Sarah. Hi." She appeared as freshly starched as she had earlier, making him glad he'd pulled on a clean T-shirt before he'd left the house.

"Are you settling in?"

"Getting there. Still haven't tackled the kitchen, though, and the gas for the barbecue hasn't been turned on yet so we have to settle for takeout tonight."

"You won't be disappointed. Paolo's pizzas are incredible. Best in the world, according to my daughter."

"Sarah!" A middle-aged man in a white chef's apron waved at her from the other side of the pass-through. "Your pizzas will be outta the oven in a coupla minutes."

"Thanks, Paolo." She set her handbag on the counter and pulled out her wallet. "I always call ahead," she said. "Casey and I have pizza and watch a movie together every Saturday night."

Something akin to envy washed over him. Saturday movie-and-pizza sounded like the kind of routine a family should have, although his never had.

The woman who'd been clearing tables approached the counter. "Sarah, good to see you. How's your beautiful daughter? She is getting ready to go back to school, yes?"

"We're all set, Maria. This is her first year of high school so she's excited and a little nervous, too."

"Tell her she has nothing to worry about. That girl of yours, she can do anything."

"That's sweet. Speaking of high school, I'd like to introduce my neighbor. This is Jonathan Marshall, the new teacher at Serenity Bay High. Jonathan's daughter is the same age as Casey."

Maria's scrutiny was intense. "You live next door to our Sarah? This is good, yes?"

There was no mistaking the suggestive sparkle in those dark eyes, and he didn't have to look at Sarah to know her self-consciousness matched his.

"Paolo!" Maria angled her head in the direction of the kitchen. "This is the new teacher."

"*Benvenuti* to Serenity Bay! You like it here, no? And for you today we give you your first pizza on the house."

"Oh, no," Jon said, taken aback by the unexpected display of generosity. "That's not necessary."

"*Si, si.*" Maria wiped her hands on a towel. "Any pizza you like. You a teacher, you work hard. That's good, yes?" It was more a statement than a question, and it was directed at Sarah.

This time he did glance down to see her reaction, and he liked what he saw.

"Just you and your daughter? You are not married, yes?" Maria's question was directed at him, although she hadn't taken her eyes off Sarah.

Paolo's leisurely amble out of the kitchen broke the tension. "Here you go. One for you and one for Casey," he said, setting two extra-large pizza boxes on the counter in front of Sarah.

"You're each going to eat a whole pizza?" The question slipped out before Jon could stop it, but Sarah simply laughed.

"Not all in one sitting." Sarah handed her credit card to Maria. "We'll save a couple of pieces for breakfast tomorrow."

"Pizza for breakfast?"

"You've never had cold pizza for breakfast?"

He shook his head.

"You don't know what you're missing."

And he could live with that.

"Here's an idea," Maria said. "You and Casey, you're having pizza. And you are taking pizza home for your daughter, yes?"

He could see where this was going. Judging by Sarah's reluctant nod, so could she.

"You all should have dinner together." Maria waggled her finger from one to the other. "And your girls, they get to know each other, be good friends, yes?"

He liked the idea more than he had any right to.

Sarah tilted her head. Her eyes, more green than gray in this light, were serious but the creases at their corners hinted at an uncertain smile. He'd initially thought she was standoffish, even a little uppity. Not so, he realized. More on the shy side, and because of that she was going to say no way, not in his wildest dreams was he insinuating himself into her evening. He shouldn't care but he did, because an evening in the company of another adult suddenly had a lot of appeal.

"It's not a bad idea," she said, the smile now real. "For the girls, I mean. And it'll give you and your daughter a break from unpacking."

Okay. Not the reaction he expected, but she was right. Getting his daughter out of the house, having her spend time with someone her own age, would be good for her. "Sure," he said. "Your place? Mine's still full of boxes."

Maria and Paolo stood shoulder to shoulder on the other side of counter, each sporting a mile-wide grin.

"*Buona idea.*" Maria sounded surprised, as if the *good idea* hadn't even crossed her mind. She was a sly one, Jon thought. He had a hunch he was going to like this woman and her husband, and their food, if the warm aroma wafting from Sarah's pizza boxes was anything to go by.

She tucked her credit card back into her wallet and picked up the boxes. "I'll see you when your pizzas are ready. It's a nice evening, so we can sit out on the deck."

He watched her walk away, again noting the sensible flat shoes. This time he also noticed how she managed to walk like a woman wearing stilettos, and then he wished he hadn't.

"You have decided what you want, yes?"

Jon swung around. "Ah. Yes. Two pizzas, please. Extra large."

Paolo was back in the kitchen, throwing dough as he chuckled to himself, and Maria's eyes sparkled with mischief as she jotted his order on a notepad. "*Bella donna*," she said. "*Una buona mamma*."

His Italian was far from fluent but he knew enough to know that the softly spoken phrases did not translate to Neapolitan or prosciutto with caramelized onions. And pizza was all he wanted. Just pizza.

SARAH PARKED IN the driveway between her place and her new neighbor's. Jonathan's place. Randomly stacked cardboard boxes, empty, she presumed, littered the porch, and a pair of bicycles leaned against the rail.

Maria and Paolo were about as subtle as a ton of bricks. While she'd stood there in the restaurant, with the pair of them grinning shamelessly and Jonathan waiting expectantly, the suggestion that they share a meal had seemed like a good one. Mostly she'd been thinking about her daughter. Sarah loved that Casey was content to march to the beat of her own drum, but a mother always wanted her daughter's adolescence to be different from hers. Sarah had been the quiet kid, the wallflower. The first one everyone thought of when they needed help with homework or the gym decorated for a school dance. The last one considered when sleepovers were planned and party invitations sent out.

Sarah knew she couldn't arrange "play dates" for a teenager, but it might be good for Casey to have someone close to her own age, a classmate, living next door. And maybe for Kate, too. The poor girl had looked lost and sullen, like a kid who could use a friend.

So far today, Eleanor Bentley and Maria Donatelli had not-so-subtly hinted about how nice it was for Sarah to have a handsome, eligible man living right next door. Silly romantics, both of them. Yes, Jonathan seemed to be a nice man, and yes, he was one of the most attractive she'd ever met. Did that mean she would toss common sense out the window, risk everything she'd worked so hard for? Absolutely not. She and Casey had a good life, a secure life, and she wouldn't jeopardize that for anyone, no matter how dazzling his cool blue eyes might be.

Sarah let herself in the front door, set her handbag and keys on the hall table, and made her way to the kitchen with the pizza. Casey had set out plates, glasses and napkins on the island, but she was nowhere to be seen. Sarah switched the oven on low, shoved the pizzas inside to keep them warm, and took two more sets of dishes out of the cupboard.

She dashed upstairs and found Casey sprawled on her bed, earbuds in her ears and head bobbing to music as she scanned the screen of their iPad.

"What are you working on?" Sarah asked from the doorway.

Casey glanced at her and smiled.

"There are so many animals at the shelter right now. It's crazy. I'm posting pictures of them on Facebook so everyone can see how adorable they are and maybe decide to adopt one of them."

"That's a great idea." Which meant Sarah would see them, too, because one stipulation of her daughter's being on Facebook was allowing her mom to have full access. A stipulation that Sarah took full advantage of, including checking the privacy settings periodically to make sure only her daughter's friends had access to the things she posted. "Is there a picture of Petey?"

"No. I'm starting with the older animals because they'll be harder to adopt."

Putting up photos of the animals was a good idea, although Sarah knew exactly why Casey hadn't included Petey's picture. She wanted to adopt him. There was no time to go there right now, so Sarah changed the subject. "We're having company for dinner tonight so I need to get changed and get back downstairs."

Casey's expression changed in an instant. "Company? We *never* have company."

"Of course we do. Your grandparents come to visit twice a year." One week at Christmastime and two weeks in early July.

"Grandparents aren't company, they're family." Wary now, Casey swung off the bed and faced her. "Who's coming for dinner?"

"The new neighbors, Jonathan and Kate. I ran into him at Paolo's. He was picking up pizza, too. It seemed the neighborly thing to do since they're not settled in yet."

"Are they going to watch the movie, too?"

"Oh, I don't know. *Twilight* might not be his thing, but you and Kate can watch it."

Casey responded with an adamant head shake. "No. You and I watched the others together and I want us to watch this one, too. Besides, she might not have seen the first three, and you can't watch them backward."

It was impossible to believe there was a teenager on the planet who had missed those movies, but her daughter's insistence on watching this one with her lightened Sarah's heart.

CHAPTER THREE

THE INSIDE OF the car now smelled every bit as good as the pizzeria, making Jon's mouth water and reminding him how many hours it had been since he'd last eaten. He pulled into the driveway next to Sarah's car, grabbed the boxes and took the front steps two at a time. Now to break the news to Kate that they were having dinner next door. Would she react favorably? He hoped so. It'd been a long day and he wasn't up for a fight, or even a disagreement.

He unlocked the front door and pushed it open. "Kate? I'm home." He held his breath till he heard her response.

"Be right down, Dad!"

Encouraged by her pleasant tone, he set the pizzas on top of a stack of boxes still waiting to be unpacked. He hoped she wouldn't make a fuss about going next door to eat, and he hoped she'd make an effort to get along with Sarah's daughter, because he was looking forward to having some adult company.

She was smiling when she joined him at the bottom of the stairs. "Mom called," she said.

Thank heaven for small miracles. "The two of you had a good talk?"

"Yeah, we did. She apologized again for not making it back to Vancouver this summer. She thinks maybe Thanksgiving or for sure Christmas."

Georgette's "for sure" was as good as a "maybe," but this wasn't the time to dwell on the negatives. "Who knows," he said. "She might make it for both."

Kate shrugged. "I doubt it. She said she'll book rooms at the Hotel Vancouver and we can spend Christmas there. You, too."

"Oh, that sounds…nice." Not. He couldn't imagine anything more excruciating than spending the holiday with Georgette and Xavier. Lucky for him, that was months away and plenty could change between now and then, Georgette's mind being one of them.

"Right now we have a more immediate invitation. I ran into our neighbor—Sarah—at the pizza place and she invited us to have dinner over there. I told her we would. I hope that's okay with you."

She shrugged again. "Sure. Do we need to take anything?"

He picked up the pizza boxes and held the door for her. “Just these.”

On their way to the house next door, she chattered about her new room and how she nearly had all of her stuff organized. She had even sent a couple of pictures to her mom, who thought the room looked great.

Jon made a mental reminder to send Georgette a text message after dinner and thank her for getting in touch with Kate. He liked seeing their daughter like this, almost effervescent, especially compared to her earlier funk.

They climbed Sarah’s front steps and rang the doorbell. The prospect of having dinner with a beautiful woman, teenagers notwithstanding, had improved his outlook, too. And his mood ratcheted up a few more notches when Sarah opened the door. Since he’d bumped into her half an hour ago, she’d undergone a head-to-toe transformation from ultrachic businesswoman to a hip-looking young mom in navy jeans and a creamy yellow lace top that flared below her waist. The diamonds dazzling her ears matched the rhinestones that studded her flip-flops.

Her smile was warm and genuine. “We’re really glad you could join us,” she said.

He smiled back. So was he.

AN HOUR LATER, Sarah watched Casey polish off her fourth slice of pizza. She said she wanted to try one of each, and to everyone's apparent surprise, she'd succeeded.

"I have to go upstairs and feed my critters," she said, tossing a balled-up napkin into one of the empty boxes. "Would you like to come with me?" she asked Kate.

"Critters?" There was no mistaking the uncertainty in the girl's voice.

"That's what I call them. My mom says she's allergic to cats and she won't let me have a dog…" During a drawn-out pause, she narrowed her eyes at Sarah. "So I have other animals in cages and aquariums."

"Any snakes?" Kate asked. "Those are gross."

Casey shook her head. "No. I mean, I don't think snakes are gross, but my mom would never let me have one of those, either."

Sarah laughed. "Creepy-crawlies make me squeamish, too, but even I'm okay with these critters. They're harmless, trust me."

Casey momentarily looped her arms around Sarah's neck. "Thanks for the pizza, Mom. You, too—" She hesitated. "Um, Mr. Marshall, I guess."

"How about we reserve the 'Mr. Marshall' thing for school?"

Casey grinned.

"And soccer practice," he added. "Otherwise it's Jon."

"Sure."

Kate pushed away from the table and followed Casey across the deck. "Thank you for having us over. This was nice." She hadn't had a lot to say while they ate, but Sarah could tell she was a sweet girl and she liked her quiet confidence.

"You're welcome. We'll have to do it again sometime."

"She's a great kid," Sarah said to Jon after the girls went inside and closed the sliding door behind them. "Nice manners, too."

"Thanks. She has her moments but mostly, yes, she's a good kid."

He seemed both reluctant to give her too much credit and pleased that someone else recognized his daughter's positive traits.

"Would you like coffee?" she asked. She hoped he would say yes. In spite of his parenting skills, which were awkward at best, she had enjoyed their conversation over dinner. "If you can afford the time, that is."

"Ah…sure. That'd be nice."

"I'll run in and make some." She gathered up the pizza boxes and tucked them under one arm, then picked up the tray with all of their empty plates and glasses.

"Let me help with those."

"Thanks, but I can manage." She gestured toward the bay. "You've had a long day. Sit and enjoy the view. I'll be right back."

Inside the kitchen, she poured water into the coffeemaker and filled the basket with grounds. While it brewed she quickly loaded the dishwasher and set a pair of bright red coffee mugs and a mismatched creamer and sugar bowl on the tray. Almost as an afterthought, she added a small plate with some of the cookies.

Jon had hesitated when she'd offered coffee. Perhaps because he still had a lot to do at home. Or maybe he'd had enough of her company for one evening. No, she didn't think that was it. She'd felt a little spark at the pizza place. She was sure he had, too, although she had to admit to being completely out practice when it came to these things. Paolo and Maria's matchmaking aside, an attractive single man would draw attention in a small town like Serenity Bay. There weren't many single women here, but she knew a few married ones who'd be wishing they were. A thought that didn't sit well, she realized.

She filled the two mugs and carried the

tray back outside. Jon stood with his back to her, leaning on the railing. The view always captivated her, and tonight was no exception. The tide was low and the bay itself was calm. Out on the strait, though, a light breeze had the surface dancing, and in the distance a cruise ship destined for Alaska glided by, lights twinkling in the dusk.

"Here we go." She set the tray on the table and he walked back to join her. "Cream and sugar?" she asked after they were seated.

"Black is good, thanks."

She scooped sugar into hers, added cream, stirred. He was watching quizzically when she looked up.

"I have a sweet tooth."

"I can see that."

She held out the plate. "Help yourself."

"Ah. Cookies. Thanks for the ones you dropped off this afternoon. They were… great." And he was a terrible liar.

"You didn't look at all guilty when you said that." His grin suggested he was onto her. "Casey thought we should bake something to welcome you to the neighborhood, but I am not a cookie-baking kind of mom. Actually, I'm not much of a cook of any kind."

"It's the thought that counts," he said, and he sounded sincere. "I was glad you stopped by. So was Kate, although she might not have let on."

Sarah set the tray on the table and handed one of the mugs to him. "Kate seems like she's got a good head on her shoulders."

"She does. But she's going through a…I don't know…a phase? At least I hope it's a phase." He drank some of his coffee. "This is good."

"Thanks. Fourteen's a tough age, especially for girls." She set her mug on the table and wrapped her hands around it. "No longer a child but not quite old enough to have any independence."

"True. Boys seem to take a while longer to get to that point."

"So I recall. I think raising girls is easier, don't you?"

"I don't know about easy, but then I never expected to be raising a kid on my own, boy or girl."

"How long has it been?"

He drank some coffee while he contemplated his answer.

"I'm sorry," she said. "That's a personal question. You don't have to answer it."

"No problem. I was just doing the math. Georgette moved out a year ago but even before that she was busy with her career, pretty much working twenty-four/seven, so we—Kate and I—were on our own a lot of the time."

Sarah gazed into her coffee cup, choosing her words carefully. "Juggling family and career is tough for a lot of women," she said. "We want to be a success at both."

"Georgette likes to live large. It's not a lifestyle that lends itself to parenting…and I'm being honest, not critical. She adores Kate, and Kate is her biggest fan."

"Your daughter's lucky to have her in her life then," she said. "Casey was only six when my…when her father died in a car accident."

He looked genuinely surprised. "Oh, I'm sorry. That must've been rough."

"It was at first." She sipped some coffee and changed the subject. "What made you choose Serenity Bay as your new home?"

She didn't particularly want to talk about herself, and she didn't want to talk about her disaster of a marriage that ended even more disastrously. Keeping the conversation on current topics should be safe enough.

"I didn't so much choose the town as it chose me. Deciding to leave the city was the first step. The town we moved to depended on where I could find a job."

"Of course, that makes sense."

"When I heard about the teaching position here, it sounded perfect. The school, the town, everything. Then I found this house, and here we are."

"I hope you like it here. After my...Jim died, my parents tried to get me and Casey to move back to Ucluelet or least someplace on Vancouver Island where we'd be closer to them. They thought it would be easier for us to be near family, but Serenity Bay was the right place for us then and it still is. Great schools, friendly people. It's a good place to raise kids."

"That's what I'm counting on." "My daughter was not happy about the move."

Sarah smiled. "Teenagers don't like change, that's for sure. Casey said she'll show her around and introduce her to some of the kids at school. Maybe that will help."

"I hope so."

"It'll be good for Casey, too, having a girl her age living close by. She can be a bit of a loner and I worry about her sometimes."

"But isn't she on the soccer team?"

"She is, and she plans to work on the student newspaper and wants to run for student counsel, but outside school she spends a lot of time by herself, doing homework, reading. Especially this summer because her best friend is away."

"She sounds grounded," he said. "Maybe some of her enthusiasm will rub off on Kate. She does what she needs to get by and then she hangs out at the mall, pores over fashion magazines, exchanges text messages with her friends."

There was no mistaking his tone when he mentioned the magazines. As close to derisive as possible without being rude.

"Sometimes a child finds her passion," Sarah said. "And sometimes that passion finds her. Our job as parents is to encourage them to keep the doors open and be willing to explore opportunities when they present themselves."

"When it comes to school, it might take a crowbar to pry open Kate's doorway to opportunity."

The comment stung Sarah's sensibilities. Did he say things like that to his daughter? If he did, then there was little wonder they had a communication problem. She stood with her cup in her hand and reached for his. "I'll get more coffee."

"Thanks." He sounded awkward, as though he'd picked up on her reaction and regretted what he'd said.

He was on his feet again and taking in the view when she returned with their mugs refilled. She set his on the metal top of the glass rail, next to where he leaned on his forearms.

The western sky was still lit by the sun that had just dipped out of sight. The harbor was quieter than it had been earlier in the day. A lone fishing trawler chugged into the marina, and a pair of kayakers paddled near the resort on the other side of the bay. For a few minutes she and Jonathan stood and gazed across the bay, occupied with their own thoughts.

She set her red mug next to his. "It's a beautiful view, isn't it?"

"I was thinking the same thing. It's why I decided on our place. We were lucky to get a one-year lease, which gives us time to decide if this is where we want to call home."

"I never get tired of this. Every time I look out here, it's a little different from the last time, depending on the tide, the angle of the sun, the marine traffic coming and going."

"The real estate agent said we'd even see whales from time to time. I wasn't sure if that was true or just a sales pitch but I put a pair of binoculars in the kitchen, just in case."

"It's true," she said. "It's quite common to see one of the resident pods of killer whales, but usually outside the breakwater. They seldom venture into the bay. Casey loves them. I'll bet Kate will, too."

"I hope so." He finished his coffee, straightened. "She and I should be getting home."

"Of course. I'll let the girls know." She took his mug and set it along with hers on the tray and carried it inside.

He followed without saying anything. She couldn't tell if he had picked up on her disappointment with his negative comments about his daughter or if something else was bothering him. In her opinion, those had been terrible things for a parent to say about a child, especially the crowbar remark. Even if he didn't say anything that harsh to his daughter's face, a sensitive kid would pick up on his attitude.

His problem is not your problem. He seemed like a nice guy and he was definitely nice to look at, but she had no time for anyone who was not fully engaged as a parent. She'd been there once and that had been one time too many.

AS BEDROOMS WENT, Casey's was a total train wreck, Kate Marshall thought. There were books everywhere. The walls were covered with World Wildlife Fund posters of a rhinoceros, a baby monkey and a bamboo-eating panda. Built-in shelves running the width of the room, beneath the window, were lined with cages and aquariums.

Casey opened the door of a tall wire cage that was filled with ramps and a wheel, reached inside and produced a small brown mouse.

"This is Jane," she said, extending her hand. "Would you like to hold her?"

Did she want to hold a rodent? In her hand? Not even a little bit. "Oh, gee, ah, no. But thanks."

The girl grinned at her as she reached into the cage and brought out Jane's identical twin. "This is Dian. Lots of people are afraid of mice, but they're actually sweet and very gentle. I named these two after famous scientists."

"Oh." Kate searched her memory for famous scientists. Other than Albert Einstein, she drew a blank.

"Jane Goodall studies chimpanzees and Dian Fossey wrote *Gorillas in the Mist*. Have you read it?"

A book about gorillas? Seriously? "No, I haven't."

Casey placed a rodent on each shoulder, giggling softly as one of them nuzzled her neck. Kate shuddered.

"You're welcome to borrow my copy."

"Oh, gee—"

"Let me guess. That's another no."

"Science books aren't really my thing," Kate said.

"That book's not really a… Never mind." Casey scooped nuts and seeds out of a glass canister and into a little dish inside the mouse cage. "I'm going to be a veterinarian some day because I want to work with animals, so I read a lot of…*science* books."

Her emphasis on science…was that a put-down?

"Most kids who haven't even started high school haven't figured out what they want to do when they graduate."

"Yeah, most people think it's weird, but I've always known. My mom says I figured it out in kindergarten when the local vet visited my class. Dr. Jacobson still runs the animal clinic in town and she does a lot of work for Serenity Bay's animal shelter. She even has three rescue dogs of her own. She helped me get on as a volunteer at the animal shelter this summer."

Casey tossed a carrot and a piece of broccoli into the cage, and then she took one mouse off her shoulder, holding it in her palm, stroking its head and along its back with the tip of one finger before setting it gently in the cage.

"Nighty-night, Jane. You, too, Dian," she said, repeating the process with the other rodent. "I've always wanted a dog, or a cat, or both, but my mom's allergic to cats and she says we're too busy to take care of a dog."

Anyone who could be this crazy about a mouse definitely should have a real pet. Kate had never had a dog, but there'd been many nights when she'd crawled into bed, snuggled up with Princess and cried herself to sleep because her mom wasn't coming home. She hardly cried about that anymore, but it still made her sad. If her dad knew, he'd freak out for sure, and she did not need that. She was glad Princess was a good listener and an even better secret-keeper. For a while she'd cried about having to move, but that hadn't made any difference, either. And she wasn't so much sad as she was totally furious with her dad for making her come to live in this stupid little town in the middle of freaking nowhere. Especially if Casey was any indication of what the other kids were like.

"Maybe you can convince your mom to change her mind about a dog."

"Oh, I'm working on her." Casey grinned and moved on to a terrarium that housed a small brownish-gray reptile. "This is Rex," she said. "He's a green anole lizard. I named him after my favorite dinosaur. Lizards aren't dinosaurs, though."

Like anyone cared.

"Birds are more closely related to dinosaurs than lizards are." Casey opened a plastic container that had small holes poked in the lid, took out a bug that was…*ew! ew! ew!*… squirming!…and dropped it into the glass enclosure with the lizard.

Kate hastily averted her gaze, not wanting to see this particular critter consume its meal. She didn't respond to the dinosaur trivia, either, but Casey didn't seem to notice.

"Rex eats crickets," she said. "I buy them at the pet store."

The only thing creepier than keeping live bugs in your bedroom? Picking them up with your bare hands and feeding them to something even creepier. Ew.

"What do kids do in Serenity Bay?" Kate asked, hoping to shift the conversation away from the science of Casey's critters. "Besides school, I mean."

Casey sprinkled fish food into the aquarium next to the lizard tank, and they both watched the multicolored fish dart to the surface. Finally, some normal animals.

"That depends. I'm on the soccer team and I've always been involved in a bunch of activities at school."

"What about after school? Is there someplace kids like to hang out?"

Casey shrugged. "At Paolo's, the place where our parents bought the pizzas, or at the after-school drop-in at the community center. The boys like to go there because there's a pool table and video games."

She made it sound lame, and Kate sort of agreed. Except for the part about boys. In the city, she and her friends usually went to the mall after school. Lots of boys hung out there, too, but she mostly loved to check out her favorite clothing stores. Recently she had been paying attention to the window displays and she already had a ton of ideas. When she was old enough to have a part-time job, she wanted to work in one of those stores and wow shoppers with her displays.

"Do you spend much time at the drop-in center?" she asked.

Casey scrunched her nose, making her freckles stand out more than ever. "I usually come home and do my homework, but sometimes I stop at the library on my way. I read a lot."

No kidding, Kate thought. The only room

she'd ever seen that had more books than this one was a library.

"You said you're not into science books," Casey said. "What do you like to read? Or do you like to read?"

Kate hesitated, having a mental debate about whether or not to confess her dreams. Why not? It's not as if they were as lame as living with rodents and lizards and dinosaurs.

"Magazines, mostly. Fashion magazines. *Seventeen*, *Teen Vogue*. I want to work in the fashion industry someday." She couldn't believe she'd said it out loud. She'd never revealed this to anyone, not even her closest friends in the city. They were only interested in goofing around or gossiping on Facebook, and they would either shrug off her ideas as totally not going to happen or, worse yet, make fun of her.

"Cool," Casey said. "You should talk to my mom. She lives and breathes fashion trends, and pretty much everybody in town shops at her store. Except me." Casey grinned. "She doesn't sell the kind of clothes I like to wear."

Kate had already noted the other girl's attire, the same outfit she'd been wearing when she and her mom had delivered the cookies earlier that day. Faded denim cutoffs with rolled-up cuffs just above the knee, the soccer

T-shirt, black-and-white high-top Keds. Ponytail. No makeup. Total tomboy. Still, Casey might not get where people like her mom and Kate were coming from, but she understood what it meant to have a dream.

"I can't wait to see your mom's store, but what I really want to do is work for a big fashion magazine someday as the editor in chief."

"Oh, wow. Like in *The Devil Wears Prada*," Casey said.

Kate laughed at that. "You saw that movie?"

"Yeah, my mom and I have a movie night every Saturday. Except tonight," she added. "Since you and your dad came over. Have you seen it?"

"Yes. I loved the clothes, but I'll be nicer when I'm the editor."

"More like Anne Hathaway," Casey said. "Although I liked her better in *The Princess Diaries*. You sort of look like her, actually."

"Lots of people say that. It's mostly the hair, before Anne cut hers. My mom interviewed her once when she was in Vancouver for something."

"Really? Wow, that must've been so cool. Did you get to meet her?"

"No." Not a chance. Her mom used to go on and on about the famous people she met, but whenever Kate asked to tag along, the answer had always been a firm no.

"She didn't even let you watch from backstage, or whatever they call it in a TV studio?"

Kate gave her best careless shrug. "Those interviews were part of her job and it wasn't appropriate to have a kid hanging around." At least that had always been her mother's excuse. But the cold, hard truth, as Kate eventually realized, was that her mother didn't want those people to know she was a wife and mother.

"That's too bad. Almost every summer we get a few famous people who bring their yachts into the marina here. Sometimes they'll even stay a few days, do some shopping. Once in a while they go into my mom's store, too. I'm never around to meet them, but it's pretty cool that they like her store enough to shop there."

"I'll definitely check it out, especially if it's the only good place in town to shop."

"Be sure to tell her about the magazine stuff, too. If she knows you're interested in more than just shopping, I'll bet she can teach you all about the business end of things, too."

This was the first positive thing Kate had heard about Serenity Bay since she'd arrived.

But was she brave enough to share her dream with an adult? "I wonder if she needs help with displays and stuff like that."

"She might. She's always super busy so if you're interested, you should ask her."

"I will. There's just one teensy little hitch."

"What's that?"

"My dad." Okay, not so teensy. "He'll have a cow if he hears about it."

He was always going on about how she needed to get a good education, and by that he meant math and science and history, and then get a good job doing whatever people did when they knew math and science and history. She had never told her mother any of this, either, because by the time she figured it out, her mother was gone. Now, when they were on the phone, her mom spent a lot of time talking about the places she and Xavier had been, the celebrities they met. Just as she did this afternoon when she called. Kate tried not to let it bother her, but it did.

"It's not like you're doing anything wrong if you talk to my mom about her business," Casey said.

True. And Sarah did seem super nice.

"We've always had soccer practice every Tuesday and Thursday after school. If your dad doesn't change the schedule, then you could drop by my mom's store on one of those days and he'll never have to know."

Huh. For a kid who came across as a Goody Two-shoes, Casey might be pretty cool after all.

"I might do that." Maybe living here wouldn't be so bad after all, Kate thought, watching Casey remove a circle of cloth that had been fastened over the top of a gigantic glass jar with an elastic band. She dropped another cricket inside. "Is there something in there?" she asked.

"Manny lives in here."

Kate leaned in for a closer look. All she could see was a bed of moss on the bottom of the jar and a dead tree branch angled against the side. "I don't see—"

A twig on the branch suddenly moved and caught the squirming cricket.

Kate squealed and jumped backward. "What on earth is that?"

"A praying mantis. She'll eat crickets when that's all I have, but she really likes it when I catch houseflies for her."

Okay, this was just plain disgusting. Seriously, no normal person kept a giant bug in a jar, especially not a bug that ate other bugs that she had to catch and feed to it. Gross, gross, *gross*.

Casey only laughed. "Last spring my science teacher had praying mantises in our classroom. I thought they were interesting, so she let me bring one home. I've had her all summer."

"Your mom really doesn't mind you keeping all these, um, critters in the house?"

"No. She gets that I love animals, and I think she's trying to make up for not letting me have a dog."

"Your mom seems really nice." And then another idea popped into Kate's head. "Is she seeing anyone?"

"You mean…dating?" Casey carefully fastened the fabric over the top of the bug jar. "No, she's either at work or at home so I'm sure she's not."

"Would it bother you if she was?"

Casey narrowed her eyes. "I don't know. Why?"

If Kate had learned one thing from her mother, it was how to choose her words carefully. "My dad hasn't dated anyone since he and my mom split, and he and your mom seem to be hitting it off."

"So you think they'll start dating?" Clearly, Casey was not warming up to the concept.

"I'm not saying they will, but I wouldn't

mind if my dad had someone to focus his attention on besides me."

"Really? Your dad seems nice and everything, but I don't know. I think my mom must have really loved my dad because ever since he died, it's just been the two of us."

Kate shrugged. "Whatever. I just thought it'd be nice if my dad could be happy again. And otherwise occupied."

"You want him to start dating so he'll pay less attention to you?"

"It wouldn't be the worst thing that could happen. And I'll bet if your mom was dating someone, you'd be able to use that to your advantage."

"How exactly?" She seemed interested in spite of sounding skeptical.

"You said you want a dog, right?"

That got her attention. "More than anything."

"Well, if your mom feels guilty because she's seeing someone and not spending as much time with you, then she'll want to do whatever it takes to make it up to you."

Casey was grinning now. "And that something would be Petey."

Kate shrugged. "It's worth a shot."

And then Sarah called to them from the bottom of the stairs. "Casey? Kate's dad is leaving now but she's welcome to stay a while longer if she'd like."

"Thanks, Mom!" she yelled back. "Do you want to?"

"I should probably go, too. We haven't finished unpacking."

Casey followed her downstairs and they joined their parents in the foyer.

Sarah was smiling. "Kate's dad offered to give you a ride on the first day of school. Isn't that nice?"

"Thanks," Casey said. "But I always go with my friend Henry. He lives across the street."

"Henry's welcome to get a ride, too. The more the merrier. Right, Kate?"

Dad, don't be lame. "Sure," she said. "More is totally merry."

She watched her dad exchange a look with Casey's mom. "Thanks for having us over," he said.

"Anytime," Sarah replied.

Kate liked the way they were looking at each other. She winked at Casey, Casey winked back, and she gave herself a mental high five. This plan might work, she thought. It just might work.

CHAPTER FOUR

SARAH CLOSED THE door after saying good-night to their new neighbors and turned to her daughter.

"That was okay, don't you think?"

"Yeah. Kate's dad seems pretty cool. Do you like him?"

That was an odd question, she thought, although Casey probably didn't intend for it to sound the way it did. "He seems nice. I'm sure they'll be good neighbors."

Casey gave her an odd smile that suggested the question wasn't so innocent after all. Best to let that go, especially since her conversation with Jonathan had ended on a sour note.

"How about you and Kate?" she asked. "Did you hit it off?"

"I think so. She doesn't like my critters, though."

Sarah laughed at that. "She's not alone. A lot of people aren't fond of rodents and reptiles."

"True. She's really into clothes and stuff."

"She certainly seems to be. That was an expensive outfit she was wearing."

Casey climbed two steps and draped herself over the banister. "I think her mom pays for a lot of her things but at least she wasn't all, 'oh, look at me and all my fancy stuff' like some of the girls at school. She's actually the only kid I've ever met…well, aside from Henry…who's already figured out what she wants to be."

"Really? And what's that?"

"The editor of a fashion magazine."

"Does she? That's an ambitious goal." One her father seemed to know nothing about, and given his scathing comments about fashion magazines and the mall, it was no surprise that she hadn't told him. Poor kid. "Speaking of Henry, have you heard from him?"

Casey's enthusiasm waned. "No. I was hoping he'd be home by now. He's been gone all summer and school starts in a few days."

"I'm sure he'll be home soon."

"I sure hope so."

Sarah reached up and gave her a hug. "Why don't you go upstairs and send him a text or an email? I want to clean up the kitchen."

"Good idea. I also need to post the rest of the pictures I took at the shelter this morning."

"I'll pop in and say good-night when I'm done." And there was no doubt she'd hear more about Petey when she did.

Back in the kitchen, she finished loading the dishwasher and turned it on, tossed paper napkins in the trash, stuffed the empty pizza boxes in the recycling bin, filled the sink with hot water and detergent. She swished the dishcloth in it and wiped every square inch of every surface in the kitchen. Take-out dinners meant she didn't have to cook, and she loved that they made cleanup so easy. Now everything was spic 'n' span, just the way she liked it.

Jonathan had not lived up to her first impression of him, and she found that more disappointing than she had any right to. Yes, he was way better-looking than any man needed to be, but looks weren't everything, and it bugged her that she found him attractive.

There was a chance that she wasn't giving Jonathan the benefit of the doubt. Moving was stressful, changing jobs was stressful, getting divorced was stressful, and he had hinted that Kate's mother didn't have much time for her. Casey had been young enough when her father died that the loss hadn't seemed to have had an adverse effect on her, although there were times when Sarah wondered if losing her dad explained why her daughter didn't form a lot of close personal attachments.

She strolled back out onto the deck and leaned on the railing where she and Jonathan had stood a short time ago. He was floundering with single parenthood, and tonight she'd been tempted to offer a little sage advice. Now she was glad she hadn't. It wasn't her place to interfere. She didn't even know these people.

She felt sorry for Kate, though. In spite of her polished exterior—the girl certainly knew how to put an outfit together—and an outward air of confidence, Sarah thought the girl could use a healthy dose of self-esteem. There was also an underlying sadness to her, which was not a surprise. Between the hormones and impending womanhood, the early teen years were a confusing time for girls, and there was probably never a time when a girl needed her mother more than at this age. All the phone calls and text messages and lavish gifts in the world couldn't replace a warm hug and a shoulder to lean on.

Sarah hoped the girls would become friends. She cherished the close bond she had with her daughter, but she also understood the importance of having close friends, and Kate might be as good for Casey as Casey could be for her. That would also provide a chance for Sarah to offer a shoulder once in a while, encourage Kate to pursue her dreams.

What about Jonathan?

What about him? Sure, she had concerns about his daughter, starting with his attitude, but she had no intention of interfering.

She glanced over her shoulder and saw that the lights were still on in his kitchen, but there was no sign of anyone in it. Apparently the man could cook, and that intrigued her. Over dinner tonight, he'd said he would like to reciprocate by having her and Casey over for homemade pizza next Saturday. Paolo's were good, but his were better. She had accepted, thinking it would be good for the girls, and she was curious about the man's made-from-scratch pizza. And her curiosity ended there. Letting herself ponder any of his other attributes was simply too risky.

CASEY SWITCHED ON her laptop and went back to work, posting the rest of the photographs she'd taken of the dogs at the shelter. She wasn't posting Petey's picture, though. Instead, she clicked on it and set it as her desktop background. After Kate hinted that she should guilt her mother into letting her have a dog, she couldn't stop thinking about it. She wouldn't have thought that up on her own, that's for sure. Her mom was just her mom. She didn't go on dates and it was weird to think of her having a boyfriend.

Casey barely remembered her dad, wouldn't know what he looked like if it weren't for the photograph on her dresser. She'd been sitting on his shoulders and they'd been laughing about something when her mom had taken the picture. Even though she didn't remember him or anything about the day that photograph was taken, he was still her dad. She'd always thought it would be fun to have a sister or a brother, but another dad? The idea had never crossed her mind.

Casey liked her new neighbor, though. Kate wasn't like any of the other girls in Serenity Bay. Not even the coolest ones were as cool as Kate. Her clothes were super trendy and her manicure was crazy cool. All the girls at school who were into those kinds of things would have gone on and on and on about them—seriously, sometimes they made her want to scream—but Kate hadn't said a thing. Instead of talking about clothes and hair and makeup, she said she wanted to work for a big fashion magazine someday, probably starting as a photographer and maybe writing articles, too, but eventually she'd be editor in chief.

She'd also seemed interested when Casey told her she was going to be a veterinarian, even though she'd been squeamish about some of the critters. Not everyone was comfortable with rodents and reptiles, but she'd said Manny the praying mantis was the grossest thing she'd ever seen.

Casey leaned in for closer look at her terrarium. "Good thing I didn't feed you a fly while she was here."

If Kate thought Manny eating a cricket was gross, watching her tear a housefly apart and gobble it up would totally freak her out.

They'd talked about their families, too, since having only one parent was something they did have in common. Kate's mom was alive and well and living in Europe with her new and disgustingly rich husband. They traveled a lot so Kate couldn't live with them. Then she'd said she didn't think they wanted her anyway.

Casey had a hard time believing that. Her mom was strict about some things, like homework and curfew and not friending strangers on Facebook, but they also had fun doing things together. Like Saturday movie-and-pizza night, which had still turned out okay tonight even though Kate and her dad had been here and they hadn't watched a movie.

Kate had confessed to being mad at her dad for making her move away from her friends in the city. Casey had tried to sympathize, but she hadn't told Kate that she didn't have many friends, mostly because other kids thought her obsession with animals was weird and her determination to get straight A's was completely lame. If Kate thought she was weird or lame—or both—she hadn't let on.

Casey's phone whistled and she grabbed it off her nightstand. A text from Henry! He must be back at home, finally.

How R U?
Good. U?
Also good. Won't B back 4 school tho.
No way. We R supposed 2 go 2gether.
Still visiting the fam. Back Fri.

Rats. This was not how things were supposed to go. Henry was her best friend. They always went together on the first day of school, and *this* was the first day of high school. She needed him there.

UR loss. Getting a ride to school with new neighbor anyway.

The new teacher?
Yep & daughter Kate.
Is she hot?

Let's just say some of the girls at SBH were going to freak when they saw their new competition. Instead she typed:

Don't be gross.
Ha! She is!
But UR not so 4get it.
Ouch. How R things with U and Dex?
There is no me and Dex.
That bad huh? U still haven't made a move?

No, she had not, and even if she had wanted to, she had no clue what the moves were.

I said don't be gross.
Gotta go. Mom's yelling lites out.
What time is it in Montreal?
After 11.
K. G'night.
TTYL.

She set her phone back on the nightstand, slid off the bed and walked over to the window. It was getting dark and across the driveway she could see the light was on in Kate's room. No sign of her, though. Maybe she was helping her dad unpack.

Casey had never considered the possibility that Henry wouldn't make it back in time to start school. Good thing she'd accepted Kate's dad's invitation to get a ride with them. The first day of high school seemed like kind of a big deal, and she'd never imagined having to go alone.

Casey was looking forward to high school because she would finally have science classes with real labs, but she wasn't looking forward to some of the other stuff. Like not having anyone except Henry to hang out with after school. But maybe that would change. Maybe she'd be heading to high school, not just with a friend but with one who was totally cool. That'd sure make people sit up and take pay attention. Maybe even Dexter would notice her.

Her uplifted spirits took a sudden dip. Would Kate still want to hang out with her once she realized Casey wasn't one of the cool kids? Better question. Was there even the remotest of chances Dex would notice Casey, or would he only pay attention to Kate?

CHAPTER FIVE

ON THE MORNING of the day school started, Jon was up before dawn. He pulled on running shorts and a T-shirt and, with a pair of socks in hand, padded downstairs to the kitchen in bare feet. He started a pot of coffee and checked that the bread maker was doing its thing, then sat on a kitchen stool and pulled on socks and laced his running shoes.

Princess strolled into the room, meowing loudly to announce her presence and to indicate it was time someone served her breakfast.

"Good morning, girl." He rubbed the top her head and she started to purr as she did a sideways sashay around his legs, back arched, tail in the air.

He retrieved a can of cat food from the fridge and scooped some into a bowl, dumped kibble into a matching bowl and returned the can to fridge. After he fulfilled his role, Princess promptly lost interest in him.

He poured himself a glass of water and

stood at the kitchen counter while he drank it. He would never tire of this view. The bay would soon reflect the sunlight, but in the faint light at this early hour, the surface was flat and dark gray. A lone sailboat slowly motored past the end of the breakwater, on its way to open water where the sailor would hoist the sail and catch a breeze.

After letting himself out the back door, he locked it and tucked the key in a pocket inside his waistband. He spent a few minutes warming up before he set off down the driveway at an easy jog. Early morning was his favorite time of the day. Even in the city he'd liked the quiet, cool stillness, but here it was magnified, exaggerated in the best way possible. At the end of the block he turned right and took the steep road that led downhill to the beach, where he picked up the walkway that paralleled the seawall. He nodded at another man jogging in the opposite direction, passed an elderly woman walking a small dog, but otherwise he had the beach and his thoughts to himself.

He ran past the quaint little downtown business district that stretched for six blocks along Shoreline Boulevard and three blocks away from the beach. There it gave way to a mix of old cottages, newer homes and low-rise condominiums. Over the years, residences had slowly crept up the hillside, biting chunks out of the rain forest, affording homeowners spectacular views of the bay and the breakwater. His house was one of those. Moving here felt right, as though he'd finally come home to a place where he belonged instead of being someplace biding his time. Convincing Kate that this was her home, too? That would take some doing.

For the past few days he had pretty much worked from morning till night, and now the furniture was in place, the boxes unpacked, the closets and cupboards full. Kate had hated her bedroom curtains so they'd driven down to Sechelt yesterday afternoon so she could choose new ones. She had asked if Casey could go with them, and he had agreed, although he'd also recalled what Kate had said about their new neighbor after the cookie delivery. *She's probably a geek.* Now he wasn't sure if she actually wanted to be friends with the soccer-playing tomboy next door or if she simply hadn't wanted to be seen alone with him in public. Either way, he was glad Casey had agreed to join them. She was a nice kid, and unlike some of Kate's friends in the city, she seemed as though she'd be a positive influence.

And there was no ignoring the fact that her mother was pretty nice, too. Easy to talk to. Very easy on the eyes. Her parenting skills were as enviable as her culinary skills were deplorable, and he had no idea why but he found that charming. Over the past few days, though, he'd only caught rare glimpses of her, and he suspected she might be avoiding him. He regretted his blunt comments the other night. He'd been comparing his parenting to Sarah's, his daughter to hers, and had fallen short on both counts. He hadn't meant to sound critical of Kate but he had, and Sarah probably thought he was a jerk. She was right, and he hoped she would accept an apology the next time he saw her.

At the end of the seawall he exchanged a wave with a young couple on the beach whose golden retriever was hauling a stick out of the water. He swung around to make the return trip, laughing as the pair narrowly avoided a shower of seawater as the dog shook out its fur.

Not only did Kate seem to get along with Casey, she liked Sarah, too. She had even hinted that if Jon thought he might like to start dating, then maybe he should think about asking Sarah out. The idea had already crossed his mind, not that he would admit that to his daughter, at least not yet. What if Sarah said no? He would still have to live next door to her and that would, at best, be awkward. Better to wait till he had some sense of what her answer would be.

And then Kate had dampened his enthusiasm by pointing out that it's not as if her mother were ever coming back. She was right. Georgette was never coming back and the truth was, he didn't want her to. But dating someone else? Until now he hadn't been ready to consider it. Kate needed to have one parent who was there for her, and for better or worse that parent was him. He couldn't focus on being a parent, and maintaining a home for them and reestablishing a career, if he was back in the dating game. There was also the not-so-insignificant matter of figuring out how and where to meet eligible women. But then, on their first day in Serenity Bay, there one was, standing on his porch with a welcoming smile and a plate of really awful cookies. That had immediately been followed by a pizza dinner. Sharing a couple of pizzas with their teenage daughters was not a date. It was simply…a simple dinner. And still he'd managed to mess it up.

During the drive down the peninsula to Sechelt, he had to admit he'd listened shamelessly and with interest to the questions Kate asked Casey.

Did she help her mom at the store?

No. Sometimes Casey went there after school and sat in her mom's office to do her homework, but working in the store was boring.

Did her father live in Serenity Bay?

No. He'd died. Jon already knew that.

Did her mom have a boyfriend?

No.

If Kate hadn't already dropped a less-than-subtle hint about him asking her out, he would have thought it a strange question. Casey didn't seem to think it was but she didn't elaborate and Kate didn't ask her to, so he couldn't very well ask her to expand.

He left the seawall walkway and tried to maintain his pace as he ran back up the hill, turning onto his street, winded, perspiring and ready to take on a new day just as the sun lit up the eastern sky above the Coast Mountains. He still had plenty of time for coffee and a shower before Kate would be up and getting ready for school. He slowed to a walk as he approached his driveway, and pulled up the hem of his shirt to wipe sweat from his forehead. As he let it drop, he glanced at the house next door and was sure he saw a curtain flutter in a second-floor window.

He spent a couple of minutes stretching muscles that hadn't had a decent workout in a couple of days. While he did, his thoughts remained on the woman next door.

Was she a morning person? Was she a runner as well? She was in great shape for someone who admitted to eating a lot of takeout. Maybe instead of asking her out to dinner, he should invite her to run with him in the morning. Running wasn't a date, and if she said no, she still might accept an invitation to dinner.

"And you are way overthinking this," he said, letting himself into the house, inhaling the aroma of newly brewed coffee and the cinnamon scent of whole-grain raisin bread. This weekend, he and his daughter had started a new life. Today he was starting a new job. The other firsts—whatever those might be—would happen in good time. And if a first date was going to be one of them, he had to apologize to Sarah for being a jerk and somehow convince her that he wasn't.

SARAH PARTED HER office curtains just enough to watch her neighbor return from his run but not so much that he could see her watching him. His dark-colored knee-length running shorts revealed the muscular calves of an athlete, exactly what one would expect of a high school gym teacher and soccer coach who ran for half an hour in the morning. She'd been downstairs and had caught sight of him as he left and headed down to the beach, and from her deck, coffee mug in hand, she had glimpsed him running along the seawall. Impressive.

Impressive also came to mind as she watched him now through the narrow slit in the curtains. His light blue T-shirt hung loose over the shorts, sweat-darkened in places that emphasized just how fit he really was. And then he pulled up the hem and swiped it across his forehead, briefly revealing strongly rippled abs. Her breath caught, her insides started to hum, then the shirt fell into place and he was gazing up at her window. She took a hasty step back, still a little breathless, still humming, the vision of those delectable abs etched in her memory.

"Mom?" Casey was awake.

Sarah jolted, realizing she'd been frozen in time, one hand pressed to her chest as though that might slow her heartbeat, stop her heart from pounding through her rib cage. The sound of her daughter's sleepy voice snapped her back to reality. She swung around, quickly turned on her desk lamp and picked up a file folder, fanning through the contents as though searching for something. She glanced up when her daughter appeared in the doorway in purple plaid flannel pajama pants and an old yellow sweatshirt.

"Good morning, sweetie. Excited about school starting today?"

"Yes, but kind of nervous, too. I mean, it's *high school*. And Henry isn't back so I'm kind of bummed about that. He and I always go together on the first day of school."

Henry, whose family lived across the street, and Casey had been friends forever and they did have a lot in common—straight-A honor students, academically competitive, seasoned bookworms. Outside the classroom, though, their interests couldn't be more different. Casey was athletic and crazy about animals. Henry was into photography and creative writing. He was also two inches shorter than Casey, and he was the only kid Sarah had ever met who could, and often did, trip over absolutely nothing.

Poor Henry. To say the kid was a klutz was an understatement. Sarah was also quite sure he'd had a crush on her daughter for the past year, and she was equally certain that the feeling was not mutual. If Casey was interested in a boy, it was a carefully kept secret. Henry had been away at photography school all summer and had gone straight from there to a family reunion in Montreal. According to Casey, he was missing the first few days of the school term and was due back on the weekend.

"What about Kate? I thought you were going with her."

"I am. They're giving me a ride, and I promised to show her around and introduce her to everyone."

"You're sure you don't want me to take you?"

"Mo-om. It's high school, not kindergarten."

Casey's horrified tone made her laugh. "You're right. Tell you what. We'll go out for burgers tonight and you can tell me all about your first day."

"Deal. What's for breakfast?"

"There's juice in the fridge and waffles in the freezer. Or we could scramble some eggs. Those would probably be better for you."

Casey scrunched her nose. "Waffles are good. Do you want some?"

"Sure. I'll be right down."

"Okay, I'll put enough in the toaster for you, too."

Sarah set the folder back on her desk and switched off the lamp, then peeked between the curtains again. There was no sign of Jonathan, so she flung the curtains wide, briefly admiring the early-morning sky, now deep blue and streaked with pink, before cinching the belt of her robe and returning to her bedroom to lay out clothes for work. Today's to-do list was long, and getting lost in thought about her buff new neighbor would only get in the way.

"Besides, it's your daughter who's heading off to high school this morning, not you." She was too old and certainly too jaded to let a man distract her from the things she needed to do to take care of herself and her daughter. Especially a man who wasn't doing a very good job of taking care of his.

"Hold that thought," she advised herself. *Hold. That. Thought.*

"WHAT'S FOR BREAKFAST?" Kate asked when she came downstairs and plunked an oversize leather satchel on the end of the kitchen counter.

"There's cinnamon-raisin bread on the island," he said. "It's still warm, and I left out the butter and honey. Fresh fruit salad in the fridge."

"The bread smells good," she said.

He wasn't used to compliments so early in the morning. Or at all, for that matter. Was she working up to asking for something? Or, he thought, eyeing her attire, maybe she hoped he'd be too flattered to notice what she was wearing. Her narrow-legged brown jeans ended well above her ankles and had front pockets that were closed with chunky metal zippers. Her silver-gray off-the-shoulder sweater revealed several straps that were attached to garments that were not intended for public viewing. On her feet, gray patent stilettos.

He resisted the urge to ask, "That's what you're wearing?"

This was why girls need mothers. Fathers knew nothing about fashion and they didn't have a clue how to talk to their daughters about what was appropriate for the first day at a new school.

While Kate applied a scant layer of butter and honey to a slice of bread, he took out the fruit salad and scooped some into a bowl for her. She slid onto a stool at the island and he set the bowl in front of her, resisting the urge to hitch her sweater up over her shoulders. Instead, he poured her a glass of milk.

"Is there any coffee left?" she asked.

Heaven help him. “You’re a little young to be drinking coffee.”

Judging by the eye roll, she didn’t think so. “Me and my friends drink coffee when we go to the mall.”

Of course you do. You did, he corrected himself. No mall here, and he hoped she would find better things to do with her time. Maybe her new friend next door would be a stabilizing influence. Casey was studious, athletic and, according to her mother, had a plan for the future. All the things he hoped for Kate.

As if on cue, there was a tap on the sliding glass doors and there was Casey, her wave as vigorous as her smile was wide. Jon gave her the sign that the door was unlatched, so she slid it open and immediately filled the kitchen with her energy.

“Wow,” she said. “It smells awesome in here.”

“My dad made raisin bread this morning.”

“What?” Casey’s wide-eyed response was amusing. “You baked it yourself?”

“I did. Help yourself.”

Casey slathered a slice with butter and honey and took a huge bite. “Mmm. This is good,” she mumbled around the mouthful.

Kate picked up hers and took a dainty nibble. "What did you have for breakfast?"

"Waffles." Casey's single-word answer was muffled by her second mouthful.

"Cool. Your mom made them?"

Casey swallowed and laughed. "No, my mom doesn't cook. We buy the frozen ones that go in the toaster."

Jon met Kate's gaze, and for one brief moment he detected what might have been gratitude. In addition to recently announcing she was a vegetarian, she had also declared the importance of going organic. Apparently she hadn't realized she'd been eating healthy food all along. Rather than let her appreciation go to his head, he changed the subject.

"Do you know which classes you're taking this semester?" he asked Casey.

"Science, social studies, math and English. What about you?" she asked Kate.

"Science, French, math and art."

"We'll have some classes together, then. And my friend Henry is taking art, so I'll bet he'll be in your class when he gets back from his holiday."

"He's into art?"

"He is. He's been away all summer, first for a month at the Emily Carr University in

Vancouver to study photography, and then he went to Montreal for a family reunion."

"He was at a university? How old is he?"

"Same age as us. They have a summer program for high school students. I think it's totally unfair that there's so much stuff for kids in the arts, you know, photography, art, music, dance. But do you ever hear about a summer veterinary program for teenagers? Never."

Jonathan turned off the coffeemaker and loaded the dishwasher as he listened with interest to their conversation. There wasn't even a slim chance that any of Kate's friends in the city would consider spending their summer vacation studying and learning something new. That would have seriously put a kink in their hanging-at-the-mall-drinking-coffee time. But here, already, she'd met one kid who aspired to do just that, and would soon meet another who already had. When it came to his daughter he was naturally leery of teenage boys, but he liked Henry already.

"Are you girls ready to leave?" he asked.

Kate slid off her stool and snagged her bag off the counter. Casey, who'd been leaning on the island next to her, straightened and hitched her backpack higher on her shoulders.

"Cool outfit," Casey said.

"Thanks. I did all my back-to-school shopping before we left the city." If she noticed that Casey's tan-colored T-shirt, jeans and high-top sneakers seemed more appropriate for the first day of school than something that had just stepped off the runway, she wasn't letting on.

Jon latched the sliding deck doors, grabbed his sports bag and followed the girls through the foyer where Princess, curled in a tight little ball, occupied a ray of morning sunshine streaming through the sidelight.

"Aw, your cat is so sweet," Casey said. "I still have my heart set on a dog, though." The girls grinned knowingly at each other, suggesting something was afoot. "Cats are great," she added. "But a dog would be more…" She paused, seemed to choose her words. "Lively."

Given Princess's penchant for catnapping, a sloth might be more energetic. And that's what made her so perfect for their household. She was demanding at mealtime, but otherwise she quietly prowled from a patch of sunshine here to a couch cushion there. She had an affection for laundry hampers, especially those filled with clean clothes, a fondness for high queen-of-the-castle places, and a weakness for windowsills from where she watched the outside world with thinly veiled disinterest. Ever since Georgette had moved out, his goal had been to create stability and routine with an absence of drama. In spite of her name, Princess was a perfect fit for them.

The girls were settling into the backseat of the SUV as he descended his front steps and saw Sarah walking down hers. In a slim navy skirt with a matching jacket over a soft pink shirt, she looked businesslike, professional and absolutely stunning. She unlocked her car, set her briefcase inside and came around to where he stood by his open car door.

"Good morning." She forced a smile.

"Good morning. You're getting an early start," he said, wishing he didn't sound so lame.

"I like to go in early whenever I can." She tipped her head, fluttered her fingers at the girls who were already fastening their seat belts in the backseat. "Have a good first day of high school. They grow up so fast, don't they?" she said to him, straightening. "Too fast."

"Mo-om."

Sarah laughed. "See you after school, sweetie."

"I've decided to get the soccer team together for a quick practice as soon as school is dismissed," he said. "I hope that's okay."

"That's not a problem. Casey's been looking forward to soccer season, and I'll be at the store until closing time. After that we're going out for burgers."

"Right." He thought of the dinner plans he'd made for himself and Kate, the fresh salmon that would go on the grill, the makings of a salad in their fridge, and contemplated extending an invitation to Sarah and her daughter. No, it was too soon. He had already offered to make pizzas on Saturday, and she had accepted. That would have to be soon enough. "Well, have a good day."

He slid behind the wheel and backed out of the driveway and onto the street. As he drove away, he glanced in the rearview mirror in time to see Sarah gracefully tuck those long, shapely legs into her car, and he knew it was an image that would stay with him all day.

CHAPTER SIX

TUESDAYS WERE SARAH'S catch-up days, the days she dusted and vacuumed the store, dealt with correspondence, shopped for office supplies, and took care of anything else that been added to her to-do list throughout the previous week. She switched on the computer in the office at the back of the store, and opened her calendar and scanned her task list.

This was always a slow day for business, particularly in the morning and especially now that tourist season was winding down and the back-to-school rush had ebbed to a trickle. This morning she would reorganize the storage room, including the corner that served as her office. And since today was Casey's first day back at school and she'd be having lunch in the cafeteria, Sarah was off the hook for having to come up with a meal at home. Instead, after Juliet started her shift at one o'clock, Sarah would dash across the street and grab something from the deli, and then she'd work right through the afternoon until it was time to go home. By then her Tuesday to-do list would be no more and she'd be ready to start Wednesday with a clean slate.

She'd been encouraged to see Casey leave for school with Kate and Jonathan that morning. Her daughter was the only girl she knew whose best friend was a boy, and until recently it hadn't concerned her. But one of these days, and Sarah suspected that day might be sooner rather than later, either Henry would fall for some other girl, or Casey would develop a romantic interest in another boy. Then what? Henry was a great kid but when the inevitable happened, Sarah secretly hoped her daughter wouldn't be the one left on the sidelines.

Sarah's cell phone trilled and she answered it as she opened her email program.

"Sarah, it's Juliet." A child wailed in the background and her efficient young shop assistant sounded uncharacteristically harried.

"Hi. Is everything okay?"

"No, yes, I mean, I hope so. Alexander was up and down all night, and now he's running a fever."

"Aw, the poor little guy. He sure doesn't sound happy." Sarah adored Juliet's three-year-old son, and Casey was his favorite babysitter. "Did you call the clinic?"

"As soon as they opened, but they can't squeeze us in until later this morning. Brian offered to stay home and help out, but we can't afford for him to take the day off."

Juliet's husband worked at the marina, doing odd jobs and helping with boat maintenance and repairs with the hope of becoming an apprentice mechanic. Between that and Juliet's part-time job here at the store, they struggled to make ends meet. Juliet's Tuesday shift normally started after lunch and her mother looked after her son for the afternoon. But in Sarah's book, family came first, always. And yes, she kept a careful eye on finances, but she didn't scrimp on payroll. Juliet was worth her weight in gold, and her next paycheck wouldn't be short the few hours she would miss today.

"I don't want you to worry about a thing. Take that darling boy of yours to the doctor, and then let's hope he has a nice long nap this afternoon so you can get some rest, too. I can manage on my own."

"What about your lunch break?"

"I'll call the deli and order something. If they can't deliver, I'll lock up for a few minutes and run across the street to pick it up."

"But what if—"

There was more crying, followed by a muffled, "Mommy, my froat hurts."

"No more buts," Sarah said. "You need to stay home and take care of your son. Give him a hug for me, okay? Everything will be fine here. Call me after you've seen the doctor and let me know how he's feeling."

"Okay. Thanks, Sarah. I really appreciate your being so understanding."

"I'm a mom, too, remember? Been there, done that. Many times."

She said goodbye, thinking how lucky Juliet was, in spite of having a sick kid. When Casey was little, Sarah's mother lived two ferry rides and a four-hour drive away, and even before her husband's accident, he hadn't been any help in the child care department. Juliet and Brian were a cute couple, crazy about each other, doting parents. Sarah considered herself lucky to have them and their young son in her and Casey's lives.

Not that your life is lacking, she reminded herself. She slipped off her suit jacket and hung it on the back of her desk chair, squaring the shoulders neatly as she consulted her list. After spending Saturday evening with her new neighbors, the push-pull of her annoyance with and unexpected attraction to Jonathan had left her feeling that maybe, just maybe, her life wasn't as full as she believed. After her guests left that night, she assured herself the feeling would be fleeting. Now, Tuesday morning, she was dismayed to discover it wasn't.

Years ago she had publicly grieved the loss of her husband, even though he'd all but become a stranger, but even before that she had privately mourned the loss of a marriage that had never lived up to its promise. "To love, honor and cherish" hadn't lasted much longer than the honeymoon. Then it was only the "till death do we part" part that made any real sense. And she had known then that marriage wasn't all it was cracked up to be. It might work for other people, but it didn't work for her. What she'd had while she was married wasn't a life. What she had now, what she and Casey had, the security, the serenity, those were the things that mattered. No way would she jeopardize them, not for anything.

Sure, Jonathan Marshall was easy on the eyes. It had been hard not to fixate on those abs until she'd seen him leaving for school that morning, dressed in casual khaki pants, a navy short-sleeved polo shirt and dark blue cross-trainers. His height gave him an air of authority and his shoulders looked athletic, and she knew, based on what she'd seen earlier that morning, that he was even fitter than he looked. But she didn't do casual, and if she was any judge of character, he wasn't in a place to do commitment. What he did do was struggle with parenting, and he had a ton of baggage when it came to his ex-wife, both of which excluded him as relationship material.

She shouldn't be thinking along those lines anyway. She certainly didn't want to be. He would be a good neighbor, possibly a good friend once they became better acquainted, and she hoped he'd be a good teacher. For now, for herself and for Casey, those things were important. Letting herself fall into the trap of believing a committed relationship was the way to go? No way. As she'd just said to Juliet, been there, done that.

Being busy was the only way she knew to dispel these unwelcome ponderings, and if she hoped to get through today's list on her own, she needed to get started. She dragged the vacuum cleaner out of the storage room, plugged it in and spent ten minutes working her way from one side of the store to the other. Once that was done, she unlocked the front door and hauled the folding sign onto the sidewalk so passersby would know she was open for business.

For the next hour she sorted through a

week's worth of accumulated clutter in the drawers of the sales counter, refolded and stacked cashmere sweaters on a table near the entrance, and straightened and untangled a rack of belts. With the store neat and tidy, she turned her attention to the two window displays. She usually redid them every other Tuesday, and today she had planned to swap out the back-to-school displays for some activewear in new fall colors. Should she tackle this while she was here on her own or wait till Juliet was back to help with customers?

Probably best to wait. Then again, she hated having her weekly work plan thrown off schedule.

Do the displays. If she couldn't finish by the time she closed up shop, she would call Casey and ask her to come to the store after school. No, make that after soccer practice, she corrected herself, because Jonathan wanted to get the team together this afternoon for their first practice. To his credit, the man didn't waste time. Casey could work on homework, if she had any, and they could go for burgers after Sarah finished the windows.

By eleven o'clock she had the mannequins stripped down and the back-to-school clothing put away, and had just started to select items for the new display when the back-door buzzer sounded. A delivery?

"What could it be?" She did a mental inventory of recent orders and couldn't think of anything likely to arrive this week. She unlatched the back door and swung it open.

"Hi, Tom. What do you have for me?"

"A shipment of…" He gave the waybill a quick once-over. "I have no idea."

She spotted the logo on the large cardboard carton. "Oooh, the DKNY handbags," she said as she signed for it. "This order was delayed and I wasn't expecting it for a couple of weeks."

He feigned interest with a nod and a smile, separated her copy from the rest of the paperwork, and handed it to her. "Can I bring this inside for you?"

"That would be great." She stepped aside and held the door so he could wheel the large box on the dolly into her storage room.

"There you go."

"Thanks, Tom. How is your dad doing?" Tom's mother had recently passed away after battling breast cancer. Three weeks later his father suffered a minor stroke, so the elderly man had moved in with Tom and his wife, Angela.

"Better. It was a big adjustment, but he's

settling in. Eating better, too, now that he doesn't have to cook for himself."

"I'll bet he loves Angela's cooking. Everyone does."

Tom's wife worked at the deli across the street, and her daily soups and stews were a Serenity Bay staple for many townsfolk.

Tom beamed as he hitched the waistband of his pants and patted his belly. "Best cook in the world, that gal of mine. In fact I'm going to swing by the deli right now, seeing as how I'm already in the neighborhood, and grab a coffee and one of her cinnamon buns for the road."

"Good plan." Tom's arteries would probably thank him if he skipped the pastry, but the man loved to eat as much as his wife loved to cook. "Tell Angela I'll see her at lunchtime."

"Will do."

After he left, she flipped the dead bolt on the back door, took a knife from her desk drawer and slit the tape on the box. Every shipment felt a little like Christmas, but handbags were her favorite. She had unpacked and inventoried half the order when the fluorescent light above the cash desk started to flicker.

"Seriously?" It was almost lunchtime and so far this day had yet to go as planned.

BY LUNCHTIME, CASEY had decided she loved everything about high school. So far they'd been assigned to homerooms, and both Kate and Henry were in hers. After getting their timetables and a rundown of the student handbook, the Grade Nines had been given a tour of the school and wrapped up the morning with an assembly in the gym. This afternoon they would attend each of their classes for an abbreviated session to meet their teachers and pick up textbooks and course outlines. Everything felt fresh and new and very grown-up.

Now she was making her way to the cafeteria with Kate and Alycia, a girl from the soccer team. The three girls hit it off right away, which was a good thing because in homeroom Alycia had whispered that over the summer she'd started hanging out with Brody, and Brody's best friend was Dexter.

The packed cafeteria was abuzz with first-day-of-class excitement by the time they arrived, but they managed to nab an empty table for six. Casey took a corner seat, Alycia sat next to her, and Kate took a chair across the table.

"So, Kate," Alycia said. "Do you think SBH is as good as your school in the city?"

Kate shrugged, lifting the top layer of her sandwich to examine the filling. "It's okay.

I didn't see my dad, not even once, so that's a good thing."

"That'd be weird, all right," Alycia said. "I'm glad my parents aren't teachers."

Casey didn't think having her mom around would be the end of the world, but she kept that to herself.

Alycia jumped up abruptly and waved an arm in the air. "Brody! Over here. I told him I'd save seats for them," she said after she sat down again.

Them? Casey scanned the room and felt her heart soar and then sink. Dexter was with Brody and the two boys were heading for their table. Brody plunked down next to Alycia and Dexter sat across the table beside Kate.

Alycia took on the introductions, which was just as well because Casey was suddenly tongue-tied.

"You guys both know Casey. This is Kate. She just moved up here from West Van. This is Brody. We're..." She giggled. "We're sort of going out. And this is his friend Dexter."

Dex nodded at Casey. "Hey."

"Hey."

She should say something else, but what? *Ask him how his summer was.*

But he had already turned to Kate. "Good to meet you. When did you get here?"

"A couple of days ago." She was smiling at him, just as Anne Hathaway had smiled at that boy in *The Princess Diaries*, and Casey's heart settled in the pit of her stomach.

"Cool." Dex leaned back in his chair and unwrapped his sandwich while he gave Kate a head-to-stiletto once-over.

Rats. She'd known this would happen.

But then his gaze swung back to her. "I haven't seen Henry around. Do you know if he's back yet?"

"Oh. Um, no, he's still in Montreal. He'll be back on Friday."

"Cool. We'll have to hang out after he gets home."

We? What did that mean? Just the guys? The girls, too? Did Dex assume that because she and Henry were friends, the two of them were going out? That he and Kate would make another twosome?

She didn't know how to ask without sounding lame, and then the conversation meandered in other directions as they compared timetables and talked about class assignments, about which teachers were cool and which were not so much. She'd like to share her excitement about the science classroom, but they'd think she was a total geek to be so enthusiastic about the lab benches and stools instead of desks, the hookups for Bunsen burners, the shelf of microscopes under plastic covers. She would tell her mom about them tonight.

For now she couldn't think of a single thing to say, so she sat and listened to Alycia's stories about her and Brody's summer exploits, watched Kate chatting easily with Dex. To her surprise, Dex seemed to be the only one who noticed she was there, glancing at her from time to time, giving her a weird little smile.

Did she have something stuck in her teeth? Ink on her face? Gunk in the corner of her eye? Ugh. She finished her sandwich and was ready to excuse herself when he gave her his full attention.

"What'd you do this summer, Casey?"

"Oh, um, not much." She'd looked up the novels they'd be reading in Grade Nine English and borrowed them from the library. Found out what the science curriculum covered and read everything she could get her hands on. She was so *not* confessing that to anyone.

"Casey's been working at the animal shelter this summer," Kate said.

Don't tell him that! Casey shot her a warning look. But Dex leaned on the table, looking at her with genuine interest.

"Wow. That sounds pretty interesting. Did you get paid?"

"Oh, no. I'm just a volunteer. I'll still be helping out on Saturdays now that school's started."

"Cool. I've always liked being around animals. If they need more volunteers, could you let me know?"

"Oh. Sure." Was he serious or making fun of her? She had no idea, and before she could figure it out the warning bell sounded, giving everyone five minutes to get to their first class of the afternoon.

"See you at soccer practice," Alycia said to her before strolling off with Brody. Kate and Dex were in the same French class, so they were going in search of their classroom, leaving Casey on her own to find her English class.

Kate slung her designer bag over her shoulder and whispered in Casey's ear on their way out of the cafeteria. "He's very cute, don't you think?"

Yes, as a matter of fact she did! But she only smiled and gave a casual nod in response. Only three more days, she reminded herself. Henry would be home and life would get back to normal. Unless he decided to go gaga over Kate, too, leaving Casey the odd one out. No way, she decided. She'd rather be alone in the library than be the fifth wheel with her friends.

SARAH HAULED A replacement fluorescent tube and the stepladder out of the storage room, snagging her pantyhose and gashing her calf in the process.

"Ow! Seriously?" She surveyed the damage. "*Seriously*!"

After she stanched the bleeding, changed the lighting tube and put the ladder away, she dug out the spare pair of hose she kept in her desk drawer. She was wriggling into those when the door chime sounded. A customer.

She smoothed her hair, straightened her skirt and put a smile on her face before she returned to the front of the store, in time to greet three silver-haired women she'd never seen before.

"Good morn—" She checked her watch. One o'clock? How had that happened? "Make that good afternoon. Can I help you find something or would you like to browse for a bit?"

"We're only in town for a couple of hours," one of the women said. She was wearing an expensive-looking tan leather jacket over tailored black slacks and had a Kate Spade bag on her arm.

"We're on a bus tour from West Vancouver," another added. "We spotted this place from the restaurant across the street and thought we'd check it out." This woman wore a cream-colored blazer and sweater of the same color with navy pants. Her only accessories were the Coach handbag hung from her shoulder and the strand of pearls looped around her neck.

"Welcome to Serenity Bay," Sarah said. "And thank you for stopping by To the Nines. If you see anything you like, feel free to try it on, and please let me know if you have any questions."

The third shopper was already skimming the rack of fall dresses that Juliet had unpacked on Saturday. Sarah had recently seen this woman's wide-lapelled tweed jacket in a magazine. Chanel.

"Margaret," the woman said, holding up a Marc Jacobs dress. "You have to look at this teal-blue dress. Didn't you say this is one of your granddaughter's wedding colors? You always look stunning in it and the style is perfect for the grandmother of the bride."

The woman in the leather jacket rushed to

take a look. “You’re right, Jasmine. It’s gorgeous! Lindy, what do you think?”

The three conferred on the dress and agreed Margaret must try it on. Sarah was settling the woman and the dress in a fitting room when the door chime sounded again. Four more women strolled in and waved to Jasmine and Lindy, each of whom already had several garments slung over an arm.

Sarah greeted the newcomers and offered to start a fitting room for the other two while they browsed. So much for a quiet Tuesday afternoon, she thought, hoping Juliet’s little guy would be well enough to stay with his grandma so his mom could come to work.

But an hour later, after ringing up purchases for all the tour bus customers, including the teal-blue grandmother-of-the-bride dress, and thanking them for shopping at To the Nines, there was still no sign of Juliet. Sarah slipped into her office, took several thirst-quenching gulps from her water bottle, and checked her phone. She had a text message from Casey, reminding her about soccer practice after school, and a voice message from Juliet. Alexander had an ear infection and was still running a fever and she needed to stay home with him. Sarah texted her back, assuring the young woman that she needed to stay home until her son was feeling better, and that everything at the store was under control. If there was one thing she was used to doing, it was managing on her own.

JON BLEW THE whistle for the kickoff and watched two team members rush for the ball. He'd called this a practice but he really just wanted to meet the girls and check out their skill level so he could start assigning positions. A number of them had been playing for several years and demonstrated a lot of potential. Several were new to the game but already showed promise, and several more would need a little extra coaching.

This was the part of the job he loved best. He didn't believe in tryouts at this level. As far as he was concerned, a willingness to play was the only prerequisite for being on the team. Rather than leave weaker players sidelined, though, he encouraged the more experienced players to work with the newer ones, and share their knowledge and love of the game. It was the best way to promote a positive team spirit, and invariably each girl was a better, stronger player for it.

He'd started coaching girls' teams when Kate was little, always with the thought that someday she would play, too. That day had never come, and he knew now it never would, but that was okay. He wasn't one of those parents who forced kids into activities they didn't want to do, and he had always encouraged Kate to explore as many new things as she liked. Recently that had dwindled to two main interests—drawing and photography. She excelled at both and he was proud of her for that, but he sure wished she would devote the same passion to academics. Last year he'd had to hire a tutor to get her through the year. The divorce plus having her mother leave the country had hit her hard, that was a given. Now he hoped the change of scene and some new friends, especially kids like Casey, would influence her in a way that he hadn't been able to.

Speaking of Casey, he watched her streak down the field with the ball, which sailed into the net in spite of the goaltender's aerodynamic attempt to make a save. She swung around, grinning widely, blond ponytail flying, fist pumping the air. He blew the whistle and jotted "forward" next to her name on the team roster on his clipboard. Then he waved them all into a huddle in center field.

"Great job today, everyone. I'll post the lineup outside the girls' locker room tomorrow afternoon. Our next practice will be after school on Thursday."

"Is that when we find out if we made the team?" a girl by the name of Melissa Merriweather asked.

"Everyone's already made the team." That announcement generated a loud cheer and a round of high fives. "On Thursday we'll also vote for a team captain and an assistant captain, so between now and then I'd like you to think about who you'd like to nominate."

"When's our first game?" a girl named Alycia asked.

"The schedule hasn't been finalized yet, but it won't be for a couple of weeks. That gives us lots of time to practice, work on some plays, build some confidence. Any other questions?"

There weren't.

"Then I'll see all of you on Thursday."

Some of the girls set off toward the school gym at a leisurely pace; others ran ahead, Casey in the lead. The girl was an incredible athlete. After Saturday night pizza, Sarah had talked about her daughter's career aspirations, which were impressive for a kid her age. He had no idea what their financial situation might look like, but he would make a point of mentioning to Sarah that she and her daughter should keep athletic scholarships in mind. If the girl could get her undergraduate degree funded and still planned to pursue higher education, she'd be set.

He flipped through his notes as he followed his team back into the school. It had been a good first practice and he looked forward to working with these kids this year. In his office, he sat and put his feet up on the desk, crossed them at the ankles and wove his fingers together at the back of his head. His first day at Serenity Bay High had exceeded his expectations. It was a good school, the kids he'd met so far were great, and from the few glimpses he'd caught of Kate throughout the day, he'd been encouraged to see her talking with other students, mostly Casey and several others.

With any luck she'd be willing to have a conversation about it over dinner tonight, the kind where she would talk without him having to feel as though he was conducting an interrogation. There had to be a first time for everything, right? Of course there was.

SARAH SAT AND EASED tired feet out of shoes that had stopped feeling comfortable several hours ago. What a day. It had flown by, but her to-do list was still almost as long as it had been that morning. Half of the new handbags still had to be unpacked and entered into the computer inventory, and the window display was still in total disarray.

"On the plus side," she reminded herself, "you've made record sales for a Tuesday, and that is always a good thing."

She sipped some more water and was debating whether or not to force her feet back into the shoes when the doorbell jangled.

"And here we go again." With shoes on her feet and a smile on her face, she returned to the front of the store. Jonathan's daughter stood there, looking both hesitant and curious.

"Kate. Hi."

"Hi, Sarah. I hope it's okay I'm here. My dad and Casey are at soccer practice or something, and you said it was okay for me to drop by."

"Of course it's okay. You're welcome anytime. Casey sent a text to remind me about the practice this afternoon."

"It seemed like a good time to check out your store." Kate took a careful look around, then seemed to zero in on the window display Sarah had dismantled that morning.

"Sorry about the mess," she said. "My assistant had to stay home because her little boy is sick. I've been here on my own all day and it's been super busy, so I haven't had time to redo the display."

"Oh." Kate's gaze lingered on the undressed mannequins, as though she had something to say.

"How was your first day at Serenity Bay High?" Sarah asked.

"It was good. Casey and I have two classes together, and she introduced me to some of her friends."

"That's good. I'll bet it's a lot different from the high school you would have attended in the city." Reminding her about the school and friends she hadn't wanted to leave behind was the wrong thing to say. What was she thinking? "I mean, I hope it's different in a good way."

Kate shrugged. "School's school."

Sarah recalled something else Jonathan had said on Saturday night after the girls had gone upstairs.

She's going through a...I don't know...a phase? At least I hope it's a phase.

He might be right, but Sarah suspected he had a tendency to overreact to his daughter's attitude, and Kate knew exactly what she needed to do to push his buttons. So instead of reacting to the girl's dismissive comment, Sarah changed the subject.

"I still have lot to do before I leave this afternoon. A shipment of handbags came in today and I haven't finished unpacking them yet, and then I still have to do the window displays. Why don't you take a look around? The younger styles are on this side of the store," she said with a wave. "Accessories—belts, scarves, handbags—are here in the center and the more mature styles are on the opposite side." Old-lady clothes, as Casey referred to them.

"I don't think I've ever seen a store that caters to both," Kate said.

"Small towns generally don't offer a lot of shopping options, so I decided it made good business sense to provide them." And she was glad she'd gone with her instincts, because it had paid off in spades.

Kate briefly surveyed the racks, but then her gaze strayed back to the mannequins. "Can I help with the window? I mean, I've always wanted to do one."

"Oh. Really?" It seemed odd that a fourteen-year-old would rather work than shop. Casey had mentioned that their new neighbor wanted to work in the fashion industry, and the girl definitely had a sense of style. Her off-the-shoulder sweater, skinny jeans and heels created a eye-popping combo. Not exactly typical for the average SBH student, but the clothes suited her to a tee and she wore them with quiet confidence and enough flair to make people notice. And probably turn the heads of every boy at school, she thought, including the seniors. Maybe her father had good reason to worry.

"You are welcome to tackle the window, but are you sure you wouldn't rather look around? You can feel free to try things on, if you'd like."

"I'd rather do the windows. And if you hate them, I'll put everything back."

Sarah laughed. "You go right ahead. And you have great taste, so don't worry about whether or not I'm going to like them. I'm sure they'll be great."

Enthusiasm brightened Kate's eyes. She swung her bag off her shoulder and glanced around as if looking for place to put it.

"You can put your bag in my office," she said. "But before you do, you need to let your dad know where you are and what you're doing, okay? I don't want him to worry."

Her eyes dimmed, but she took out her phone and tapped out a text message on her way into Sarah's office. She returned, still looking at the screen, nodding. "He says it's fine."

"All right then, let's get to work. I'll bring my laptop and the new inventory out here so I can work at the sales counter in case you want to ask questions."

They both went to work, Sarah keeping an eye on the girl, amazed by the transformation. Kate moved purposefully from rack to rack, choosing items, holding them up together, changing her mind, returning a scarf, sweater or jacket to a shelf or rack, selecting something else. Her focus was intense and her choices were bang on. When she was finished, one window had a youthful, spirited feel to it. The other was as chic and understated as any of Sarah's more mature patrons. Somehow Kate had picked up on exactly who her customers were, even though no one had come into the store while she dressed the mannequins and staged the windows.

Sarah shut down her laptop, put the last of the handbags on the display rack, and joined Kate at the windows "Great job. This looks incredible."

For the first time since she'd met the girl, she saw what she felt was a genuine smile. "You really think so? Thanks!"

"Let's take a look from the sidewalk."

In front of the store, Kate pulled her phone from her jeans pocket and snapped a couple of photos.

"Does your store have a Facebook page?" she asked.

"No, I've never taken the time to set one up." And never saw the point to having one.

"I can make one for you. Is it okay if I take some pictures inside the store?" Kate asked as they went back inside.

"Of course. Photograph anything you like."

For the next few minutes, Kate wandered around the store, eyeing displays, angling her phone this way and that. Then she must've checked the time.

"Omigosh, I seriously have to go. I need to be home before my dad gets there. I, um, told him when I texted him that I'd be home before he was. So he'll…he might worry if he gets there before I do."

"I'll be closing the store in half an hour," Sarah said. "If you want to wait, send your dad another message to let him know when you'll be home. You can get a ride with me."

"Oh. Thanks, but that's okay. I'll walk."

Sarah was tempted to say half an hour shouldn't make a difference, especially since walking uphill in those shoes wasn't going to be easy. *Not your place*, she reminded herself. Kate was now as anxious to get home as she'd been to help with the shop windows, and that parent-child relationship was none of her business. There was something she could do, though.

"You've done a wonderful job and your help means I won't have to stay late tonight. How would you like to pick out one of these new handbags?"

"You mean I can take one? Like, for free?"

"Yes, you're welcome to take one, and no, it's not free. You've already earned it."

Wide-eyed, Kate surveyed the new inventory. "I really like this one." She ran a hand over a large black-and-white DKNY logo tote.

"Then it's yours."

"Oh, wow!" Kate surprised her with a hug. "Thank you so much. I'll get my bag out of your office and then I'd better get going."

Poor kid, Sarah thought, as she watched the girl leave the store, her own bag slung over her shoulder and her new one tucked inside a To the Nines shopping bag. There was a big hole in that girl's life, and it seemed to her it was a gap only a mom could fill. Not that Sarah could replace Kate's own larger-than-life mother, but she could be there for her with a female perspective and an understanding shoulder to lean on from time to time. And since Jonathan had all but admitted to being overwhelmed, he would probably be okay with that.

She turned her attention back to the task of closing up the store for another day. Although it had started as something of a disaster, it had turned into a good day after all, and now it was almost time for some real mother-daughter time.

CHAPTER SEVEN

ON THE WAY home from school, Jon swung by the grocery store to pick up a few things for dinner. He'd had a very good day and he hoped Kate had, too, so he decided to celebrate with one of her favorite meals.

He wheeled a shopping cart through the produce section and selected fresh tomatoes, parsley, basil. He knew there was garlic in the pantry, but onions? Better buy a few in case they were out, and the makings for a salad, too. He moved on to another aisle and chose a package of whole wheat penne, a nod to Kate's current healthy eating kick.

"Jonathan? Hi." That was a familiar voice.

"Sarah, hi." Her silky pink shirt, almost an exact match to the blush on her cheeks, and the slim navy skirt were as runway perfect as they'd been that morning. She'd shed the jacket, though, and a small cream handbag dangled from her shoulder on a gold chain.

"How was your first day?"

"Good. It was good. I think it's a great school."

"It is, isn't it? How was soccer practice?"

"It went very well. There are some excellent players on the team, and your daughter is one of them."

She smiled as only a mom could. "I'm very proud of her."

"Are you picking up things for dinner?" he asked, changing the subject before it segued from her daughter to his. He wanted to talk to Kate and hear firsthand about her day before he had to answer questions about her or discuss how she was settling in.

"We're going out for burgers tonight, but I needed a few things for breakfast this week."

He glanced into the basket she had on her arm. Frozen waffles and a box of breakfast cereal that promised very few calories while delivering a boatload of vitamins and minerals. A quart of skim milk.

"What are you making?" she asked. "Whatever it is, it looks healthy."

"Spaghetti with marinara sauce, salad, garlic bread. It's one of Kate's favorites."

"I can see why. It sounds delicious."

She was a great mom who had an enviable relationship with her teenager but didn't know how to cook. Give him a handful of ingredients and he could whip up a meal, but he couldn't figure out how to connect with his daughter. The irony didn't escape him, but he had a feeling it was going to haunt him, especially given Sarah's cool demeanor. Since this wasn't the place to launch into an apology, he decided to use the marinara sauce as way to open the door. He would make extra, and after dinner he would run a container of it next door. Would she think he was being pushy? Desperate? He hoped not.

Sarah's phone went off and she pulled it out of her handbag and read the screen. "We're out of microwave popcorn so I need to pick that up. Good to see you, and I'm glad everything went well today."

"Thanks." He watched her walk briskly down the aisle. At the far end, she stopped to chat with someone. He realized he was still staring at her legs and pulled himself back to the task at hand. Dinner. He surveyed the contents of his cart and set off for the dairy and bakery sections for Parmesan and French bread. He liked to start from scratch whenever he could, but there was no time to bake bread. A whole loaf would make a lot of garlic bread, so he'd wrap up some of that and take it over to Sarah's with the sauce.

Seriously? You need to get a life and stop worrying about feeding the family next door.

Twenty minutes later he had made it through the checkout and driven home and was in the kitchen unpacking the groceries. Back in the city, the rush-hour commute alone would have taken way more time than that.

Kate wandered downstairs and into the kitchen.

"Hey," he said. "How was your day?"

"Fine."

He grabbed a bottle of sparkling water from the fridge, took out a pair of tumblers and filled them, adding a lime wedge to each.

"Here you go." He leaned across the island and set hers in front of a stool, a silent invitation for her to join him. To his surprise, she accepted.

He set out a cutting board and knife and went to work on the vegetables for the sauce.

"I hope your classes went well," he said, deciding it best to avoid questions if possible.

"Yeah, they're okay. Mr. Balcarres, my art teacher, is really awesome. Our first project's going to be a mixed media collage. I've already started sketching out my ideas for that."

Huh. More words in one stretch than he sometimes heard in a whole day.

"Good for you. I'll look forward to seeing that when it's done."

"He said everyone's piece will be on display because he's set up an exhibit wall near the main office. All through the term he'll be choosing everyone's best pieces for a show at the art gallery. Isn't that cool?"

"That's very cool." He'd met Emile Balcarres in the staff room at lunchtime and immediately liked the man's calm and thoughtful demeanor. Now that it sounded as though he was the kind of teacher who went the extra mile for his students, Jon liked him even more.

He pulled a couple of saucepans from the pot drawer next to the stove, set one on an element and poured in a generous glug of olive oil to start the sauce, then filled the other with water for the pasta.

Kate sipped water and checked her phone for messages. "Have you heard from Mom today?"

"No, I haven't. I know she's been really busy, but she knows this is your first day at a new school. I'm sure she'll call." If she didn't, he'd send a discreet message to remind her.

"Whatever." Kate set her phone down and picked up her water. Better to focus on the positive, he decided.

"Did you meet Casey's friends today?"

"Some of them. Her best friend who lives across the street will be back on Friday."

"Right. She mentioned that when we were on our way to school this morning." He tossed chopped onions into the pan and stirred till they were coated with hot oil. While those softened, he minced the garlic and measured oregano into the pan, then added a pinch of hot pepper flakes.

"Mmm. That smells good," Kate said.

"Thanks. I thought it'd be good to celebrate with one of our favorite meals."

"My all-time favorite."

He didn't know what had changed, but whatever it was, he was glad for it. He opened a can of tomatoes, dumped it into the pan, added the fresh tomatoes he'd chopped because he liked the texture they added to the sauce and gave the whole thing a good stir.

"I'll let that simmer for a bit before I cook the pasta." Meanwhile, he'd start on the garlic bread.

"Soccer practice went well," he said, hoping to keep the conversation going but shift the topic away from her for a bit. "Lots of great players."

"I'll bet Casey's pretty good. She told me she's been playing for three years."

"She is." And her experience showed. He hoped the rest of the team would give her the nod as captain, or at least assistant captain, but he couldn't reveal that to Kate.

"We had lunch with Alycia. She's on the team, too."

Right. Another good player, if memory served. He unwrapped the French bread and set it on a cutting board. "What did you do after school?"

"Oh." A guarded look flickered across her face and was gone again a split second later. "Not much. Nothing, really. I walked home and then I worked on some ideas for my collage."

"Good for you. You know, if you want to stay at school on the afternoons the team has practice, you could work in the library and then we could drive home together."

"I'll see. I don't mind walking, though."

"Sure." Since these kinds of conversations were few and far between, he resisted the impulse to remind her that wherever she was after school, she needed to spend time on her other homework, too. He'd save that confrontation for another day. Besides, she was likely to change her mind about walking when the still-mild weather turned to rain.

He sliced the bread into two lengthwise

halves and set them on a baking sheet. In a small bowl he whipped a stick of butter, added minced garlic and chopped parsley, and slathered the mixture onto the bread. After generously sprinkling both halves with freshly grated Parmesan, he moved the sheet to the counter next to the stove.

"On my way home, I ran into Sarah at the grocery store."

Kate raised her gaze from scanning the phone screen, momentarily wary. "You saw Sarah?"

"I did."

"Did she say anything?"

"Just that she and Casey are going out for hamburgers tonight, and we chatted a bit about school."

"Ah."

"They seem to eat out a lot, or fix fast food at home, so I thought I'd run over later with some leftover sauce and garlic bread. Sort of a thank-you for the cookies, and for having us over for pizza on Saturday night."

"I can take them over," Kate said. "I didn't see Casey after school and I wanted to ask her some stuff about the…um…about our science class." Abruptly, she slid off the stool. "I'll just run upstairs and take a look at my notes."

He stared after her as she raced out of

the room. What on earth was that about? He loved his daughter more than life itself, but that wasn't enough to skew his perception of what was real and what was, well, not. And on the first day of school, he knew with absolute certainty that science would be the last thing on Kate's mind. If he had to guess, whatever it was that she so desperately needed to discuss with Casey had nothing to do with schoolwork. More likely it had something to do with the kids she'd met today, maybe even a boy.

Right now, it didn't matter. He was so happy about having a pleasant conservation with her, and so relieved that she seemed to be making friends, he'd let her deliver the sauce and garlic bread and find another excuse, make that an opportunity to talk to Sarah. She was right next door, after all. That should provide plenty of chances to see her, whether by design or otherwise.

BY THE END OF THE WEEK, Jon had not had plenty of opportunities to run into Sarah. He hadn't had any, unless he counted fleeting glimpses of her leaving for work in the morning or returning home at the end of the day. And it wasn't as if the glimpses were the result of spying on her. They weren't. But he had been hoping for a face-to-face encounter that looked as though it happened by chance, like the way she'd shown up at the Paolo's after he went in to pick up pizza, and the way she'd bumped into him at the supermarket. Apparently the only way those things happened by accident was if they really were an accident.

Otherwise he'd had a good week. Classes and soccer practice had gone well. He had finished unpacking and hauled all the flattened cardboard cartons to the recycling depot. Best of all, though, had been his dinner conversations with Kate. Georgette had called several times and while Kate said very little about those chats with her mother, he had the impression they weren't terribly satisfying. His ex had a tendency to talk about her life rather than delve into anyone else's, even her daughter's, but that no longer felt like his problem. For the first time since the divorce he felt as though his relationship with Kate was on a solid footing, and he hoped to keep it that way.

This afternoon she had stayed after school with Casey to help set up for Club Day on Monday, an event that would feature all of the school's extracurricular activities and give them an opportunity to solicit new members. He had offered to wait and drive the girls home when they were finished, but she had insisted they could walk. Now that she seemed willing to take on some responsibility, she was proving herself worthy of a little independence.

He went into the kitchen, poured himself a cup of coffee and carried it out onto the deck. That morning he'd gone for a run in the dense fog that had blanketed the bay. He'd liked the stillness, the silence intermittently broken by the foghorn from the lighthouse on an island off Shelter Point. By mid-morning the fog had lifted, and now bands of high clouds streaked the sky. The temperature warmed and cooled as clouds periodically obscured the sun, and the breeze off the bay hinted that fall wasn't far away.

Sarah's deck was unoccupied. She would still be at her store, and she didn't seem to spend a lot of time out there anyway. If he had to guess, he'd say she was a bit of a workaholic, although in spite of that she made time for her daughter. Come to think of it, the girls should be here soon, although it would be a while before Sarah came home.

He debated running to the grocery store later on to pick up things for dinner—if he timed it right, he might even run into her there—but this was one of those rare days when he wasn't inspired to cook. Maybe he and Kate would go out for a meal instead. Besides, the invitation for Sarah and Casey to come over for homemade pizza tomorrow night still stood. The girls could occupy themselves after dinner, and that would give him and Sarah a chance to talk. He was still on the deck, empty coffee mug on the rail in front of him, when he heard Kate come in. He went inside in time to see her toss her bag on the island.

"Hi, Dad."

He placed his mug in the dishwasher. "Hey, how was your afternoon? Everything all set for Monday?"

"Yeah, it's all good. We set up tables in the main hallway and helped hang up posters. It was fun, and I found out there's a photography club. Mr. Balcarres is the sponsor so I'm definitely going to join that."

"That's a great idea." In truth, he couldn't be happier. After the first week of school, she was fitting in, had made friends, was getting involved. And as always, she looked a little like a photograph herself. In white jeans, short black boots, a long silver-and-white print top and a cropped black jacket, she could have stepped off the cover of a fashion magazine.

Even her oversize purse was a perfect match for the rest of the outfit. He took a closer look at it and registered the DKNY logo. Kate had a sizable handbag collection but he'd never seen this one before.

"That's a new bag, isn't it? Where'd you get it?"

"Oh, yes, right. It is." She seemed surprised that he noticed. "It came in the mail yesterday. Or maybe by courier. I'm not sure. Mom sent it to me."

Really? That was out of character for Georgette. She was more inclined to transfer funds into their daughter's bank account, to which, at his insistence, Kate had restricted access. Ditto the credit card she'd given to Kate and that he had promptly confiscated. Money, that Georgette had no problem throwing around, but her time was closely guarded.

"That was nice of her. I'm surprised you didn't mention it."

She snatched the bag off the counter, shrugged as she slung it over her shoulder. "I guess I forgot. And, you know, I assumed she probably told you herself."

Georgette revealed little to him, and he was okay with that. "I haven't spoken to her in a while. Have you?"

"Day before yesterday, I think."

Was it just him, or did she sound less disappointed than usual. "You should send her a text or an email to thank her, let her know the bag arrived."

"Sure, maybe later. I'm going up to my room now. What's for dinner?"

"Not sure. I thought we might go out."

"Can Casey come?"

"Of course, if it's okay with her mom." Or maybe Sarah would want to join them, make it a family night. Or he could order takeout for the girls and invite Sarah to have dinner with him. Right. He'd gone from family night to date night in point-zero-eight. Like that was going to happen.

"I'm sure it's fine with Sarah. She has a business meeting or dinner or something tonight."

Did she? Or maybe *business dinner* was a euphemism for a date.

"She's, I don't know, like on the Chamber of Commerce or something. Casey says they have meetings once a month. Anyway, she usually stays home and her mom orders takeout for her, so I'm sure it's okay for her to come with us. I'll text her and let you know."

So much for date night, he thought after she left the room. It wasn't as though he'd had a shot at that anyway, but he liked knowing Sarah wasn't on a date, either. And if he couldn't spend the evening with an attractive woman, he'd rather spend it with a pair of teenagers than a roomful of stuffy businesspeople.

KATE TOSSED HER bag on her bed and plopped herself next to Princess, who was curled up with her nose resting on her back paws. She unzipped her ankle books, toed them off and shrugged out of her jacket.

"Life can be *such* a drag sometimes."

The cat opened sleepy eyes.

"Not your life. Mine."

Princess's eyelids slid shut again. Kate wrapped her arms around the cat and brushed her cheek against Princess's soft fur.

"When Mom calls, she always talks about what she's doing and never asks about my new school. My dad never stops talking about what's happening in my life, and he even noticed the DKNY bag Sarah gave me."

Who knew he paid attention to those things? *Not me.*

"So I lied and said Mom sent it. She could have, right?"

Except her mom never sent things like that. She'd given Kate a credit card so she could buy whatever she needed, but her dad wouldn't let her have it because there was no reason he could think of for a kid to have a credit card. He had let her use it to buy school clothes before they left the city, and even then there'd been a spending limit because he was covering half the cost himself.

"Which makes no sense, since Mom has way more money than he has," she told Princess. "And she doesn't care how much I spend on clothes, but that's my dad for you."

The cat stood, stretched and curled up again, this time on her other side.

"Dad just doesn't get it and it's totally unfair."

That was why she'd had to lie about the bag. He thought designer clothes and "fancy" handbags and salon manicures were a waste of money. She could tell he liked Sarah, but if he saw all the amazing things in To the Nines, he would say Kate was wasting her time. She needed to go to the library and do homework and study and get good grades in stupid subjects that had nothing to do with what she wanted to do.

She sat at her dressing table, ran a brush through her hair, checked her makeup.

Sarah had invited her to take a look around, but then she'd complimented Kate's outfit and had actually let her help in the store. No one had ever done anything like that for her before. Sarah listened to her ideas, had told her to go ahead with the displays, and when Kate went back on Thursday, she'd made a point of telling her about all the great things her customers had said about the windows.

Sarah was cool. She had great taste in clothes, there were fashion magazines on her coffee table, and she didn't just work in a clothing store, she *owned* one. It was weird that Sarah and Casey were so completely different but still got along so well. Kate had never met a parent and a kid who were such good friends. In a way it wasn't fair that Casey, who had no fashion sense whatsoever, had such a cool mom who totally did "dress to the nines," even when she was serving up pizza and hanging out on the deck.

If anything, Casey seemed more like the kind of kid her dad wanted. When Sarah and her dad suggested she go with Casey on the first day of school, there was no polite way to say no. Besides, there were advantages to being friendly with a Goody Two-shoes, not the least of which was getting her dad off her case. Now she was glad she'd agreed. Casey knew everyone, and although she didn't seem to have any close friends, all the kids seemed to like her. Especially Dexter, who was easily the cutest boy in the whole school. She was pretty sure Casey liked Dexter, too, and she was equally sure the girl didn't have a clue he liked her back. Kate didn't know why, but she hadn't mentioned it to Casey.

Kate slid off the bed and sat at her dressing table. She sorted a handful of lip gloss tubes, debated between Really Raspberry and Iced Coffee, decided on the pink and swiped it on. Good choice. This color worked better with her white-and-silver Diesel T-shirt and the orange-and-white striped scarf she'd paired with it.

She stood and wandered around the bed to the window. Her dad had suggested she start on her homework, but she had all weekend for that. She could work on Sarah's Facebook, though. This week she'd taken enough photographs to schedule several posts a day until the next time she went in and could take some more. Her dad still didn't know she was helping Sarah. She had to figure out a way to tell him, though, and it had to be a way that didn't make him freak out.

This afternoon hadn't been the right time, but she'd have to do it soon, before Sarah let something slip. Kate had been tempted to ask her not to tell him, which might have worked if she hadn't already sort of lied to Sarah by pretending to text her dad to let him know she was there. Looking back, that had not been a smart move. Now she'd lied to Sarah about having her dad's permission, she'd lied to her dad about the bag, and by not telling him where she was going after school she was sort of lying by omission. Some would argue that wasn't really lying, although she knew her dad wasn't one of them.

She opened the curtains wider and was wondering what Casey was up to when she saw her sprinting across her front yard. The front door of the house across the street opened and a boy raced down the steps two at time. The two met in the middle of the street. Casey flung herself into his arms and he twirled her in a circle before setting her down.

This had to be Henry. He was taller than Casey, with light brown hair that was short on the sides and combed into wavy spikes on top. She'd bet anything that his eyes were blue. He was wearing black jeans and a gray pullover sweater with the sleeves scrunched up to expose his forearms. Wow. He was the cutest boy she'd ever seen.

Casey had said they'd been best friends since first grade. She'd been surprised, shocked even, when Kate asked if he was her boyfriend.

"Henry?" She'd laughed at that. "No way. That would be too weird. He's just a really good friend, practically like a brother."

Well, he wasn't Kate's brother.

She quickly pulled on her boots and zipped them, checked her hair and makeup again, and dashed down the stairs and out the front door. Outside, she slowed to a casual saunter across the yard. Casey, eyes bright with excitement, waved to her.

"Kate, looks who's back! This is my friend Henry."

He watched her walk toward them, and she congratulated herself on being right about the eyes.

"Hi, Henry."

"Hey."

She liked the way he held her gaze, even as Casey pelted him with chatter about school and a barrage of questions about what he'd been doing all summer.

"My dad and I are going out for dinner tonight," Kate said. "He says it's okay if you want to come with us. Both of you."

"That'd be great," Casey said. "What do you think?"

"Sounds good. My parents are still unpacking," he added. "They won't mind if I'm not here."

"All right, then. I'll go let my dad know."

"What time?" Casey asked.

"I'll text you when I find out. It's good to meet you, Henry. Casey's told me all about you."

"You, too."

Did that mean Casey had told him about her, or just that it was nice to meet her? Seriously, who cared? Not her. She had a feeling life in Serenity Bay was about to get interesting. And it was time to let Casey know Dexter was all hers.

CHAPTER EIGHT

BY MID SATURDAY MORNING, Sarah congratulated herself on having caught up on all of her paperwork. No more frittering away half a day spying on her new neighbor. Today she was in control. Her books were in order, all the invoices paid, and she had even checked the new To the Nines Facebook page Kate had created. In just a few days, the shop had close to a hundred likes.

Kate suggested having a contest when they reached a certain number of fans, or drawing a name from among the people who posted comments and giving the winner an in-store discount or maybe a scarf or a belt. For someone so young, the girl had some business savvy, and several customers, including Mrs. Bentley, had raved about her window displays.

Casey liked her, too, and the girls were getting along well in spite of having such different interests. Or maybe because of it. Tonight they'd get to spend more time together because Jonathan and Kate had invited them over for Jonathan's homemade pizza.

All week she had done her best to avoid him, and aside from that brief encounter at the grocery store, she had succeeded. In spite of her initial reaction to the way he talked about his daughter, she had to admit that her impression of the man was starting to soften.

According to Casey, he was already one of the favorite teachers at Serenity Bay High, and the best soccer coach ever. Granted, Casey's views might be somewhat skewed since he'd named her as the team's first-string forward and her teammates had voted her assistant captain. But the man also had some serious cooking skills. The pasta sauce and garlic bread he'd sent over with Kate had been to-die-for delicious, and Casey hadn't been able to say enough good things about the raisin bread he'd baked. Clearly there was more to the man than a pretty face and killer abs. So had she misjudged him? Caught him on a bad day? Could someone so well-rounded really be the hopeless parent she'd taken him for?

Maybe she'd find out tonight, she thought, tucking a bundle of envelopes into her briefcase. She would drop those at the post office on her way to the store. She was turning off her computer when the front door was flung open and banged shut.

"Mom? I'm home!"

"Up here, sweetie. In my office."

Casey pounded up the stairs, more energetic and even more excited than usual after putting in a shift at the animal shelter.

"You'll never guess!" She burst into the room, breathless, face flushed, eyes wide.

"You're probably right."

"A water main broke and there's water *everywhere*. The shelter has to close for a couple of days, maybe longer. They have to dig up the parking lot and everything."

"That's too bad. What will they do with all those animals?" Sarah zipped her laptop into its protective sleeve and tucked it into her briefcase along with her paperwork.

"Well, that's the thing. I was hoping—"

"Oh, no. Casey. No. We've talked about this. We're in no position to leave an animal alone all day while I'm at the shop and you're at school."

Her daughter went quiet and looked sheepishly down at her shoes.

Uh-oh. "Casey? What have you done? Please tell me you didn't make a promise we can't deliver on."

Her daughter's guilty shuffle told her that's exactly what she had done.

"You did." Sarah strengthened her resolve. A dog was simply out of the question.

"I didn't actually make a promise," Casey confessed. "I sort of made a decision."

"You *decided* we would take one of those animals?"

Casey's nod was barely perceptible. "I decided, and then I sort of…brought him home."

"You…what? Where—?"

"Mom, I didn't have a choice! The animals had to go right away and I couldn't leave him there."

Him? *Let me guess.* "Petey."

This time the nod was more vigorous.

"Where is he?"

"Ah…" She looked up and finally made eye contact. "In his crate. On the front porch."

"Oh, sweetie. You brought him home? Without checking with me?"

"I had to, Mom. It was crazy. There was water everywhere. They called Dr. Jacobson at the vet clinic and she came and took three of the bigger dogs to her place."

Sarah's sigh was heavier than intended. "Okay, let's meet this guy who has stolen your heart."

Casey's eyes filled with unchecked emotion.

"No promises," Sarah said. "Seriously. No. Promises."

Undaunted, Casey whipped around, ponytail flying, and dashed down the stairs. Sarah followed, unable to match her enthusiasm.

"Wait'll you see him, Mom. He's so cute, so adorable, I know you're going to love him."

And I know nothing of the sort.

Casey flung the door open and held it, waiting for Sarah to join her. She knelt in front of a pet crate that seemed impossibly small for a dog, that's for sure, and pulled a red canvas leash from the plastic bag sitting next to it. She opened the crate, snagged the little dog's red collar as he wriggled his way out, belly to the porch floorboards, and clipped on the leash.

"Good boy," she crooned. "Good boy, Petey. You're going to live with me now." She shot Sarah a look. "For this week, anyway. Yeah, you are. That's a good boy."

Petey's little pink tongue darted across the back of Casey's hand that gripped the leash. Her other hand stroked the smoke-gray ears. The rest of him resembled a shaggy white dust mop.

"They gave me everything he'll need for a week. Food, treats, his food and water bowls, a ball, his squeaker toy…" She produced a yellow plush duck and squeezed it, producing a high-pitched squeak from the toy and an even higher-pitched one from the dog. “His tennis ball squeaks, too.” Her demonstration had the same effect as the squeaky duck.

“Look how cute he is, Mom. Isn’t he cute?” Casey gently tipped his head up so Sarah could see for herself.

“He’s very sweet.” He was, with his glossy black eyes and the little black button nose. She struggled to harden her heart and failed, dismally.

Casey picked him up, scrunching her nose and giggling as he tried to lick her face. “No thanks, Petey. No puppy kisses.”

“What kind of dog did you say he is?”

“A shih tzu-Maltese cross.”

“And he’s finished growing?” she asked. Not that it mattered.

“For sure. He’s two years old so he’s full grown, and he’s really well trained. He used to live in Gibsons but then the lady who owned him got sick and couldn’t keep him, so he had to be surrendered.” She hugged the dog closer. “Poor Petey. It wasn’t because she didn’t want you, it’s because she couldn’t keep you.” She talked to him as though he knew exactly what she was saying. “But we can. For now.”

"For now," Sarah repeated. She appreciated her daughter's boundless enthusiasm, but she needed to understand that this couldn't be a permanent arrangement. "How long before the water main is repaired?"

"By the end of the week, probably. Maybe."

And a week, in Casey's mind, was long enough for her mother to become so attached to the animal, she couldn't bear to part with him. Well, that wasn't going to happen.

"You'd better bring him in," she said. "We can't leave him out here."

"Did you hear that, Petey? You get to stay!" Casey set him down and picked up the crate and the bagful of canine accoutrements. The dog wagged his stub of a tail and dashed into the house ahead of her, tugging on the leash. "He won't be any trouble, I promise. I'll look after him. You won't even know he's here."

Sarah doubted that, but she followed the pair inside and closed the door. "Where is Petey going to sleep?"

"He can stay in my room."

Sarah raised her eyebrows at that.

"He's crate-trained, Mom. It's not like he'll be sleeping in my bed."

"I certainly hope not, but what about your critters?"

"They won't be a problem. They're all

caged, and Petey's used to being around other animals. Poor guy's been at the shelter for two whole weeks."

Poor Petey? He looked healthy, happy and perfectly adoptable. By someone else.

"Keeping him in your room is your call," Sarah said, wishing he looked less adorable, that those bright eyes were a little less heart-melting.

"He'll be fine, Mom. I'll feed him, walk him, clean up after him—"

Sarah couldn't stop her eyebrows from going up again.

"Not that he'll make a mess. He's totally not messy, I promise. I've been looking after him since he came to the shelter and he's a really good dog."

"I'm sure he is." She hated making her daughter defend something she was so passionate about. "He's lucky to have you looking after him."

Casey set the crate and the bag on the floor and hugged her while Petey wound the leash around their ankles. "Thank you, Mom. I won't let you down."

"I know you won't, sweetie."

Casey untangled them and unclipped his leash. "There you go, little guy. Check out your new home."

Sarah let that one go. "We should have lunch, and then I need to get the store. Juliet's been by herself all morning and she'll need a break soon."

"Okay. I'll put Petey's things away and open a can of soup."

"Thanks. Give me a few minutes to finish getting ready for work and then I'll join you."

Casey toed the crate into the closet and hung the leash on a hook, then she picked up the bag of supplies. "Come on, Petey. Let's check out the kitchen." The dog scampered after her, ears flapping, tail wagging.

Casey had soup heating on the stove when Sarah came back downstairs a few minutes later. She kept up a steady stream of chatter to the dog sitting at her heels, gazing up at her, head to one side.

Sarah set out bowls and spoons and a box of crackers. It was usually right around this time every Saturday that they talked about what kind of pizzas to order for dinner, which movie they'd watch. "Did Kate say what time we should be there for dinner?"

Casey stirred the soup. "No set time. Her dad said to come over after you get home from work. He won't put the pizzas in the oven till we get there."

Sarah sat at the table and couldn't help

smiling as the little dog approached cautiously and nudged her leg with his nose. She stroked his head, then the soft, shaggy ears. Darn little dog. *Do you have to be* this *adorable*?

"Do you think we should take anything?"

Casey shrugged. "I don't think so. I asked Kate's dad what kind of pizza toppings he was using. He said he'd surprise us."

Sarah had never cared for surprises but they'd been popping up all week. Unexpected changes to her routine, a dog, a man who offered to cook for her. The same man whose morning routine she knew almost as well as her own. She knew what time he left for his run along the seawall and she knew when she would see him return in a sweat-soaked T-shirt if she happened to be looking out her window.

"Mom?"

"What?"

Casey looked puzzled. "I said lunch is ready and I'm taking mine out to the deck. Do you want yours out there, too?"

"No thanks." Her face felt warm. Was she blushing? "I'll take mine to the store with me. Is that okay?"

"Sure. Come on, Petey. Let's go outside. After lunch we'll play ball."

Sarah put her bowl away and ladled chicken noodle soup—Casey's favorite—into a small thermos. The store was always busy on Saturday afternoons and she would have plenty of work to do. All she had to do was stick to her routine and not let herself be distracted by a man who had thrown her off her game.

CASEY QUICKLY CLEARED away the lunch dishes after her mom left for work, then she snapped a picture of Petey and sent it in a text message to Kate. Having Petey here was one thing but getting her mom to let her keep him was a whole other matter. What she needed was a plan, and since she and Kate sort of already had one, it was time to put that plan in motion.

My new dog!
Srsly? BRO!

The doorbell rang a few minutes later. She scooped Petey into her arms so he couldn't run outside, and opened the door.

"Omigosh, he's adorable." Kate stepped inside and shut the door behind her. "I can't believe your mom is actually letting you have a dog."

"Well, that's the thing." Casey set him on

the floor and he raced circles around them. "She didn't let me have him. I just brought him home."

"He's a stray?"

"No, this is Petey. The shelter dog I told you about." She filled Kate in on the flood and the broken water main. "So now I only have a week, maybe a little more, to convince my mom to let me keep him."

Kate grinned at her. "Then we'd seriously better get to work on our plan."

Problem was, how were they going to get Kate's dad to ask Casey's mom out on a date? "I'm not sure that's going to work."

"Of course it will. When my parents were splitting up and my mom starting seeing Xavier they let me have anything I wanted." Kate cupped her hands around Petey's face. "You are so cute."

Her friend might not see the flaws in this plan, but Casey did. "You were just taking advantage of a situation. That's not the same as creating the situation and then taking advantage of it. I just don't see how we're going to get our parents…you know…together."

Kate was grinning again. "You're still coming over for dinner tonight, right?"

Casey nodded.

"And Petey will need to be walked, won't he?"

"Um, yeah."

"Well…" Kate said, drawing out the word for dramatic effect. "Something will come up, something very last-minute, and you and I will have to go out after we eat. You won't be able to walk the dog, so you'll ask your mom to do it. *Beg* her if you have to, and I'll convince my dad he should go with her."

"I don't know. What's going to 'come up'?" Nothing in her life ever happened at the last minute.

"Well…" she said again. "What if you get Henry to call you? He can say he has friends coming over because he's been away all summer and wants to get everyone together. Your mom knows you missed having him around. I guarantee she's enough of a softy to walk the dog so you can hang out with him."

Casey had never attempted anything so devious, but Kate was right. If she asked, her mom would definitely let her go over to Henry's after dinner.

"I don't want to tell him about our plan, though. He might tell his parents." Or even worse, let something slip to her mom.

"We'll figure something out," Kate said, with the self-assurance of someone who'd had plenty of practice at deceit. "All he needs to do is send you a text after dinner so it looks totally last-minute. We don't have to tell our parents what's in the text."

"Okay. We can talk to him this afternoon and see what he says." And she would leave most of the talking to Kate.

"Is Henry friends with Dexter?" Kate asked.

"They're pretty good friends. Why?"

"Maybe we can invite him to come over, too."

Seriously? Last night it had been glaringly obvious that Kate was flirting with Henry, and it was just as clear he was flirting back. And that was okay. She could handle that. But Dexter, too? No way.

"I don't know..."

"Oh, come on. I can tell you're totally into him."

"I'm not...I mean, how..." If her dumb crush was obvious to Kate, did that mean everyone knew? Even Dexter? Casey felt her face heat up.

Kate rolled her eyes. "Yes, you are. And the feeling's mutual. He likes you, too."

"He does? I thought...I mean, he spends more time talking to you than me."

"That's because boys are clueless about this

stuff, but this'll be fun. You and Dexter, me and Henry. Not to mention your mom and my dad. What's the worst that can happen?"

Casey couldn't begin to imagine anything worse than her mom's reaction if she found out about this crazy plan. But as she looked into the little dog's big dark eyes, she knew she had to go for it. Petey was worth it. And hanging out with Dex was totally worth it.

"Okay. This is going to work. I know it." Kate grinned and held up her hand for a high five, and Petey barked excitedly when they slapped their palms together.

This better work, Casey thought, because if their plan backfired, her mom was going to kill her.

JON WAS AT the kitchen island arranging pizza toppings on plates when the doorbell rang.

"Kate?"

"Got it, Dad."

A moment later, Sarah and Casey followed her into the kitchen.

He looked up and caught Sarah's smile as she and her daughter set bottles of cola on the counter.

"Thank you," he said. "Kate, would you put those in the fridge, please?"

"Sure. What kind of pizzas are you making?"

"One is vegetarian," he assured her. "Tomatoes, peppers and artichokes."

"Mmm, my favorite."

"Is there anything I can do to help?" Sarah asked.

"Thanks, but everything's ready. I just have to roll out the dough and then we can get them ready to go in the oven. Can I get you something to drink?"

"I can do that. Just point me in the direction of the glasses."

"Thanks. They're in the cupboard over the dishwasher, and there's ice in the freezer."

Casey looked around the kitchen. "Where's Princess?"

"She's sleeping in my room," Kate said.

Jon cut the pizza dough into four portions and centered one of them on a floured board. "I hear you got a dog this afternoon," Jon said.

Sarah set four glasses on the counter. "We did not 'get' a dog. We are dog-sitting for a few days."

Undaunted, Casey launched into an animated description of Petey, how he was the cutest, smartest dog in the world, how he needed to find a forever home. While he listened to the girls chatter about pets, he watched Sarah pour drinks for everyone.

Earlier he'd seen her come home from work in one of those elegant business suits she always wore. Now wearing slender-legged jeans with cuffs rolled above the ankle, yellow-and-blue flower-patterned espadrilles, and a sweater the color of butter, she looked fresh and youthful, too young to be the mom of a teenager. She handed glasses to the girls and smiled at him as she set one on the island counter close to where he worked.

"Thanks," he said, picking it up, raising it toward her.

"You're welcome." She lightly touched her glass to his, ice clinking.

The girls giggled. To his chagrin, he realized their laughter was directed at him and Sarah. If Sarah noticed, she didn't let on. He set his glass back on the counter and, head down, went to work on the pizzas. He knew Sarah was watching as he rolled and fitted rounds of dough to the pans, brushed them with olive oil, spread them with sauce, layered on the toppings. He heaped both pies with generous handfuls of grated cheese and was sliding two of them into the oven when someone's phone let out a wolf whistle.

"That's me," Casey said, digging her phone

out of the back pocket of her jeans. "It's a text from Henry. Oh, cool. Some of the kids from school are coming over to his place around seven o'clock. He wants to know if we can go over." She gave her mom a hopeful look. "Can we? I haven't seen him all summer and this'll be so much fun."

"Can we, Dad?" Kate chimed in.

He and Sarah exchanged a look. "I'm okay with it," he said. "As long as you're home by nine."

"Will they have time to eat before they go?" Sarah asked.

"These will be out of the oven in fifteen," he said, setting the timer on the stove. "I made one vegetarian and one with ham and pineapple…I remembered that's Casey's favorite…so they'll have plenty of time to eat before they have to leave."

"Thanks, Coach," Casey said.

He'd noticed that she preferred to call him that instead of using his first name, and he quite liked it.

"So can I go, Mom?"

"What about Petey?" Sarah asked. "Doesn't he need to be walked?"

The girl looked deflated. "He does. Sorry, I forgot."

Hmm. The dog just might give him a

chance to extend the evening, spend a little extra time with Sarah. "If you want, we can walk him after we've finished eating. I could use some exercise, too."

"Oh. Okay, I guess we could do that." Sarah didn't sound overly eager.

Jon hadn't even met the dog and he liked him already.

Kate and Casey grinned and winked at each other over the tops of their sodas, obviously ecstatic about the prospect of hanging out with Henry and most likely one of the other boys from school. Sarah didn't seem to notice and that was just as well, since he had his own selfish reasons for wanting to spend alone time with her. Finally, he had opportunity to apologize for his behavior last Saturday and, he hoped, to convince her that he was not the loser dad she thought he was.

SARAH BUNCHED HER napkin and set it on her empty plate. "I think I ate too much," she said, groaning just a little. "Those pizzas were so good, especially the last one."

Which surprised her because she'd watched Jonathan make it—a layer of provolone topped with fresh sliced pears and sprinkled with gorgonzola and chopped pecans—and thought it had to be the strangest pizza combo ever. She had sampled it cautiously and discovered it was also the most delicious.

"Glad you liked it." He gathered up the paper napkins, stacked their plates and reached for the ones the girls had abandoned when they'd rushed out to meet their friends.

"I'll help." She collected the glasses, dumped chunks of ice into the sink and loaded them into the dishwasher.

The conversation had been easy and relaxed while the girls laughed and talked and gossiped. But then they'd left in a flurry of back-and-forth text messages with their friends, leaving the kitchen quiet and Sarah feeling awkwardly tongue-tied. She hadn't anticipated being alone with him tonight.

Jonathan gave the table and counters a quick swipe and tossed the cloth over the tap. "That should do it."

"So…I'll run home and meet you out front with the dog?"

"Sounds good."

Back at her place, she let a very excited, tail-wagging dog out of his crate.

"Sit still," she said.

He sat immediately, tongue still in action, eyes alert with excitement.

"Good dog. And you can stop being so cute. That works on Casey but not me."

She clipped the leash to his collar, determined not to let the cuteness of the little upturned face get to her.

"Come on, you rascal," she said, being tugged along as he bolted for the front door.

Jonathan waited at the end of the driveway and he laughed when he saw Petey. "He is pretty cute, no question about that."

"Casey's counting on that to soften me up. She thinks that by the time the repairs at the shelter have been completed, I will be as much in love with him as she is and will want to keep him."

Jonathan fell into step beside her. "You're saying that won't happen?"

"It can't. We're both out of the house all day so it's not fair to the dog."

He didn't respond and they walked in silence for a moment or two.

"I've never been much of a cat person," he said. "Kate had her heart set on having one, though, so a few years ago we gave in and adopted Princess from the SPCA. After my wife and I separated, Kate spent a lot of time in her room. The cat is in there most of the time, so I was glad then that she had a pet."

Sarah tipped her head so she could see his face. "You think I should let Casey keep him?"

"Oh, geez, I have no opinion. I have a hard enough time making the right decisions for my own daughter. I'm just saying what worked for us."

"Well, we're not getting a cat. I'm allergic to them."

He looked down at her, eyebrows curved up like a pair of question marks.

"What?"

"You just spent a couple of hours at my place. Did our cat bother you?"

Huh. No, it did not. "Usually my eyes itch and I start to sneeze when I'm around a cat. And that's the truth. I'm not making it up."

Jonathan smiled. "Just as well, then, that your daughter didn't notice."

"That's for sure."

They walked half a block without saying anything, the silence growing more awkward by the step until Jonathan broke it.

"I owe you an apology," he said. "A few of the things I said about Kate last Saturday night were uncalled for, and I'm sorry I made you uncomfortable."

Sarah had wondered if he would bring that up and now she was glad he had decided to clear the air.

"Apology accepted. I figured you must be pretty stressed, what with moving, starting a new job, helping your daughter adjust to a new home."

"I appreciate the benefit of doubt, but I was out of line. It won't happen again."

She believed him. He'd seemed much more at ease tonight, and he and Kate were definitely more at ease with one another.

They were halfway down the hill and on their way to the beach—Petey leading the way on little legs that were, as Casey had described, going "a mile a minute"—when it dawned on Sarah that they hadn't started out with a destination in mind. "We can walk along the seawall, if you like."

"I was hoping you'd say that. I run down there and back almost every morning."

Oh, I know you do. I see you almost every morning. Not the time to confess to practically being a stalker.

"You must like to stay in shape," she said instead. "For teaching, I mean. And coaching." Not for the sake of curious neighborhood women peeking through their curtains at dawn. When had she become *that* woman? The answer was obvious When *this* man had moved next door.

"It definitely helps me keep up with my students and the kids on the teams I've coached,"

Jonathan said. “I’ve been running since I was in high school. What about you?”

“Me? A runner? Oh my goodness, no. Yoga and aqua-fit are more my speed.”

“Also great ways to stay in shape.”

She glanced at up at him, saw he was watching her and liked what she saw in those blue, blue eyes. Humor, the prospect of friendship. Possibly the promise of something more. Startled, she looked away. That had been a moment and he’d felt it, too. Did she want this? Was she ready?

For several minutes they walked in awkward silence, crossed Shoreline Boulevard and turned onto the walkway that hugged the seawall and wound its way around the bay. Petey led the way on his fully extended leash, ears flapping, short little legs scissoring along the pavement.

“So.” She tried to inject a little less awkwardness into the silence, only to discover she didn’t know what to say.

“So,” he echoed. “This is a great town.”

“It is. I love it here.” She was grateful to have the conversation shift to safe, neutral ground, too. “Especially at this time of year, after the tourists leave. Don’t get me wrong, though. I love tourists. They bring a lot of business to Serenity Bay. But once school starts in September, those of us who live here year-round get our town back. Then it feels like home again, like a real community."

"Tourists only come during the summer?" he asked.

"Oh, no. We get visitors all year, but the majority are here in July and August. That's when all the hotels and campgrounds in the area are at capacity, every berth at the marina is occupied. A lot of downtown businesses have sidewalk sales, and restaurants and even the deli across the street from my store set up outdoor patios."

Petey stopped to sniff a small piece of driftwood that someone had dropped on the path.

"That's what it was like when I was here in July," Jonathan said. "When I signed the lease for the house. The real estate agent assured me that by the end of the summer, it wouldn't be so busy."

The dog picked up the stick and gave it a shake and a toss and snatched it up again as though it were something alive.

"Come on, Petey. Let's go." Sarah urged him with a gentle tug. The dog pranced ahead again, proudly carrying the little bit of wood like a prize catch. "Silly dog."

"He's a cute little guy, that's for sure."

"Have you noticed how everyone smiles as they walk by?"

"Oh, yes. You know how this is going to turn out, don't you?"

"You mean with Casey wanting to keep him?" she asked.

"I was thinking more along the lines of Casey's mom wanting to keep him."

She looked up at him, caught the laughter in his eyes and sighed. "I really want to not want to keep him."

He laughed at that and let it go. "So, about Serenity Bay. When did you move here?"

She was glad to revert to the previous topic of conversation and grateful not to be put on the spot about keeping the dog. She suspected he might be right, but that didn't mean she was anywhere even close to admitting it.

"Right after college, almost fifteen years ago. Even then it was a bustling little tourist destination, but there've been a lot of changes, too. Like the new subdivision we live in, and this resort."

They stopped in front of the sprawling two-story log structure, shoulders almost touching. Petey stopped, too, and sat obediently without even being told.

"I wouldn't have guessed it was new," Jonathan said. "It blends into the forest and the beach, as though it's always been here."

"It does, doesn't it? But that wasn't part of the original plan. The developer wanted to build a second marina, add on a casino. Almost everyone in town was opposed to it, including a handful of lawyers and one Supreme Court judge who retired here. They came to Serenity Bay to get away from all of that. So after a lot of petitions and town meetings and environmental studies, the original plan was scrapped and we now have the Serenity Bay Resort and Spa."

She couldn't bring herself to tell him it was the original scheme that had brought her and Jim here in the first place. He had been hired by the developer's accounting department to handle the company's finances, and he'd never recovered from the bitterness of that defeat. And because of the animosity around that, Sarah had never really felt as though she fit into the community, either. And she'd hated that because she liked so many of these people, and once she realized what the impact the developer's original plan would have had on the town, she had silently agreed with them. It wasn't until Jim died that she'd been able to forge friendships and truly make this her home.

"Do you ever come here?"

"Not often. The dining room is very formal, not at all the sort of place you'd take a family."

"Expensive, too. I checked it online."

That was true. "The same goes for the spa. As tempting as it is, it's not the sort of thing I've budgeted the time or money for."

"You budget your time?" He seemed to think that wasn't possible.

"I have a routine I like to stick to and..." Oh, what the heck. "Hello, my name's Sarah and I'm a list-aholic."

His laugh was deep and genuine. "Hello, Sarah. I'm Jon and I'm a basket case when it comes to being organized."

He held out his hand and she put hers in it. It was less of a handshake and more of a hand-hold, and then they were having another moment. After several seconds he let her go, and his warmth was replaced by the cool evening air.

"I'm sure you're not as bad as that."

"Would you ever pack up a house and move without labeling any of the boxes?" he asked, laughing when he saw her expression.

"You did that?"

"I did. And if you're thinking it was chaos, then you'd be right."

"We all play to our strengths." Casey was already raving about what a great teacher and coach Mr. Marshall was, and Sarah imagined that being an instant hit with the students had a lot to do with his casual, easygoing nature. "I would never have the patience to teach high school or coach a sports team."

"Thanks. I'll try to remember that next time I get home from the grocery store and realize I forgot to buy milk and eggs."

"You don't even make grocery lists?"

"I jot things on a notepad on the fridge when I notice we're running out of something. Then when I'm at the store, I try to remember what's on the list. Does that count?"

Um, no! But he sounded so hopeful. "Of course it does."

"You're a terrible liar. Anyone ever tell you that?"

"My mother. I could never pull one over on her." Petey tugged on the leash. He had abandoned his stick and was ready to go again. "What do you think? Should we carry on to the point or go back?"

"I'm okay to keep going."

So was she. Adult conversation was good, Jonathan's light banter was even better, and she felt more relaxed than she had in ages.

"Unless you think it's too far for the dog," he added.

"He seems fine for now. And he's so small, I can always carry him if I have to."

"Good plan."

The walk from the resort to the end of the seawall at Outlook Point took them past a handful of luxury beachfront properties, and Sarah knew one of them belonged to Eleanor Bentley and her husband. Directly across the bay was the marina, angled between Shelter Point and the protective arm of the breakwater that kept the bay relatively calm during storm season. Boats of various sizes, mostly pleasure craft, were moored here, and tonight there were also two commercial fishing boats and a floatplane. She'd been locking up the store that afternoon and had heard the low drone of the plane as it swung low over the bay and landed. The passengers were most likely business executives up from Vancouver or Seattle for meetings or a weekend retreat at the resort.

She and Jonathan kept up what now felt like a comfortable conversation, and in what seemed no time at all, they'd reached the point. The walkway widened into a small parking lot, now empty for the evening. For several minutes they leaned against the stone wall that formed a half circle between the lot and the rocks below. Petey, panting slightly, sat on the ground next to her feet. The breeze was stronger, whipping the water in the strait into a light chop. In the distance, an Alaska-bound cruise ship, one of the last of the season, glided by, its lights and white hull gleaming against the sunset.

Sarah shivered. “It’s starting to cool off. I should have brought a jacket.”

“I didn’t think to bring one, either, or you could have worn that.”

“Next time I’ll remind you,” she said before she could stop herself. Would he think she was flirting with him? *You* are *flirting with him.*

He looped an arm around her shoulders. “Next time you won’t need to.”

His warm breath brushed over her hair and she shivered again for an entirely different reason. This was beyond flirting. Part of her, the part that been alone for a very long time, considered exploring how far this could go. Her sensible side knew it needed to go no further.

He straightened and dropped his arm. “We should go back,” he said, hinting that he knew what she was thinking.

“We should.” The shivers were back, partly

from the evening air blowing across her recently warmed shoulders, and partly due to freshly awakened sensations now tumbling around her insides.

They walked back along the seawall at a brisker pace, mostly in silence that was companionable but now emotionally charged as well. Halfway up the hill, a panting Petey stopped and sat down and no amount of coaxing could get him going again. Sarah knelt to pick him up and he eagerly jumped into her arms, trying to lick her face.

"Stop," she said, but she couldn't help laughing. "Silly dog. Hold still, we're almost home."

"Would you like me to carry him?" Jonathan asked.

"I'm okay. He hardly weighs anything, and he helps to keep me warm."

Moments later they'd reached the end of their driveway. They'd been gone longer than she'd expected and the sky was nearly dark. Sarah set the dog down and turned to face Jonathan. "Thanks for joining us. I wouldn't have gone so far on my own."

"Any time," he said. "I enjoyed it."

"Me, too."

Their gazes locked for a heartbeat. Two… three…four. The only way to break the tension was to kiss him, or get him to kiss her. He leaned in and so did she; their lips met, lingered, and the lightness felt surprisingly intimate for a first kiss. She wasn't sure who had initiated it and couldn't say who ended it. Maybe neither, maybe both, but they were suddenly apart, staring at each other again, and Jonathan was smiling.

"I guess that's good-night."

"I guess it is." She was now acutely aware that they were still on the street in plain view of anyone who might be watching, and now that the streetlights were on, anyone could be. "I should go in. We should. Into our own houses, I mean. Before the girls come home."

"Right." He checked his watch.

Sarah fished her house key out of her jeans pocket. "Come on, Petey. Let's get you inside."

"After that walk, he should sleep well tonight."

That would make one of them, Sarah thought. "Good night."

"Good night, Sarah."

Inside, she leaned against the door and closed her eyes, still shivering from the combination of the cool night air and Jonathan's bone-melting kiss. She wouldn't sleep a wink that night, but that was okay. She would still be up early enough to see him leave for his morning run, and this time she wouldn't feel guilty for watching him.

ACROSS THE STREET, from her friend Henry's living room window, Casey stood with Kate, both girls watching their parents. The girls laughed and shared a high five.

"Your mom is so going to let you keep that dog," Kate said.

"And your dad is so not going to be on your case about every little thing."

It was weird to think of her mom going on dates with Kate's dad, Casey realized, but she would get used to it. Petey was worth it. After their parents went inside, they sat back on the couch with the boys, who were finishing a video game. Dex grinned at her, and she smiled back. She could definitely get used to this.

CHAPTER NINE

JON SPRAWLED IN his favorite chair in the living room, feet up on an ottoman, laptop on his lap, catching up on sports news in the *Vancouver Sun*'s online Sunday edition. The house was quiet, even quieter than usual since Kate had announced she was going out with Casey and Henry. That she already referred to them as friends was a huge relief for him. He had reminded her that her homework had to be finished before she went out, and she'd assured him it was. She liked her art class, of course, but after the first week of school she was already behind on writing up a lab report for her science class, and she had received a D on her first English assignment. So yes, he was pleased to see her adapting to a new school, but schoolwork had to come first.

This afternoon they had taken Casey's dog for a walk downtown and planned to hang out at a local coffee shop that had dog-friendly tables on the sidewalk. The weather was decent enough for it, overcast but no rain in the forecast.

A week had passed since he and Sarah walked Petey along the seawall. He had hoped a similar opportunity would present itself. No luck. All they'd had were two end-of-day encounters in the driveway, once while Kate was with him and the other when Casey was with her mother, plus some brief interaction on Thursday afternoon when Sarah picked up her daughter after soccer practice. If he wanted to spend time with her—and of course he did—he would have to create an opportunity. Problem was, he couldn't decide what he should do. Suggest they take the dog for a walk? Invite her out for coffee? Suggest they drive down to Sechelt for dinner?

She was a self-confessed list maker who had no interest in sports and hated to cook. He would like to be organized but wasn't, and at one point years ago had fleetingly considered dropping out of kinesiology to enroll in a culinary school. He'd thought about their conversation since that night, and about her, but mostly he'd thought a lot about the kiss. The lead-up to it was a blur—who had initiated it?—and he'd lain awake running the instant replay in his head. All he remembered was her. Her firm mouth, her sweet taste, her real-woman scent rather than some lavishly expensive, artificially scented fragrance that made his head ache. Her glamorous appearance—and let's face it, even in jeans and a casual sweater the woman was a knockout—seemed natural, effortless. Unlike…

But there was no point in going there. Georgette was part of his past, a past that he was finally ready to put behind him because the future was suddenly filled with promise. Sarah shared many of the same qualities—intelligence, self-confidence, drop-dead gorgeousness—but she didn't need or want to be the center of attention. And she was a great mom. It was too soon to speculate where this might go, or if it would go anywhere, but he hoped it would.

His phone rang then, and as he followed the sound to the kitchen where he'd left it, he had a hunch it was Georgette. This was the time she usually called Kate on weekends and if she couldn't reach their daughter, she called him by default. He grabbed his phone off the counter and the display confirmed his suspicion.

For a split second he considered not answering. It would be the smart thing to do since he really didn't want to talk to her. But she would keep calling until he answered. So he manned up and took the call.

"Hello, Georgette."

"Is Kate there?" she asked.

"It's nice to talk to you, too."

"Very clever. We both know we're past the point of having to chitchat about the weather."

Her words could still cut like a knife, swift and sharp and deep enough to drain the life out of him.

"Kate is out with her friends. She has her phone with her, though."

"I already tried that. She didn't pick up."

Kate checked obsessively for missed calls and messages. She looked forward to her conversations with her mother, but it didn't surprise him that she wouldn't take a call from her while she was out with her friends.

"I'll ask her to call you when she gets in."

"When will that be?"

"She'll be home in an hour or so."

"It's already after eleven over here, and Xavier and I are on our way back to our hotel. We're in London."

He didn't care where she was, or why, but she always found a way to work it into a conversation.

"We're here for fall Fashion Week here, and then we're off to Milan."

"That sounds…nice. Speaking of fashion, I hope Kate thanked you for the purse you sent her."

There was an uncharacteristic pause. "I didn't send her a purse."

"Oh. She said…huh…never mind. I guess I misunderstood."

Mom sent it. It came in the mail yesterday. Couldn't be less ambiguous, and now it turned out to be a bold-faced lie.

"Apparently you did. Listen, I have to go. Our driver just pulled up with our car and Xavier's waiting."

"I'll tell Kate you called. If she can't get through to you later today, I assume you'll call before she leaves for school in the morning?"

"Of course I will. I always do."

"Okay, I'll let her—"

But Georgette had already disconnected.

He stared at his phone. "Nice talking to you. I'll be sure to tell her you called." Right after he found out how she'd acquired the purse and why she lied about it.

He understood why a woman wanted to look and feel attractive, and he had a healthy appreciation for beautiful women. He had resented Georgette's obsession with fashion, though. Not because of the clothes themselves, but because of the implication that if an item wasn't expensive, if it wasn't sporting a designer label, then it had no value. He would never understand the concept, and he resented the influence it'd had on their daughter.

But right now he had a more immediate problem. If Kate's mother hadn't given her the handbag, then where did she get it? There was a chance she had used the credit card Georgette had given her to order something online. He fished the card out of his wallet and dialed the number on the back to check the activity on the account. No recent purchases.

He had recognized the logo on the bag; it was one of Kate's favorite designers, and those bags weren't cheap. There was no way she could afford one on her monthly allowance. He put the card away, strode into the kitchen and poured himself a glass of water from a bottle in the fridge. Maybe she bought the bag before they left the city, when she'd shopped for back-to-school clothes. But then why lie and say it was a gift from her mother?

He slammed the fridge door harder than he should have and immediately felt guilty. He needed to get a grip. But what if she'd…? No, no way. She could give him some attitude, but she was a good kid. She would never take something that didn't belong to her. Would she?

What were the options? She didn't have the bag when they lived in Vancouver. The thing was huge, and it was distinctive enough that he would have remembered seeing it. She hadn't bought it online. So where in Serenity Bay would she—

Sarah's store?

No. Kate wouldn't have shoplifted a purse from their new neighbor's business. Heaven help her if she did. Maybe he should go next door, find out if Kate had been to the store, if Sarah had noticed anything missing.

Bad idea. He needed to wait till Kate came home, give her a chance to explain. He owed her that much.

He went out on the deck and leaned his forearms on the railing. He'd been congratulating himself for making this move, finding this great house, figuring a small town was a good place to raise a teenager. Was this a mistake? Was Kate so unhappy that she would act out like this?

"You don't know that she took the purse." He needed facts before he passed judgment. Surely Kate would have an explanation for the bag and why she lied about it.

"She better have," he said to himself. "And it better be a good one."

SARAH LOVED SUNDAY AFTERNOONS. This was her "me" time. Casey, usually occupied with one of her many projects and interests, had taken the dog and gone out with friends, leaving Sarah with the whole house and several hours to herself. She consulted her afternoon to-do list, smiling because it reminded her of her last conversation with Jonathan. Among other things.

She had already given herself a manicure, and because she was in such good spirits, she'd chosen a pale shade of pink instead of the clear polish she usually wore. The blush color satisfied her desire for something a touch more feminine and at the same time wouldn't clash with this week's wardrobe choices. The six days of outfits that now hung in an orderly row in her walk-in closet.

She sat at her desk and crossed off "clean the bathrooms"—which qualified as me-time because there were few things she liked better than a clean bathroom—and surveyed what was left. Figure out what to have for dinner. Check out the To the Nines's Facebook page.

Dinner was hours away and she already knew there were frozen dinners in the freezer.

Or she could run to the market and pick up something, or they could grab takeout at Wharfside Fish 'n' Chips.

That left Facebook. She turned on her laptop and opened the browser, found the link Kate had saved for her, and logged in. The girl had done an amazing job in such a short time. The banner at the top of the page was a photograph Kate had taken of the storefront after she'd set up the windows a couple of weeks ago. They needed to be done again this Tuesday and she had promised the girl she could help after school. Kate had agreed to photograph each new window display and use it to refresh the banner.

Sarah should learn how to do these things herself, and she would, someday, but for now she was thrilled to have help. Kate had an eye for design and a head for business, no doubt about it. Sarah had lost count of the number of customers who had raved about the windows. Kate had also suggested they reward customers with a gift after the page had 250 "likes" and they were now at…

Wow. Two hundred and twenty-seven.

She clicked on a button to see who all these people were. Kids from the high school, their mothers, other businesswomen. But Eleanor Bentley—who would have guessed she was using social media?—and a woman from Boise, Idaho, were completely unexpected. Kate had set the page to like other local businesses and many had already reciprocated. Earlier in the week, she photographed individual items and somehow programmed the page to post one photo every day along with a description.

Sarah understood almost nothing about social media, but she knew effective advertising when she saw it. The photographs were great, and every item, including the one Kate had posted yesterday morning, had sold. This was one business-savvy fourteen-year-old.

She might even have mentioned this to Jonathan while they'd walked the dog last week, except she'd had other things on her mind. Instead of talking about kids, about being parents, they had spent the time getting to know each other. She already liked what was on the outside, and now she was drawn to the man on the inside, too. He was funny, easy to talk to, and he made her feel…

He made her feel. She put her hands to her face to cool her cheeks with her palms.

The front door banged shut and was followed by Casey's customary, "Mo-om, we're home."

"Be right down, sweetie." She shut down

the computer and checked her list. The only thing left on it was tonight's dinner. Frozen entrees had no appeal. They would go for fish and chips instead. If the rain held off, they could walk down and eat at one of the nearby picnic tables. With fall almost here, there wouldn't be many more opportunities to eat outside. They could even invite Jonathan and Kate to join them. She was sure he wanted to spend time together as much as she did, and she was beginning to realize that it was up to her to make it happen.

But first she wanted to hear all about Casey's afternoon. Now that she was spending more time with friends, some of whom were boys, Sarah intended to keep the lines of communication wide open. After they talked, she would run next door and invite Jonathan and Kate to join them for dinner.

JON WAS WAITING inside the front door when Kate returned, the new bag casually slung over her shoulder.

"Hi, Dad." She eyed him suspiciously. "What's up?"

"I'm not sure. I was hoping you'd tell me."

"Oh-kay."

"Did you talk to your mother?"

She at least had the grace to look uncomfortable. "No. My friends and I went for coffee and then we hung out at the beach. It wasn't a good time to talk."

"You couldn't have answered, let her know when she could call you back?"

She shrugged. "I guess. Did she call you?"

"Yes, she did. She wanted to know why you didn't pick up."

Kate rolled her eyes. "I'm sure she's not mad because I missed a call. I talk to her pretty much every day."

"She wasn't mad." Not at Kate, anyway. "But you're always wondering when she's going to call, checking for text messages, so I was surprised you didn't take her call."

"Fine. I'll text her to let her know I'm home and she can call me if it's not too late over there." She unzipped one of her high black leather boots and pulled it off, removed the other one, and headed for the stairs. The bag still swung from her shoulder.

"Not so fast," he said.

She turned around, her sullen expression easy to read. *Now what?*

"I asked your mother if you'd thanked her for giving you that bag."

Her defiance waned.

"She said she didn't send it."

Kate lowered her gaze to the floor.

Keep your cool, he warned himself. "I have a pretty good idea how much it cost and I know you didn't have enough money to buy it. Where did you get it?"

She kept her head down, her eyes low, but it was the indifferent shrug that made him lose it.

"You don't know where it came from? You expect me to believe that?"

Her head snapped up and the defiance was back, in spades. "Duh. Of course I know where it came from. I got it at Sarah's."

Duh? Not a good way to respond to a man whose patience was worn dangerously thin. "You…borrowed it?"

"Not from her house, from her store. And I didn't borrow it, she gave it to me."

He walked away from her, drew a long breath as he raised his hands and jabbed his fingers through his hair. Heaven help him. He exhaled slowly, turned to face her again.

"Sarah gave you an expensive handbag? For no reason, she just gave it to you?"

"No, she didn't just give it to me." She hiked her nose in the air, hitched the bag higher and held one arm against it, as if protecting it from him. "I earned it."

He wanted to believe her. If this was true, then she hadn't shoplifted the bag, but it still didn't make any sense. "You 'earned' it. How, exactly?"

"I've been going to her store after school on the days you have soccer practice. I went that first day because I didn't have anything else to do. The woman who works for her had called in sick that day and Sarah was super busy so she let me do her window display while she unpacked a shipment of handbags. She said I did a really good job so she let me choose one, you know, as payment. I liked this one, and I didn't feel right about taking one of the really expensive bags."

While he tried to process this new turn of events, he recognized the last statement for what it was—an attempt to turn the table in her favor.

"So let me get this straight. For the past two weeks you've been going there after school on Tuesdays and Thursdays?"

Her nod was almost imperceptible.

"The days you said you were at the library or at home doing homework."

That question garnered another halfhearted acknowledgment.

"That explains why you're already behind in your school work and failing assignments."

"You've been checking up on me?"

"Of course I check up on you. I'm your father. That's my job." He was finding it hard to keep his reactions in check and not raise his voice. "You have a job, too. You need to keep up with your schoolwork and get decent grades, not waste time decorating store windows."

"It's not a waste of time. I knew you wouldn't understand. Because of Mom you think being interested in fashion and wanting to wear nice clothes is totally lame, but it isn't. Sarah said a lot of her customers told her how much they liked the displays I put together, and the Facebook page I set up for her is already really popular, too."

Facebook? Not that he had any experience with it, but that had to be an even bigger waste of time than window-dressing. And what was Sarah thinking, letting his daughter do these things without asking him first? She'd had plenty of opportunities and hadn't even hinted at it.

"So, you lied about the purse, you lied about what you've been doing after school. Anything else? Did you ask Sarah to lie to me, too? So she wouldn't tell me—"

"I never asked her not to tell you. If she didn't mention it, it's because she didn't think it was a big deal. And it isn't!" She'd resorted to the high-pitched yelling that was the precursor to a full-on meltdown. "Seriously, I can't believe you're so…so *not* cool about *anything*."

"Believe it. From now on, when I have soccer practice you will remain at the school, do your homework and study. There will be no more working at Sarah's store, no more hanging out with your friends."

"So I'm grounded?"

"If that's what you want to call it, yes."

"For how long?"

"Until your assignments are caught up and your grades improve. Then we'll talk."

"This is not fair! If I was on your stupid soccer team or if I'd joined the stupid chess club, you'd be fine with that. But you think the stuff I like to do is a waste of time, so I'm grounded?"

"You're grounded because—" No. The increased decibel level reminded him that he was more than a dad, he was a teacher, too. He knew better than to let a situation get out of hand, and this one was. Time to bring it down a notch.

"We both need a time-out. Go up to your room. I'll start dinner and call you when it's ready. We can talk after we've both calmed down."

"Oh, I'm going up to my room all right."

She stomped up the stairs. "But I will *not* be down for dinner," she shouted over her shoulder. "And I'm not talking to you. Ever."

He could still hear her footfall after she disappeared down the hallway.

And here we go. Wait for it.

Wham!

These abrupt reversions from nearly adult to petulant child and back again always caught him off guard and left him floundering. He doubted that slamming the door made her feel any better, and it probably scared the daylights out of the cat. Best to give her time to cool off and wait for the return of the nearly adult phase so they could have a conversation that involved less shouting and more listening on her part.

He went into the kitchen, debated what to fix for dinner, and decided on tomato soup and grilled cheese sandwiches. Kate had loved both since she was little, and since he knew from experience that she was stubborn enough to stay in her room until well past dinnertime, he could take some up to her and feel reasonably confident she would eat something.

While he chopped, sliced and stirred, he thought about Sarah. Hiring a kid to work in her store, not telling her father…why would she do something like this? How would she feel if someone sabotaged her daughter's academic success with what was little more than frivolous volunteer work? She'd be as furious as he was, and justifiably so.

So what are you are going to do about it?

He slapped the wooden spoon on the counter. He would go over there and talk to her, that's what he'd do, as soon as his soup was ready.

As soon as your soup is ready? No wonder Kate thought he was lame. He was.

CHAPTER TEN

SARAH CAME DOWNSTAIRS to find Casey and Petey already curled up together on the sofa. The little dog was well trained and well behaved, but he had no understanding of the no-dogs-on-the-furniture rule. After only one day, Sarah had given up and decided to let it go. He was only here for a week. Then she would have the furniture shampooed, or least thoroughly vacuumed.

The dog was asleep and Casey had a book in her hands.

"What are you reading?"

"My science textbook. This week's lab assignment is all about cell biology so I'm reading up on the parts of a cell."

"Good idea."

"Look at this diagram." Casey angled the book so she could see a labeled drawing of a cell. "Did you know the human body has trillions upon trillions of cells? They're not all the same, but they're all this complicated. That's crazy. We'll be using microscopes, too.

I've never used a microscope before, so that'll be cool."

As she often did, Sarah gave silent thanks for being blessed with such an awesome kid. "How was your afternoon?"

"Good," Casey said.

Hmm. Details were usually more forthcoming.

"Just good? Who did you hang out with?"

"Kate and Henry and some other kids from school."

A sleepy-eyed Petey popped his head up when Sarah sat down. She gave him a scratch behind the ears but kept her gaze on her daughter's face.

"Do these other kids have names?"

"Alycia was there. She's on the soccer team and she's in Kate's and Henry's art class. And Brody and Dexter."

Three girls, three boys, and there was no mistaking the color that bloomed in Casey's cheeks.

Sarah decided to try a different approach. "What did your friends think of Petey?"

That was all it took to brighten her eyes and dissolve the evasiveness. "Everybody loved him! Henry had his camera with him and he took some awesome pictures of the guys throwing sticks for Petey. He made a video, too, and he'll post them on Facebook tonight."

Aha. Sarah would discreetly log in and check those later. She knew Alycia and Brody, but until now Casey had never been particularly good friends with either. Dexter's name was new to her, and she had a hunch he might be responsible for her daughter's telltale blush, not to mention the unwillingness to talk about him that actually spoke volumes. For now, this was all the information she needed.

"For dinner tonight, I thought we'd go to Wharfside for fish and chips." After pizza, it was Casey's favorite.

"Sure."

"We could invite Kate and her dad to join us."

Casey grinned at that.

"What's so funny?"

"Nothing."

"Should we invite them or not?"

"Sure. I'll text Kate and see what she says." Casey closed her textbook and picked up her phone just as the doorbell rang. She jumped up and Petey followed her. "Maybe that's her. Oh. Hi, Coach. Come on in," she said after she opened the door. "Mom, it's Kate's dad."

Sarah stood, smoothed her hair and pressed

her palms to her cheeks for a moment before walking into the foyer.

Casey, textbook in one hand, phone in the other, gave her a broad wink. "I'll be up in my room. Come on, Petey."

"Hi," she said after Casey was out of earshot, trying to get her emotions under control.

"Hi." He looked tense, upset about something.

"I was going to run over to your place and invite you and Kate to join us for dinner. We're going down to the wharf for fish and chips."

"Not tonight."

"Okay. Is something wrong?"

He didn't respond right away, but she could see he was angry.

"Jonathan? What's going on?" He was starting to alarm her.

"Did you give my daughter a handbag?"

That's what this was about? "Yes, I did. She helped me at the store one day and I—"

"Just one day?"

"Well, no. She's been there on the days the soccer team practices after school."

He just stood there and stared at her, arms tightly folded across his chest, feet planted on the runner.

"Is there a problem?"

"Yes, there's a problem. Didn't it occur to you to get my permission?"

"Of course it did. She seemed to be at loose ends that first day she came to the store. I told her she was welcome to stay as long as she let you know where she was and what she was doing. She sent you a text message and a few minutes later, you replied and said it was okay." And then the penny dropped. "She didn't send the message, did she?"

"No, she didn't, but that doesn't let you off the hook, does it?"

"Excuse me?"

"You could have checked with me, but instead you didn't even mention it."

He was angry with her because *she* had been duped by *his* daughter? "I didn't mention it because it didn't come up. I wasn't trying to hide anything, and I certainly haven't done anything wrong." And aside from lying about having her father's permission to be there, neither had Kate. She'd spent a few hours helping Sarah and she'd been very fairly compensated for it. So why the overreaction?

"Thanks to you filling her head with nonsense about working in a clothing store, she's already falling behind and getting failing grades on assignments."

"Wait just a minute." She was no longer shocked, she was angry. Maybe angrier than he was. "I filled her head with nonsense? Your daughter lied to me, doesn't do her homework, and that's my fault?"

"She's impressionable. Of course she'd rather think about things that don't matter rather than getting good grades at school."

"Things that don't matter? Well, let me tell you a thing or two. Those 'things' you find so frivolous have put a roof over our heads, paid off my mortgage and helped me set up a college fund for my daughter."

He started to speak and she cut him off.

"I'm not finished. If your daughter isn't interested in school, if she feels she can't be open and honest with you, then that reflects on you, not me. If you want to know why she told me she had your permission when she had nothing of the sort, then you need to take stock of your relationship with her."

"I'm trying. It's hard to get her to focus when there are so many outside influences."

Sarah refused to back down. No way was he pinning this on her. "I sympathized with your struggle to raise a kid on your own because I thought you were really trying, but not anymore. Not if you're going to be such a narrow-minded jerk. Kate's a smart kid with a real eye for design and a good head for business. My customers are impressed with her displays, she set up a Facebook page for the store and it's already bringing in business, and I—"

"Oh, well, why didn't you mention that sooner? Who needs an education when they know how to set up a Facebook page?" His sarcasm cut deep. "Don't expect her to be back. She's grounded until she catches up at school and improves her grades."

"Good luck with that." She opened the door and flung it wide. "You need to leave." Tears threatened to spill and her voice was as shaky as the rest of her.

He hesitated.

"Now," she ordered.

He backed out and she firmly shut the door. To make sure her message hit home, she clicked the dead bolt into place. Then she turned her back to the door and leaned against it, trembling, eyes squeezed shut.

Was she really such a bad judge of character? There'd been no question she found him attractive, but she'd also been drawn to him as a person, and she was already fond of Kate. If he couldn't manage his kid, that was his problem, and if he thought he could use her as a scapegoat, he could darn well think again. She wasn't sure she would ever forgive his behavior, but she hoped this disagreement wouldn't affect her daughter's friendship with the girl next door. Poor Kate needed a friend, and Casey…

Oh, no. Casey! Had she overheard this ridiculous exchange? She certainly hoped not. Explaining why they'd be going to dinner alone would be awkward enough.

KATE WAITED TILL her dad went jogging on Monday morning before she put her plan in motion. She started by sending a message to Casey.

Am walking 2 school 2day OK?
Why?
Why not?
It's raining

Rats. She peeked past her curtains and sure enough, it was. Not pouring though. She would take an umbrella, wear her Hunter rain boots, and she'd be fine. Besides, anything, *anything*, even walking in the rain, was better than having to spend even one minute in the car with her dad.

I'll share my umbrella.
R U going to tell me wuz up?

Had a fight with my dad.
So did my mom.

She knew he'd stormed over there, probably to tell Sarah not to let her hang out at the store anymore. How could he?

Sry. CU in 15?
OK.

Ugh. This was so typical. Just when things were going great for her—just when she'd made new friends, met grown-ups who believed the things that interested her were worthwhile, found a supercute boy who wanted to hang out with her—her super-lame dad had to ruin everything.

She made a quick tour of her bedroom, opening and closing drawers, tossing things into her bag. At least he hadn't made her give the DKNY back to Sarah. Having it now strengthened her resolve. She carefully opened her door. The house was quiet. She slipped down the hall to her dad's room, slid the credit card out of his wallet—it was hers, after all—and scurried back to her room.

Princess sat on the foot of her bed, all four paws tucked out of sight beneath her. Kate knelt and buried her face in the cat's soft fur and listened to her purr.

"Sorry, girl. I can't take you with me but don't worry. He'll take care of you."

Her father had soccer practice after school so he wouldn't miss her for a couple of hours. By then she'd be…well, that was the thing. She had no idea where she would go, not yet, anyway, but she wasn't coming back here. And by the time he came home and realized she was gone, it would be too late for him to do anything about it.

AFTER THE LAST BELL, Casey dashed down to the locker room and changed into her uniform. She pulled thick blue socks over her shin pads and was all set to lace up her cleats when her phone whistled. She pulled her locker open and dug it out of her backpack.

Need to talk. Now.

Now what?

I have soccer practice, rmbr?
I only need a minute.
Where RU?
My locker.
OK. BRT.

Casey felt bad about Kate's fight with her dad, and her mom's fight with Kate's dad, but she didn't want to get dragged into the drama. She knew Kate wouldn't want to go home alone, so she would arrange to meet her after practice and they would walk together. She set her phone on the shelf in her locker and snagged her blue-and-gold jacket off the hook below it, silently congratulating herself on the arm band that designated her as assistant captain as she sat and stuffed her feet back into her sneakers.

"Where are you going?" Alycia asked.

"Forgot I have to do something. It'll only take a minute and I'll be right back." She banged her locker door shut, then raced out of the change room and down the hallway.

Kate was leaning against her locker, the big black-and-white bag that had caused the whole mess slouched on the floor at her feet. "What's up?"

"I'm leaving."

"What are you talking about?" Surely she wasn't planning to…? "You're running away?"

Kate didn't answer. "You can't tell anyone, okay? Please? I'm going back to Vancouver."

"That's crazy. You can't just leave. How are you going to get there?"

"There's a bus to Gibsons that goes right to the ferry terminal. When I get off the ferry in Horseshoe Bay, I'll grab another bus into the city."

"And then what?"

"One of my friends says I can stay with her for a couple of days."

"Which friend?"

Kate shrugged.

She's lying, Casey thought. *She doesn't have the slightest idea where she'll stay.*

"This is crazy," she repeated. "You need to talk to your dad."

"No way."

"My mom, then. She'll listen and she'll help you figure out what to do."

Kate picked up her bag. "I'm grounded, remember?"

Yes, she remembered. Kate had spilled the whole story on the way to school that morning.

"He says I'm not allowed to set foot in your mom's store, and he says he and I will talk about me being grounded after my schoolwork's caught up and my grades have improved. Who knows when that'll be."

"I can help. I get good grades."

"That's all my dad cares about. If he cared about me, my grades wouldn't matter."

Casey was starting to feel somewhat panicked. What if she couldn't get her to change her mind? She could let her go, then call her mom, Kate's dad, have them go after her. But then Kate would be in even more trouble, and she'd be mad at Casey, too.

"Okay. I'll go with you."

"You? The supersmart honor roll girl who's captain of the soccer team is going to run away?"

"Assistant captain. And I'd be pretty dumb if I let you go alone."

Kate hiked up her nose as though she didn't believe her. "Let's go."

"Right now? Can I get my stuff?"

"Go ahead, but I'm leaving now."

Brat. "Then so am I." She had plenty of time between here and the bus stop to change Kate's mind, and if things got out of hand, she could always call her mom to come and get them.

By the time they reached the stop, though, Kate was still as determined as ever. Even worse, Casey realized she'd left her phone in her locker. The bus pulled up and as Kate stepped on, she tossed a defiant look over her shoulder at Casey.

"Coming?"

What choice did she have?

"SARAH?" JULIET STUCK her head into the office.

She tore her attention away from the online order screen she'd been working her way through. "Yes? Do you need help in the store?"

"I can manage, but I was wondering if Kate will be in this afternoon."

"I'm afraid not. She's…ah…I think she working on a school assignment. Why do you ask?"

"I just had a customer ask when we'll be updating our Facebook page."

The daily photos. Of course. "Good question. I'm not sure when Kate will be in again, so I'll take some pictures before I go home and get Casey to show me how to upload them."

Now that Kate had been banned from ever setting foot in To the Nines, she needed to learn this stuff anyway.

"No problem. I'll finish refolding the summer tops on the sale table…we had quite a run on those today, thanks to Kate's post on the weekend. Unless there's something else you need me to do."

"Sounds great, Jules. Once I've finished this order, I'll be out to give you a hand."

She selected three more items, as always

finding it strange to be ordering holiday party dresses in September. After she double-checked and submitted the order, she logged out, shut down her laptop and stowed it in her briefcase. Her regular customers would love this season's dresses, and she had chosen several that were sure to suit individual preferences.

And for your information, Coach Marshall, there is nothing frivolous and inconsequential about this.

So what if he thought that what she did for a living didn't matter? As if chasing a soccer ball around a field had some earth-shattering significance. No, that wasn't fair. Casey loved soccer. In addition to staying physically fit, she was learning the importance of good sportsmanship, how to be a team player and leadership skills since she'd been voted assistant captain.

The phone rang and she grabbed it without bothering to check the display.

"To the Nines. This is Sarah."

"Sarah, it's Jonathan."

The last person in the world she had expected to hear from, and one of the last she wanted to talk to. Unless…

"Why are you calling?"

"We have soccer practice this afternoon

and Casey isn't here. I know you're not happy with me, and to be honest, I don't blame you, but you shouldn't make her stop coming to practice."

What was he talking about? "I would never do that. She's probably still in her last class. Did you check there?"

"I did. And I don't want to alarm you, but some of the girls on the team saw her in the locker room, she was already in her uniform. Then she left and it seems she's…I don't know. No one knows where she went."

Sarah felt as though the wind had been knocked out of her and now she couldn't breathe. This was crazy. Kids in Serenity Bay didn't simply disappear. "Did you check the rest of the school?" she asked.

"I had the office page her over the PA system but she hasn't responded."

"Where's Kate? Maybe she's with her."

Even through the phone, his sigh was audible. "I've already called her but she's still mad at me and she's not picking up."

No surprise there. "Casey might have gone home to check on the dog. I'll call her and then I'll call you back."

"Okay, thanks. And Sarah…?"

"Yes?"

"I'm sorry about yesterday, I really am. I

was being…the things I said were uncalled for."

You've got that right. "I'll call you after I've talked to my daughter." If he thought she'd forgive this easily, he could think again. Still, she could be gracious. "Don't worry. I'll find her. I'll find both of them."

She disconnected, brought up her daughter's number and made the call.

"Come on, Casey. Pick up."

But she didn't. The call went to voice mail and that never happened. She had Kate's number so she tried that, too. The girl had no reason to be angry with her. But that call went to voice mail, too. That left Henry. He did answer, and yes he had seen both girls after school. Casey was wearing her soccer uniform and she was in the hallway at Kate's locker. The two had their heads together in conversation and hadn't seemed to notice him as he left the school. He would have talked to them but his mother had been waiting to drive him to Sechelt for a dental appointment. They were on their way there now.

Sarah thanked him and pondered what to do next. She couldn't imagine why Casey would skip soccer practice, but if she had to guess, it had something to do with Kate, who was furious with her father. She dialed Jonathan's number. He picked up immediately.

"Casey didn't answer and neither did Kate when I tried her number, so I called Henry." She relayed what he had told her.

"Thanks for that. I'm going to cancel practice and head home. Kate is supposed to be there doing homework. Let's hope they both are." There was no mistaking the worry in his voice.

In spite of her own growing concern, Sarah's heart softened a little. He had overreacted for sure, but he didn't deserve this. "I'm leaving, too. I'll be there in a few minutes."

CHAPTER ELEVEN

SARAH'S CAR WAS parked in her driveway when Jon pulled into his. He flung open the door of his SUV and took his steps two at a time. He unlocked the front door and did a quick tour of the house, calling Kate's name, hoping for a response. He didn't get one. Princess, curled in a tight little ball on the end of Kate's bed, gave him the haughty look of one who was annoyed at having her beauty rest disturbed. Otherwise the house was lifeless.

He let himself out and jammed the key in the lock. Maybe he should leave it unlocked. What if Kate didn't have her key? The city dweller in him refused to let him leave the house unsecure. Besides, if lack of a key was the only thing preventing Kate from coming home, she would have called or texted long ago. He locked the door and sprinted the short distance to Sarah's place.

She and Petey met him at the front door. She had already changed out of the black skirt and tan jacket he'd seen her wearing when she'd left for work that morning and into jeans and a mossy-green sweater that was a perfect match for her eyes.

"Come in." She held Petey in her arms until Jonathan stepped in and closed the door behind him, then she set the dog on the floor. The energetic little fellow raced into the living room, pounced on a small teddy bear, and shook the daylights and a little of the stuffing out of it.

"Have you heard from them?" he asked.

She shook her head, and the sharp movement loosened a tear that had been hovering on her eyelid. He watched it slide down her cheek, regret stabbing him like a knife. It was too soon to consider the worst-case scenario, and besides that, his gut was telling him that whatever the girls were up to, Kate was behind it. This was her getting back at him for grounding her, and she had somehow convinced Casey to go along with her. He offered his arms and Sarah walked into them with the same fluid motion as the tears that were now soaking his shirt.

"I'm so sorry. I don't know what those two are up to, but we'll find them."

Her body shook with a single silent sob. Then she seemed to pull herself together by drawing a long, controlled breath. She lifted her head and backed out of his embrace.

"This isn't like Casey," she said, swiping at her eyes with the back of a hand. "Where could she have gone?"

What they knew so far was that Casey had been on her way to practice until she talked to Kate. Now they had both disappeared, which meant Kate had talked her into…what? He had no idea.

"Kate hasn't spoken to me since last night. I know she's upset about being grounded, but I'm having a hard time believing she'd do anything rash."

"It sounds as though you were pretty hard on her."

Now that Sarah had composed herself, she wasn't going to go easy on him. He'd been hard on her, too. Actually, arrogant and unreasonable is what he'd been.

"That's generous of you," he said. "I was out of line and I owe you both an apology. I thought about this while I was out for my run this morning, decided I would talk to her before we left for school, but she had already left by the time I came home."

The hard set of her mouth softened a little. "Casey walked with her. She said they were leaving early so they could help with setup for this morning's assembly."

"I know. Kate left a note." That she'd thought to leave him a note had seemed a positive step at the time; now he realized she'd been avoiding him, as she had at school all day. "I hope she's still just avoiding me, maybe gone to a friend's place or to one the kids' favorite hangouts, but that doesn't explain why Casey missed soccer practice and isn't answering your calls."

"My daughter has a good head on her shoulders, but I'm getting scared. She always sends me a text message after school, after practice, when she's on her way home, when she gets home. Now it's almost five o'clock and…" Sarah shrugged. "This isn't like her."

"I drove around before I came here," he told her. "I checked the pizza place, the community center, even the library." Although that was the last place he'd expect to find his daughter. "I didn't know where else to look."

Unless…

He pulled his wallet out of his back pocket and flipped it open. Kate's credit card was gone.

"Oh no."

"What?"

"Before Kate's mom moved to Europe, she

gave her a credit card. There's no way I would let her carry it around with her so I keep it in my wallet."

"And?"

"It was here yesterday afternoon. Now it's gone."

"Are you sure?"

"Positive. At first I thought she might have ordered that handbag online so I took out the card and called to check on the balance."

"Any chance you didn't put it back?"

He shook his head. He clearly remembered putting it away. He knew exactly when it went missing. "I don't carry my wallet when I run in the morning. She must have taken it while I was out of the house."

"We need to call the police."

"The police? Won't they tell us we need to wait a few hours to see if they show up on their own?"

"That might be what they do in the city, but not here. Everyone knows me, and they know Casey. If I say something's not right, they'll believe me."

"Then let's call."

He followed her through the foyer and the short hallway to the kitchen, thinking, as he had the one other time he was inside, that this house seemed brighter, more welcoming than his. More of a family home.

In the kitchen, he stood on the opposite side of the island while Sarah put her phone on speaker and made the call.

"Sunshine Coast RCMP Detachment, Constable Merriweather."

"Gayle? It's Sarah Stewart."

"Hi, Sarah. Good to hear from you. I mean, as long as everything's okay."

"You, too. And no, it's not. Casey missed soccer practice after school today and she's not answering her phone or responding to text messages. No one's seen her since classes were over, and we think she's with Kate Marshall, the daughter of the new teacher at SBH."

"Does Kate have a cell phone?"

"Yes. She isn't picking up, either. Her dad has looked around town for them, and now we just discovered that Kate has a credit card with her. We're both really worried."

"Any reason you can think of why the girls would up and disappear like this?"

Sarah glanced up at him.

"Constable Merriweather? Jon Marshall here, Kate's dad. My daughter and I had a bit of a…a disagreement last night, and she was supposed to come straight home after school."

"So, grounded?" the constable asked. The tone of her voice suggested she was smiling. "You have my sympathies, Mr. Marshall. I have two teenage girls, fifteen and seventeen. I've witnessed my share of hissy fits."

"You're Melissa's mom? She's on the soccer team."

"That's right. She told me practice was canceled today. Now I understand why."

Sarah gave him an eyes-wide look that said, *seriously?* Our girls are missing and *this* is the conversation you're having?

"Right," he said. "So—"

"No need for explanations. We want to find those girls as much as you do."

He doubted that but felt somewhat reassured nonetheless.

"Give me their phone numbers. If the phones are on, we should be able to get a location for them. And if you can email recent photos of the girls, I'll circulate those to everyone who's on duty tonight."

Sarah tore a sheet from a notepad on the fridge door and jotted down the email address. "Thanks, Gayle. We'll send those right away and then we'll go out and keep looking for them."

"Sarah, I know you're worried and you want to do everything you can to find them, but the best thing right now is to stay home so you're there when the girls do show up. Nine times out of ten, they come home on their own and their reason for being 'missing' is something completely innocent."

And the one time out of ten? Jon thought. He could tell Sarah was thinking the same thing.

"Are you sure?" Sarah asked. "I feel as though—"

"I'm sure. I'll call as soon as we know anything. Just hang tight, okay?"

"Sure," Sarah said, with absolutely no conviction whatsoever.

For a minute or two after the call ended, they stood and stared at each other. Now what? Should he stay? Better question, would she let him? He hoped so. He'd hate to go home and wait alone.

The dog tore through the kitchen and jumped against the sliding door to the deck, his front paws going at the glass like a windmill. That could only mean one thing.

"Oh, Petey. That girl promised to look after you."

"Why don't you take him out while I…I mean, if you like, I could fix us both something to eat."

She pulled a leash from a basket by the

door and clipped it to the dog's collar before she replied. "I don't have much here. I'd planned to pick up Casey at the soccer field and grab a bite before we came home."

"I can fix something at my place and you can join me after Petey's taken care of business."

She hesitated.

"Come on, Sarah. You have to eat something."

"I know. But I don't want to leave this little guy on his own, he's already spent all day in his crate, and if Casey comes home…"

"Fair enough." He crouched down and scratched the energetic little mutt behind the ears. "I'll fix something at my place and bring it back here."

Her nod was less than enthusiastic.

He stood his ground. "I know I'm not your favorite person in the world right now, but our girls are out there, somewhere, and it seems pretty certain they're together. Waiting to hear they're okay isn't going to be easy. I don't know about you, but I don't want to wait alone."

"I don't, either. I'm sorry. I just never thought something like this could happen, not with Casey. She's a *good* kid."

Unlike his kid who was, at best, a handful. He reached out, touched Sarah's shoulder, wished there was something he could do other than offer to make a meal, knowing he was lucky if she let him do that much for her. On the positive side, she didn't pull away, at least not right away, and not until the dog reminded her that the situation was now a code red.

"Oh, for heaven's sake, Petey." She unlatched the door and slid it open. "Let's go."

Jon followed her outside and down the stairs to her backyard. "I'll be back in ten."

He managed to make it back in fifteen minutes, balancing a plate of sandwiches—bacon, tomato and avocado—in one hand, a bag of potato chips tucked under his arm, and the fingers of his other hand curled around the tops of two bottles of sparkling water. While at home, he had tried calling Kate again and his call went straight to voice mail, just as before. Where was she, and better question, why had she turned off her phone? Sarah told the RCMP constable that Casey's phone rang half a dozen times before going to voice mail. That meant Casey's phone was on and she wasn't picking up, and Kate's phone was off. None of this made sense, and he was going to make himself crazy trying to figure it out.

"Thank you for doing this," Sarah said, far

more graciously than he deserved. "There are glasses and plates in the cupboard next to the microwave. Napkins in the drawer right below it." She peeked at her phone, clearly willing there to be a text message from her daughter. He knew that's what she was doing because he'd been doing the same thing. "Come on, Petey. Let's get you some dinner, too."

A well-understood word in the dog's vocabulary, judging by the way he danced on his hind legs. While Sarah scooped kibble into his dish, Jon plated sandwiches, poured drinks, dumped chips into a bowl.

"Would you like to eat in here?" he asked.

"No, let's sit in the living room." She tucked her phone into the back pocket of her jeans, picked up a plate and a glass, and led the way. "The sandwiches look delicious."

"I hope you like bacon."

"Everybody likes bacon." For the first time since this afternoon, she gave him a genuine smile as she settled onto one end of the sofa.

Kate didn't, now that she'd become a vegetarian, and now he wished he hadn't let it bother him so much. He sat on the other end of the sofa, and they both set their phones on the coffee table, checking for missed calls or messages as they did.

"The bread is great," Sarah said. "Did you bake it?"

He set his sandwich on the plate and gulped some water. "I did."

Sarah nodded. "I thought so. Kate told me you're a great cook and that you bake awesome bread."

"She said that?"

"She did. One afternoon while she was at the store."

Interesting. It seemed everything she said within earshot of him was subtly tinged with sarcasm or mild disdain. If she could be positive when he wasn't around, maybe there was hope for their father-daughter relationship after all. He would work on it, he decided. As soon as she came home.

He picked up his sandwich again. "Did she say anything about her mother?"

The way Sarah quickly lowered her gaze as she thoughtfully nibbled a potato chip said it all.

"What did she say?" He needed to know and wished he could have sounded more casual. It's not as if Kate would ever volunteer anything, and he hadn't figured out how to get her to talk about her feelings.

"Not much. Just that she moved to Europe last year, and even though they talk almost every day, it's not the same as having her here."

Her tone was matter-of-fact and nonjudgmental, and he was grateful for that.

"Even when we all lived in Vancouver, she was away a lot so I don't think proximity is the big issue. Most of Kate's resentment stems from the promises her mother makes but doesn't follow through with."

"What kinds of promises?"

"She said she'd be over for Kate's middle school graduation last June, then had to cancel when something came up at the last minute. To make up for it, Kate was supposed to spend two weeks with her in Italy at the end of July. That fell through, too."

"Poor kid." Sarah sounded genuinely understanding. "She must have been awfully disappointed."

Disappointment didn't even come close. "She was devastated. I know she understands her mother's personal commitments, but it's not easy for her. I've tried to convince Georgette to make more time for Kate, but there's no talking to her. You can be sure she'll have something to say to me, though, if she hears about this."

"Aren't you going to tell her?"

Wasn't planning on it. He must have shaken

his head, because Sarah's eyes went round with surprise.

"Really?" It wasn't so much a question as an accusation.

"You don't know Kate's mother."

"Well, what if—" She didn't finish her sentence. She didn't have to.

"What if the situation was reversed?" he asked. "Is that what you were going to say?"

"Yes, it was. If Kate went missing on her mother's watch, how would you feel if she didn't tell you?"

He stared into his glass, watching the bubbles rise to the surface and escape. Sarah was right. If the tables were turned, he would want to know what was happening. He'd be furious, sick with worry, and he would place the blame, all of it, squarely on Georgette. He sighed and picked up his phone.

Time to face the music.

CHAPTER TWELVE

SARAH GATHERED NAPKINS, empty plates and glasses and carried them into the kitchen, leaving Jonathan to make his call in private. A call he was obviously reluctant to make, and she couldn't fault the poor man for that. Although his ex was an absentee mom who was either unwilling or unable to be there for her daughter, she had a right to know the girl was missing.

She could hear Jonathan's voice from the foyer.

"Georgette, please, just listen to me. Serenity Bay is a safe place and Kate isn't alone."

There was a pause, during which she told herself she shouldn't eavesdrop. She did anyway.

"The girl who lives next door is with her. Her name is—"

"I don't care what her name is!"

Jonathan must have moved closer to the kitchen or accidentally switched to speaker because now she could hear both sides of the conversation.

"How do you know this girl isn't having a negative influence on Kate?"

Because *my* daughter is not a runaway, Sarah wanted to yell back.

"Because..." Jonathan said. "Look, Kate's been having a bit of a tough time with everything and you—"

"Don't try to pin this on me. You're the one who pulled her out of her old school, moved her away from her friends, from civilization."

Sarah had heard enough. She turned on the kitchen tap, filled the coffeemaker and left the water running for no reason other than to drown out Jonathan's conversation with his ex. Calling her had been the right thing to do, but now she understood his hesitation. By the sound of things, Georgette Ogilvie wasn't accepting any responsibility for Kate's behavior. But to try to pin this on Casey? And to blame Jonathan, who, although somewhat misguided in his approach to discipline, was doing his darnedest to make a home and a good life for his daughter? While taking none of the responsibility? That was completely unreasonable.

As though sensing her frustration, Petey roused himself from his post-dinner nap, trotted across the kitchen and nudged Sarah's ankle. She picked him up and hugged him close.

"I know. You want to know where she is, too. She was supposed to take you for a walk, maybe play a game of fetch in the backyard."

The little mutt gazed at her, and she could see her concern reflected in his dark eyes, then his pink sandpaper tongue popped out and he gave her nose a swipe, and he was all but grinning at her.

She rested her cheek against the top of his head, fighting back tears. Puppy kisses, Casey called them. "Thank you, Petey. I needed that."

JONATHAN STOOD IN the kitchen doorway, listening to Sarah's conversation with the dog, wondering why the tap was running, thinking he could use a kiss himself, and not the canine variety.

"How are you holding up?" he asked.

She swung around to face him. Her tears, while perfectly understandable, whittled away at his already eroded sense of self-worth. Calling Georgette had been the right thing to do, but he still wished he hadn't.

Sarah set the dog on the floor, turned off

the tap, tore a strip of paper towel from a dispenser and used it to dry her eyes.

"I'm sorry."

"Don't apologize." He wanted to hold her, offer comfort, get some in return. Something held him back.

"How did it go?"

"As expected." But he didn't want to rehash Georgette's accusations, the threat of her calling her lawyer. What was a lawyer going to do? "I finally told her that I have to keep the phone free so I don't miss Kate if she tries to call, and that I'll call her as soon as we hear from them."

"And we will hear from them. I know we will."

He knew she needed to believe that. So did he.

Sarah took mugs out of a cupboard and filled them with coffee. She handed one to him, apparently remembering he took it black.

"Let's take these into the living room," she said after stirring sugar and cream into hers. She pulled her phone out of her jeans pocket and checked it on the way.

They sat again, on either end of the sofa, coffee mugs in hand, phones on the coffee table within easy reach.

"Thank you for making dinner," she said. "Again."

"No problem."

"So where did you learn to cook?"

He resisted the urge to tell her that making a sandwich wasn't exactly cooking.

"I guess my mother taught me, although I don't actually remember being taught. It was just the two of us, so I had to learn to be self-sufficient when she was at work."

"Where was your father?"

For a long time, that had been the million-dollar question. "He moved out when I was eight. For quite a few years my mother never talked about it, but around the time I graduated from high school she told me he'd left her for another woman."

"All those years and she never said anything?"

"Not a word."

"Did you see him, talk to him?"

Jon shook his head. "Not once. He and his new wife moved to the east coast, had a couple of kids—"

"So you have siblings."

"No. Parents and siblings are the people you grow up with. My father and his new family are strangers." And it was strange to be talking about them now because he usually didn't think about them at all.

"But you have your mother, and she taught you how to cook."

"I do have my mother." She'd also taught him the importance of having a home and a family. "She always said the kitchen is the heart of a home."

Sarah laughed. "My kitchen is definitely not the heart of my home. Not even close."

"I've never seen a cleaner or better organized kitchen than yours," he said. More like the heart of a display home, though. Beautiful cabinets, a nearly empty fridge and a pristine stove that didn't see a lot of action aside from keeping take-out pizza warm and burning slice-and-bake cookies. "But I'd have to say you are the heart of your home."

"Nice save," she said. "I wish I loved to cook but the simple fact is that I don't. I grew up in a home where food preparation took up a huge amount of everyone's time, especially my mom's. When I left for college, I swore I wouldn't eat another bowl of granola as long as I lived, let alone make it from scratch."

"Fair enough," Jon said.

"Luckily, Casey's happy with cereal and frozen waffles, and the deli makes a great breakfast wrap with scrambled eggs."

"Breakfast takeout?"

She shrugged. "When it comes to cooking, I'm more than happy to let someone else do the work."

She was one of the most capable, take-charge people he'd ever met, with maternal instincts that more than made up for a lack of culinary skills.

"What was it like growing up in Ucluelet?" he asked. "It's sure a beautiful part of the world."

"It is, and I can appreciate that now. It's also remote, and back then, especially when I was a teenager, all I could think about was getting away and living in the city."

"Vancouver?"

She pulled her knees up under her chin and wrapped her arms around her legs. "Vancouver, New York, Paris..." She shrugged. "I had big dreams in those days."

"Those cities are a long way from Serenity Bay. Well, not Vancouver, but still worlds apart."

"I know. And I've still never been to Paris, but I hope to go someday."

Jon's memory flashed to a recent photograph of Georgette and Xavier posing in front of the Eiffel Tower. She had emailed it to Kate, who had inadvertently, or maybe not so inadvertently, left it open on her laptop where he couldn't help but see it. To him, Paris now had little appeal.

"So what made a woman with big-city aspirations decide to make her home and livelihood in a quiet little place like Serenity Bay?" He knew she'd come here with her husband, but after he died she could have gone anywhere.

"It's not a terribly long story. After high school I went to Vancouver to study business administration at the University of British Columbia, and that's where I met my husband, Jim. He finished his MBA at the same time I earned my degree. Within two weeks he had been offered a job with a developer. He proposed and I accepted, and a week later we were married and moved into an apartment above the pharmacy on Hemlock Street."

Huh. He'd have never pegged her as someone who'd do something so out of character. Then again, love made people do impulsive things.

"You've certainly been successful here. Happy, too, I hope."

She appeared to give that some thought. "You know, not many people ask about the happiness factor. Everyone focuses on the success. But there was a time when I was neither. Jim was one of those larger-than-life people who loved being the center of attention. He basically swept me off my feet. Not that it was hard to dazzle a girl who'd grown up next door to the wilderness, raised entirely on organics and completely off the grid."

Off the grid? That piqued his interest, but he was more interested in hearing about her marriage and what had happened to her husband.

She checked her phone again before she continued. "After six months, Jim had landed a promotion. He was playing the stock market, too, and his investments were doing well, so we bought a house, decided to start a family. We also bought a boat and he loved to spend time on it on the weekends, but that always turned into a party. I assumed it would stop after Casey was born, but it didn't."

He took her hand and gave it a squeeze. "I'm sorry. We don't have to talk about this."

She gave him a faint smile. "It helps pass the time. I'm afraid that if I don't keep talking, I'm going to lose my mind."

He could relate. He was barely keeping it together himself, and she was very easy to listen to. He didn't let go of her hand, and she didn't seem to notice.

"If something's happened to her, to either of them—"

"They're going to be fine." They had to be. "You were telling me about your early days in Serenity Bay."

"Right. Jim was always wanting to spend time with friends, coworkers, basically anyone who was into partying. After Casey was born, she was the center of my world. So sweet and smart, I couldn't bear to leave her with a sitter. At some point I realized Jim and I had become strangers. Living under the same roof was the only thing we had in common. Then one night…it was late and he hadn't come home after work…an RCMP officer showed up at the door. And I knew. Even before he told me, I knew. He'd crashed his car into a rock cut on the Sunshine Coast Highway, and he wasn't coming home. He was drunk, of course, but he was alone in the car and no other vehicles involved, thank the heavens for that."

Jon wanted to pull her in for a hug, but if he tried to make this physical, he risked severing the emotional connection that was drawing them together.

"How old was Casey?"

"Six. She had just started first grade and I

was trying to figure out what to do with the next phase of my life."

"Sometimes life has a way of propelling us headfirst into making decisions."

"It sure does. Especially when I discovered that his investments had tanked, our credit cards were maxed out, the mortgage was in arrears and we were just barely getting by, paycheck to paycheck."

Jon suddenly had a newfound respect for a woman who had already impressed him beyond words. "How did you manage? Did your family help you?"

"They did, in their own way, at least. But I had a business degree and a good head for finances. My only real mistake was assuming that Jim did, too. Anyway, I sold the house and the boat, moved Casey and myself into a little apartment, and landed a job with the original owner of To the Nines, doing her books, taxes, that sort of thing. She was happy with my work and word spread and pretty soon I was turning down jobs. I worked from home a lot, which gave me lots of time to spend with my daughter."

"How does an accountant make the transition to owning a clothing store?"

She laughed lightly. "It's not as big a leap as you might think. Fashion had always been part of that big-city dream of mine. Living in a city didn't happen, except while I was at college, but I've always followed fashion trends."

"Off the grid?"

"Yes, even then. My mom was busy with her garden and cooking, my dad was always building something, and my older sister seldom had her nose out of a book. I was the odd one out, dreaming of owning my own business someday, maybe even a chain of fashion boutiques."

"You're amazing," he said, and he meant it. In spite of some major hardships, she was well on her way. "Doesn't living off grid mean no electricity?"

"It sure does."

"Did you have solar power? Or does it rain too much on the west coast of the island?"

"Oh, it rains all right. Believe it or not, though, solar panels work even when it's cloudy or foggy. We also had woodstoves for heating and cooking, and a diesel generator for backup."

"Wow. I'm impressed."

"Me, too. My dad's an engineer but he mostly works as an environmental consultant. And these days my family's home is no longer off the grid, it's tied to it."

"So when your dad produces excess electricity, he's feeding it into the grid?"

"That's right."

"I've heard of people doing that but I've never known anyone who's actually done it. Do you visit your family very often?"

"We spend a week or so with them every summer. Casey loves it there, the beaches, tide pools, doing science-y stuff with my dad and my older sister. She's a professor of environmental studies in Montreal.

"Science-y." He smiled at that. "I can see the appeal."

Sarah unexpectedly pulled her hand away and covered her face. "What if she's not okay?"

He was trying to think of something to say when her phone rang. They both jumped.

"It's not Casey. Not the police, either."

For a second or two, it seemed as though she might not answer it. Then she did, and her hesitation turned to jubilation the instant she said, "Hello?"

"CASEY! OH MY HEAVENS, girl! I've been worried sick! Are you okay? Where are you? Who's phone—?" Her hands shook so bad, she could hardly hold the phone.

"Mom! I'm fine. Let me talk."

"Where—?"

"Mom!"

"Okay, okay. I'm listening." Over the thunder of her pulse pounding in her ears.

Jonathan leaned in, wanting to hear, too. Poor guy. She switched to speaker.

"I'm using Kate's phone. We're at the Langdale ferry terminal—"

"What? How did you get there?"

"On the bus. We—"

"I've been calling and calling and you didn't pick up. Where—?"

"Mom! Kate went to the washroom and she forgot to take her phone with her. Let me finish before she gets back."

"Sorry, sweetie. I'm listening." This time she would.

"Kate's mad at her dad…"

He and Sarah hadn't broken eye contact since she'd answered the call. Now there was no missing the hurt, the sad set of his mouth. She touched his hand, and her heart lightened a little when he linked his fingers with hers.

"I was getting ready for soccer practice and Kate texted me. She said she was going to take the ferry to Vancouver and stay with a friend. How dumb is that? I'd put all my stuff in my gym locker when I went to talk to her. I couldn't talk her out of leaving so I thought if I went with her, I'd have plenty of time to change her mind before she actually got on the ferry."

"So your phone's in your gym locker?"

"Yup, and Kate turned hers off in case her dad tried to call."

Jonathan let out a sigh and shook his head. She could see that his relief was already morphing back into annoyance.

"What time does the next ferry leave?"

"In about twenty minutes. Can you get here?"

"Not a chance, but don't worry. I've already talked to Gayle Merriweather. I'll call her and she'll get them to hold the ferry till we get there."

"Oh, geez, Mom. You called the police?"

"Of course we did. We were—"

"Gotta go. Kate's coming."

"We're on our way."

"Bring Petey?"

"Sure."

The line went dead.

Jonathan stood and pulled her to her feet. Sliding into his arms was maybe not the smartest move, but she went anyway. She tipped her head to look up at him and sucked in a quick breath just as his lips met hers. There was nothing tentative about this kiss.

His mouth was firm, as comforting as it was demanding, and his arms created a warm shelter. She wished they could linger, and on another level was glad they couldn't. This had been an emotionally charged day, it had been a very long time since she'd experienced this kind of intimacy, and it all felt like uncharted territory.

After a few seconds, he eased away. "We need to go."

"I'll get the dog."

"We can take my car."

"And I'll call the police."

He was standing next to his SUV talking on his phone when she stepped out her front door. With her purse slung over her shoulder and Petey's travel crate clutched in one hand, she locked up and joined Jonathan in the driveway. She stowed the dog in the back and climbed in, buckling her seat belt while making the call to Constable Merriweather.

Jonathan slid in behind the wheel and tossed his phone on the dash, started the engine, and backed onto the street as he buckled himself in. She didn't have to ask who he'd been talking to. The tight set of his jaw said it all.

As they drove out of town, she updated the police with the girls' whereabouts and was assured that an officer would pick them up at the ferry terminal before the next sailing.

"I'll call as soon as we find them," Gayle said.

"Thank you."

In the backseat, Petey yipped from his carrier, excited about going for a car ride. Sarah periodically gave Jonathan a sideways glance. He kept both hands on the wheel and never took his eyes off the road, his features so rigid, they might have been set in stone.

"Kate's mom must be relieved."

He nodded.

Okay. Maybe something else was bothering him. Maybe he was thinking about how to react when they reunited with the girls. Or maybe he wished they hadn't just shared a kiss. She hoped that wasn't it. That kind of kiss shouldn't be ruined by regret. Finally, she couldn't take another second of the silence.

"Are you okay?"

"Not really."

"You're worried about Kate."

"Of course."

"But there's something else."

He nodded.

Great. Was he intentionally giving her the silent treatment? She looked away, staring out the passenger window as they whizzed their way down the coast, catching glimpses of the deep blue water of the strait. She was still trying to process the few details Casey had given her, how she had gone with Kate in an effort to talk the girl out of doing something rash. She still had a lot of questions, but those could wait till they were home, alone. For now the relief of knowing they were okay was all she needed to set her mind at ease.

Her phone rang, snapping her back to the present.

"It's the police," she said before answering. Jonathan didn't respond.

"Gayle? Hi, what's happening?"

"We got lucky, Sarah. We had a cruiser near the terminal and the officer was able get there within minutes. He has apprehended the girls and they're on their way to the station in Gibsons."

Apprehended? "Oh, I…I'm not sure what that means. Have they been arrested?"

That snapped Jonathan out of his ironman pose, and he gave her a quick glance before turning his attention back to the road.

Gayle laughed. "No, it does not. They haven't done anything wrong."

Sarah wasn't sure she agreed with that. Kate had decided to run away, and Casey had decided to go with her. Both girls had made bad decisions, but at least they hadn't made it onto the ferry. She was beyond grateful for that.

"Thank you for everything you've done, Gayle. We're so relieved to know they're safe," Sarah said. "We should be there in ten minutes, fifteen tops."

She tucked her phone into her handbag, folded her hands in her lap, and waited for Jonathan to say something, anything, but he didn't speak. A few moments ago she'd been in his arms and he'd kissed her, thoroughly and with enthusiasm. Now, as though a switch had been flipped, he wasn't speaking to her. She looked at him again and realized there was so much about him that she didn't know. Beneath his outdoorsy, laid-back exterior, there was an underlying sadness that had been there right from the start. She hadn't noticed it until now, and her heart broke just a little bit.

Of course he was sad; why wouldn't he be? His wife had left him, his rebellious daughter had tried to run away.

You shouldn't be making this about you, she told herself. *Let it go and cut the poor man some slack.*

CHAPTER THIRTEEN

JON LOOSENED HIS grip on the steering wheel when he noticed his knuckles were white. His thoughts darted from what he should say to Kate when he saw her, to the things Georgette said when he called to tell her their daughter was safe, to this beautiful woman next to him who had, moments ago, kissed him senseless. There had been more to that kiss than relief. He'd felt the heat, and he knew she'd felt it, too, and then his brief conversation with Georgette had hit him like an icy blast from a fire hose.

"Would it help to talk about your conversation with Kate's mom?" Sarah's eerily pertinent question caught him off guard and had him wondering if he had inadvertently blurted one of his scattered thoughts out loud.

"Not really."

"I'm a good listener," she said, apparently unfazed by his abrupt response.

He exhaled a sigh. "I know you are."

"But I'm also annoying."

He gave her a quick sideways glance. "Why would you say that?"

"Because you're annoyed with me."

"No, I'm not." If he'd given her that impression, he owed her an apology. "I'm sorry, Sarah. I'm upset with Kate and I'm furious with Georgette, but I am not annoyed with you."

"That's good to know, but…"

"But…?"

He could feel her steady gaze on him. "At the risk of annoying you now, would you mind my being honest with you?"

"I don't mind." He hoped.

"I think you need to lighten up with Kate."

He hadn't known what to expect, but he sure hadn't expected that. Where to even begin? "She's only two weeks into the school term and she's already falling behind."

"I know, but that means it shouldn't be too hard for her to catch up. Maybe, instead of grounding her, you should sit down and have a heart-to-heart talk with her. Ask her how she's feeling about the situation with her mother, about her new home, about her new school."

"Has she said something to you about those things?"

"It's not what she says, it's more what she doesn't say. She seems a little lost."

It killed him to think his daughter was hurting and he hadn't been there for her, but Sarah was right. That's exactly what happened. He'd been focused on her negative attitude and rebellious spirit instead of trying to find out what was behind them.

"She's been through a lot." They both had. "Her mother calls her every day, but it's not enough. Kate wants to spend time with her and Georgette promises she will, but then she always has a reason for putting it off. She has a busy life, I understand that. And I get that she's happy to finally have the life she always wanted, gadding about Europe, rubbing shoulders with royals and millionaires and Hollywood film stars, but she's still a mother. Yes, she calls Kate almost every day, but she isn't really there for her."

"And Kate knows that," Sarah said. "She's a smart kid."

"She is." But when was the last time he'd acknowledged that, even to himself, let alone told her? "She deserves more credit than I've been giving her."

"Don't beat yourself up. I'm a single parent, too. I know how hard it is."

"You make it look easy."

Sarah's light laugh eased some of the tension that had his gut tied in knots. "I've had a lot more practice than you have, and Casey was a lot younger than Kate when she lost her other parent."

"Thank you for that. Kate didn't lose a parent, though. She just has a mother who doesn't make time to be with her."

"It's still a loss, and she's grieving."

Grief. Until now, he hadn't thought of it in those terms. Maybe because his own ego had taken a major hit when Georgette told him she was leaving, and she wasn't leaving alone.

"You're right. How did I not see that?"

"Because you were grieving, too."

He pondered that for a few moments. "It'd be nice if it was that simple. Our marriage was over long before Georgette left."

"And now it's up to you to be the parent Kate can count on, the one she can turn to when life gets overwhelming, and the parent who helps her forge a better relationship with her mother." The matter-of-factness of her statement hit its intended target, but her gentle tone of voice softened the blow.

"I want to be that parent. Any advice on how I go about it?"

"Yes," she said without hesitation. "If you're sure you want to hear it."

"I am."

He could hear her draw a breath, as though she was gathering steam.

"Kate's a smart, capable kid. I know you know that, but did you know she has a genuine passion for the fashion industry and a real flair for design?"

You need to hear her out, he told himself, trying to ignore the tension that bunched between his shoulders.

"I know you think it's frivolous—"

"I've never said that."

"Yes, you did."

She was right. So much for hearing her out.

"And I can tell that you think Kate's love of clothes and fashion trends is frivolous."

He was sure her repetition of the word was meant to hammer her point home.

"I happen to share that love, and I'm here to tell you that I've worked hard to build a successful business. I'm proud of everything I've accomplished. And on this subject, I don't think Kate's the one who needs an attitude adjustment."

"But I do?"

"Yes."

Ouch. He didn't know if he could explain where he was coming from without sounding mean-spirited, but he had to say it anyway. “Kate is a lot like her mother. Georgette was…*is* all about appearances. Clothes, hair, makeup, she even has a personal stylist.”

“Earlier, you told me about your father, how he left and shut you out, how he started a new family that you were never part of. Was there ever any danger of you becoming just like him?”

He didn’t know how to answer that question, but apparently it was rhetorical because she didn’t miss a beat.

“Of course you didn’t. You’re not your father’s clone. You and I have only just met, but I think I know you well enough to say you would never turn your back on your daughter. And I don’t have to meet your ex-wife to know that Kate isn’t a clone of her mother, either.”

“What about her schoolwork? I’m not being a responsible parent if I let her do the things she likes and ignore the things she doesn’t.”

Sarah sighed. “That’s not what I’m saying. Sit down and talk to her. *With* her, not *at* her. Ask her about her hopes and dreams, listen to what she has to say. Set aside your judgments and listen hard enough so you actually hear her. And then find a way to compromise.”

Talk, listen. Hear. “You make it sound easy.”

"Well, it's not. Parenting is the toughest job you'll ever have, but it's also the most rewarding, don't you think?"

He wanted the kind of connection and mutual respect she and her daughter had, but right now he was on his way to pick up his kid at a police station. "I'll have to get back to you on that."

Could he do the things she suggested? He had to. Failure wasn't an option.

On the outskirts of Gibsons, he slowed to the posted speed limit. "Do you know where the station is?"

"I do. In another mile or so we'll need to turn right. I can't remember the name of the road, but I'll know it when I see it."

He was anxious to see Kate, to assure himself that she really was okay, but he worried about saying or doing the wrong thing. Something he had a real knack for.

You could ask an expert. He had one right here in the car with him.

"So you wouldn't happen to have any other advice for a bungling father, would you?"

"What kind of advice?"

"Ah, like how to handle things when we get there."

She reached out, and her hand on his arm was both unexpected and reassuring. "Stay calm and don't overreact. It's okay to let her know you were worried, but it's not a good time to point fingers and lay blame. Make sure she knows you're relieved to see her and that you'll talk later, once you have your emotions under control."

"Okay. I can do that." He hoped.

"And when you do get home, don't come down too hard on her."

Good advice, he thought, since it was the coming down hard that had landed them in this mess in the first place.

"See if the two of you can find some middle ground." She pointed to the intersection ahead. "We need to turn right here."

Middle ground, he thought, signaling and making the turn she'd indicated. He had a feeling she had something very specific in mind, and he had absolutely no idea what that might be. *Might as well ask,* he told himself. It's not as if he had anything to lose.

"You've probably already figured out that I'm a little dense when it comes to these things. What you mean by 'middle ground'?"

"What if Kate agrees to keep up with her schoolwork in exchange for helping out at my store a couple of afternoons a week after school? You would both have to compromise, but you would both be getting what you want, too."

Compromise. He thought that's what he'd been doing all along. In one of those all-too-rare lightbulb moments, it dawned on him that he had not been giving Kate the benefit of the doubt. Instead of asking what she needed and wanted, he had let her know, as much through his actions as his words, that he knew what was best for her. All she had to do was listen and do what she was told.

"This is it," Sarah said. "Here on the right."

He swung the car into the driveway and pulled up behind the police cruiser parked there. The two-story white clapboard building with immaculately groomed grounds could pass as a house if not for the sign and flagpole in the front yard and radio tower behind.

Sarah's door flew open the instant he stopped and switched off the ignition. She had one purpose now and it wasn't him… and he couldn't fault her for that. She released her seat belt and jumped out of the car in one fluid move. He was moving a little slower and she already had Petey's crate out of the backseat by the time he stepped out and closed the door.

Their gazes met over the roof of the SUV. And then, as though she could see the enormity of his self-doubt, she gave him a wide smile. Then she walked around the front of the car and slipped her free arm around his waist as they walked to door.

"You can do this," she said. "You know how they say it takes a village to raise a child? Well, just remember that we live in the same village."

He looped an arm around shoulders and for the first time in what felt like forever, he believed her. He could do this.

LIFE COULDN'T POSSIBLY get any suckier, Kate thought. On the drive back to Serenity Bay, she wedged herself into the corner of the backseat and stared out the window, refusing to speak to or even look at any of these people.

Her dad hadn't yelled, even though she'd expected him to go totally ballistic. Sarah hadn't reprimanded her for dragging her precious daughter into this. Casey hadn't gone all nya-nya-nya-nya-nya on her but, still, some friend she'd turned out to be.

What were they doing instead? Her dad had put the radio on her favorite station, Sarah calmly pointed out several points of interest along the highway, and Casey had taken Petey out of his carrier and had him sitting on her lap. All of this was really bugging her because she was spoiling for a fight.

She leaned her head against the window and squeezed her eyes shut. They flew open again when something cold touched her hand. Petey's nose. He was looking at her with such sad eyes, she couldn't resist petting him. He crawled onto her lap and rested his chin on her arm, and for some crazy stupid reason, that made her cry.

In the front seat, Sarah dug a little plastic packet of tissues out of her purse and passed them back to her without saying anything.

She wanted to scream. *Stop being nice to me!* But she just dried her eyes and blew her nose and tried to make herself small enough to disappear into the corner.

JON HAD SOME very mixed feelings as he unlocked the front door. He glanced next door in time to see Sarah, arm in arm with her daughter, disappear inside. *You're on your own*, he thought, stepping aside for his daughter. A sullen and still-silent Kate made a beeline for the stairs.

You can do this, Sarah had said to him. But he already wanted to play the village card because this would be so much easier if she was here.

"Hold on," he said.

She stopped but didn't turn around to face him.

"Come on into the kitchen and I'll fix you something to eat. We need to talk."

"What's to talk about? You're grounding me till I'm eighteen?"

He refrained from pointing out that, under the circumstances, her belligerence was out of line. This was about finding that middle ground, not creating an even wider and deeper rift between them.

He eyed the bulging black-and-white bag with suspicion. It was the catalyst that had precipitated this whole mess and although he normally didn't have an opinion about purses, he intensely disliked this one. Judging by its shape, she had packed for an extended time away from home.

"No punishment," he said.

She faced him then, warily, as though she either didn't believe him or didn't trust him to keep his promise.

He hiked his head in the direction of the kitchen. "Come on. I'll make some sandwiches."

She followed several paces behind him and stood at the island. He handed her a cutting board, a knife, a tomato and an avocado.

"If you'll slice these, I'll slice the bread and cheese," he said, hoping her favorite sandwich would open the lines of communication.

For a few seconds, he thought she might refuse, but then she peeled off her jacket and draped it over the back of a stool and sat down.

He unwrapped the loaf of bread he'd made that morning and took butter, cheese and condiments out of the fridge. "What would you like to drink? Is water okay?"

She only nodded. Okay, still not talking. That was fine. At least she wasn't talking to him at home instead of who knows where it was she'd been going. He still needed to get to the bottom of that, but first things first. He filled two glasses and passed one to Kate. Then he carved off thick slabs of sourdough, spread them with butter and sliced the cheese. "Would you like mayo on yours?"

Another nod. No problem. This time, no matter what, he would not lose his cool.

To keep calm, he only needed to think about those hours spent not knowing where she was, about how lost she'd looked sitting in that stark, impersonal room at the police station. About Sarah telling him she was part of his village. He had a second chance with both of them. This time he wouldn't blow it, because he might not get another.

After Kate finished slicing vegetables, he layered everything together, cut the two sandwiches on the diagonal and set them on plates. He forked dill pickles from a jar and added one to each plate, slid one in front of Kate and settled on a stool at the opposite end of the island with his. He watched her tuck into the meal and was glad he hadn't let her disappear upstairs to lick her wounds. If she'd had anything to eat since lunchtime, it had likely come from a vending machine at the ferry terminal.

He gave her a few minutes to eat while he took that time to polish off half of his own sandwich and contemplate how to approach this. The direct approach, he decided, was the only way to go.

"I overreacted yesterday and I owe you an apology for that. I'm sorry."

Kate's eyelids fluttered in surprise, suggesting that was the last thing she'd expected him to say.

He pressed on. "If I've made you feel as though you can't talk to me about the things that interest you or tell me how you're spending your time, then I haven't been doing my job as your father. I hope you know that your mother and I both love you very much," he continued. "And we've both been doing a lousy job of showing it."

She crunched a pickle, sputtered a little, then gulped some water. "Then how come she didn't let me visit this summer?"

"I can't answer that." And there was no way he would speculate, not out loud and certainly not for his daughter to hear. Besides, that's not where this conversation was headed. "But I can tell you that the problems your mother and I were having, our reasons for getting a divorce—" and there'd been plenty of them "—none of those things had anything to do with you. You've only ever been our smart, beautiful daughter and we've always been insanely proud of you."

"So why did you get divorced?"

"Because your mom and I realized we didn't want the same things anymore. Her career was taking off. She was always busy, and she was away a lot."

Kate's eyebrows shot up. "So it was her fault."

"No, it wasn't. I was proud of her, I still am. She's always known what she wanted, she knew what she needed to do get it, and she went for it." And it was those same traits in Kate that had him feeling so conflicted. "Your mom had an amazing career and there's no way I would have asked her to give it up. But that kind of hectic life, always being on the go, the long and irregular hours…I couldn't make them work for me."

"Even before she moved out, when she was out at night and working late and stuff, I used to go to bed and wonder if she was ever coming home again."

He'd thought the divorce was the low point in his life, but with this revelation his emotions spiraled to dark new depths. To think he and Kate had been worrying about the same thing and he had never picked up on it. He'd convinced himself that Georgette was the self-centered one. Not so.

He found himself wondering what sort of advice Sarah would offer.

She's grieving. You were grieving, too.

Was it possible they'd both been grieving the loss of a wife and mother before she was actually gone?

"I used to lose sleep over it, too," he admitted. "If I'd guessed you were going through the same thing, I would have talked to you about it. I guess I thought you were young enough that you wouldn't notice, and that you were too young to be dragged into the world of grown-up problems."

"Seriously, Dad? I'm not a little kid." Her tone was forceful but it was laced with humor, too, and that was the first bright spot in what had been a very dark day.

"I know you're not, and I'll try not to think of you that way, but you'll always be my daughter, in some ways the little girl who used to count on me for everything."

That netted him an eye roll. "It's still Mom's fault that we had to come here. If she hadn't moved out, then we'd all still be living in the city together. Sometimes I think maybe she'll change her mind and come back to Vancouver, and then we can all be a family again."

"You really don't like it here? I thought you were settling in, starting to make new friends."

"I am. I miss my old friends, though. And the city."

Honestly, there were things he missed, too, but Serenity Bay was already starting to feel like home. He hoped Kate would eventually feel that way as well.

"I'm sorry if it seemed as though I wasn't involving you in my decision to move here, but I thought it would be good for us, both of us, to have a fresh start. And just to be clear, your mom and I won't be getting back together."

Ever. Even if by some miracle Georgette were to have a change of heart, a reunion was never going to happen.

"It's just you and me, kid. The divorce wasn't your mom's fault. We were equally responsible. All I want now is for your mom to be happy with her new life, and for us to be happy with ours."

He was finally ready to move on, and moving on with his new neighbor felt right, especially now that she'd forgiven him for being such a jerk when he found out Kate was hanging out at her store after school. It was too soon to share *those* feelings with Kate, though.

"So where do we go from here?" he asked.

"Am I still grounded?"

He shook his head. "No. I'm rescinding that."

She brightened noticeably.

"With conditions," he added quickly. "You're not off the hook entirely."

"But I'm not grounded?"

"No."

"And I can go to the freshman dance on Friday night?"

Ah, yes. The dance. He'd been asked to

chaperone but had declined because he knew Kate wouldn't want him there. Now he tried not to think about the fact that freshman boys also went to dances, and few things interested them more than freshman girls.

"Who else is going?"

"Casey and Alycia and some of the…some of our friends."

"Some of the boys" is what she'd been about to say. Henry and Dexter, if he had to guess. He'd been trying not to monitor her activities at school, but he wasn't blind.

"Of course you can go. And you'll be happy to know I won't be one of the chaperones."

She trained her gaze on him, steady and straight as an arrow. "You should. Casey's mom is chaperoning."

That was unexpected—on both counts—and suddenly a high school dance had a whole lot of appeal. There was still a smattering of freshman boy in every man. He was no exception, and since Sarah would be there…

"You won't mind if I go?"

"Not if you're there as one of the teachers and not trying to be a cool dad or anything."

He laughed at that. "Okay. I'll be sure to leave my cool at home."

"Dad, that's lame." She was right, but she laughed, too.

"I assume that Casey will be giving her mother the same instructions."

"Sarah *is* cool."

And he was not. Well, he could live with that. "Speaking of Sarah…she and I had lots of time to talk tonight. She told me how much you've helped her at the store."

Kate stared down at the half sandwich on her plate.

"You really like being there, don't you?"

She nodded and picked up the sandwich.

"Since you're not grounded, I was thinking we might work out a compromise."

Instead of taking a bite, she set the sandwich down. "What kind of compromise?"

"That you could still work there two afternoons a week on the days I have soccer practice, and maybe the occasional Saturday."

"Really? Are you serious?"

"Yes, *but*…it's contingent on a couple of things. You have to keep up with your schoolwork, and your grades need to improve, too."

She looked a little deflated.

"You're a smart kid with a lot of talent, and I'm sorry I haven't given you enough credit for that, but school's important, too. I'll do what I can to help. We'll even hire a tutor if your teachers think it's necessary."

"Okay, I will. I promise. And I can ask

Casey if she'll help me with science. She gets straight A's in that class."

"As long as it's okay with her mother."

"I'm sure it's fine." She slid off her stool, looking somewhat timid at first, and gave him an awkward hug. "I won't let you down, I promise."

He believed her. Their father-daughter relationship had taken a giant leap in the right direction, and while he knew there were bound to be a few bumps in the road ahead, they were actually communicating.

"Are you going to finish your sandwich?"

"Can I take it upstairs? I want to call Casey. And Sarah."

"Of course. But before you make those calls, will you do one thing for me?"

"Sure."

"Call your mom and let her know you're okay. She's waiting to hear from you."

Her enthusiasm waned a little. "It's pretty late over there."

"It doesn't matter. She wants to hear your voice."

"Okay." She picked up her plate and glass and disappeared out of the kitchen.

For a few minutes he just sat there, mulling over the evening's events, then he went to work on the kitchen, putting things away in the fridge, loading the dishwasher, wiping down the counter. He was bone-tired and exhilarated all at the same time. He'd like to talk to Sarah, too, but he'd already imposed on her enough for one day. Still, a text message might be appropriate.

He tracked down his phone, retrieved a binder from his briefcase in the foyer and flipped to the page of contact information for the girls on the soccer team.

You were right about compromise. Thank you.

That should do it. It sounded formal but he couldn't bring himself to use the accepted shorthand and symbols that kids used in text messages, though, so he left it as it was, punched in her number and sent it. Her reply came a moment later.

U R welcome. Knew U cld do it. Congrats! :-)

He smiled, set the phone on the counter, picked it up, read it again. Kate was right. Sarah was pretty cool. Maybe he should reply. He typed:

:-)

Delete, delete, delete.

He didn't know why it seemed lame when he did it, but it did. Better to leave things as they were. Kate was home where she belonged. He and Sarah were on good terms. There was a school dance on Friday. For now he could finally say *life is good*, and he'd like it to stay that way.

CHAPTER FOURTEEN

ON THURSDAY AFTERNOON, Sarah was in her office when Kate arrived at the store.

"Is there anything you'd like me to do?" she asked.

"Before we get started, I'd like you to come in and sit down." Sarah took her briefcase off the spare chair and patted the seat. "The first thing we're going to do is set some ground rules." She stopped short of tacking a stern "young lady" to the end of her sentence.

Kate, who apparently reserved her derisive eye roll for her father, sat with her gaze lowered to the hands folded sedately in her lap. "My dad knows I'm here."

"I know he does. He called before he went to soccer practice to let me know you were on your way." Half expecting some attitude from the girl, Sarah softened her tone a little. "He and I were worried sick when you and Casey took off after school the other day."

Kate looked up then, and for the first time since that night, there was genuine concern in her eyes. "It wasn't Casey's fault. She was worried, too, and she wanted to go with me so I wouldn't be alone, but I shouldn't have let her."

"You're right about that, and you shouldn't have gone, either."

A spark of defiance glittered in the girl's eyes, and faded almost as fast. "I know. My dad and I talked and he said he was going to lighten up."

"He loves you, you know. He only wants what's best for you."

"I know, but he never used to ask what I wanted."

Sarah took one of Kate's slender hands in both of hers, thinking the iciness of the girl's skin was a good match for her demeanor. "Did you ever think you should tell him?"

"No. I figured he'd think my ideas were dumb. He probably still thinks I should be a lawyer or something."

"Did he say that?"

"No, but he's all about wanting me to study all the time and get good grades and stuff."

"So why don't you tell me what you see yourself doing someday." She had already heard it from Casey, but she wanted Kate to actually say it out loud to a grown-up.

"I want to work for a fashion magazine."

"What's your favorite magazine?"

"*Seventeen.*" She said it without hesitation.

"And what do you see yourself doing if you get a job there?"

The girl shrugged, as though nothing she dreamed of doing someday had any validity. "Photography, maybe. Writing articles about designers and celebrities."

"Being a journalist would be a really interesting job."

Seemingly buoyed up by a little positive reinforcement, Kate continued. "I wouldn't stay doing that forever, though. Someday I want to be editor in chief of a magazine like that."

"What sort of education do you think a person would need to land a job like that?"

Kate shrugged again.

"A college degree, for sure. Something like journalism, or maybe business administration."

"I guess."

"And good photography is all about light and angles and exposures. Remind you of anything?"

Kate scrunched her nose. "Science and geometry?"

"That's right. And the editor in chief of a big fashion magazine would need to understand budgets and finances."

"And that means math."

The resignation in her voice made Sarah laugh. "I'm afraid so."

"Did you help Casey figure out what she needs to do to be a veterinarian?"

Interesting question, and one that required a careful answer.

"Not exactly."

Sarah had always known her daughter was not like most kids, and to draw a comparison between Casey and Kate wouldn't be fair to either girl.

"Casey decided she wanted to be a vet when she was in kindergarten. I'm not sure how she came up with the idea. We didn't have any pets and so she'd never actually met a veterinarian." Her father had still been alive at that time, drinking heavily, burning through money faster than he could earn it. A pet, no matter how much Casey would have benefited from having one, would have been an extravagance they couldn't afford.

"That's so Casey," Kate said. "For someone who's supersmart, I figured she'd be a total nerd. She's not, though. She's pretty cool."

Sarah's heart swelled. These were things she'd always known about her daughter, but hearing someone else say them, especially one of her peers, was a gift. But this conversation was about another girl, one who was every bit as smart but, for reasons Sarah didn't fully understand, lacked the self-confidence to believe it.

"There's a chance I could be biased...but yes, she's a pretty cool kid. And so are you. You're smart. You're really good with computers. The write-ups you've put on our social media sites are brilliant, you're great with customers, and you have an eye for design. I've noticed the outfits you put together for yourself, and I saw how easily you put together the window display here in the store. I think a career in fashion is perfect for you, and any magazine would be lucky to have you."

Sarah was reminded of a flower blossoming as she watched Kate's features soften and her color heighten.

"Would you maybe consider telling this to my dad? He thinks all this stuff is lame."

Hearing things from Sarah wouldn't have half the impact on Jonathan as hearing it directly from his daughter. She'd been really pleased to hear he'd followed her advice and had a heart-to-heart talk with Kate after they'd brought the girls home, but it sounded as though they still had a way to go before the lines of communication were flowing as they should. Between Kate's attitude and Jonathan's opinions, she could imagine how that conversation might go.

"I have a better idea. How would you like to write a blog post for the store's website?"

"Sure, but I don't see what that has to do with my dad."

"That's because I haven't given you the topic yet."

A little of Kate's earlier wariness was back. "You make this sound like school."

Sarah laughed. "I hope it'll be more fun than that. I'd like you to write about the things we talked about this afternoon. About your goal to work for a fashion magazine someday and about the things you'll need to do to achieve that goal."

"And you think he'll read it?" Kate asked, clearly skeptical.

"I'll make sure he reads it."

"Really? What about your customers? Don't they want to read about current fashion trends, the new merchandise you're bringing in, stuff like that?"

"My customers will love finding out there's a budding fashionista in our midst, I guarantee it. And your dad will be proud of you. I can guarantee that, too."

"You really think he will?"

"I know he will."

"Okay. I'll do it! Is there anything you'd like me to do today?"

"I have to finish the accounts I'm working on. Juliet is on her own out front and it would be great if you could give her a hand with customers and the new window display."

"Sure." But the girl remained seated.

"Is there something else?" Sarah asked.

"It's just…I just wanted to say that Casey… she's lucky. You know, to have you as her mom."

Even if Sarah could have spoken at that moment, she wouldn't have known what to say. So instead she reached out and hugged the girl.

"Thank you, Kate," she whispered when she was finally able to speak. "That's the nicest thing anyone's ever said to me."

Kate wriggled out of the embrace and jumped to her feet, keeping her head turned away. Sarah knew the gesture was meant to keep her from seeing the tears.

"Okay. That's…it's…all good. I'd better get out there and see if Juliet needs some help."

Sarah watched her go, glad they'd had this talk. After dinner tonight, she would tell Jonathan about it. He was a good father, a great one, and Kate was a great kid. It bothered her that at no time during this conversation had Kate mentioned her mother's expectations. Under the circumstances, Sarah hadn't wanted to ask what those might be, but surely Georgette must have some.

CHAPTER FIFTEEN

ON FRIDAY EVENING, Sarah left the house with Casey and Kate in their freshman dance finery and drove to the school. As a teacher-chaperone, Jonathan had to be there before the doors opened. The girls hadn't wanted to be the first to arrive, though, so Sarah agreed to drive them to the school at a time that was just late enough to be fashionable but not so late that they missed anything.

Inside, the school gym looked straight out of a movie set. A disco ball glittered high above the center of the dance floor and tables draped with white cloths lined the perimeter. She couldn't identify the song that was playing although she had heard it on the radio. The dance floor was empty but that would change soon enough.

"Wow, you girls did a great job with the decorations."

Casey and Kate had volunteered for the dance committee and had stayed after school to decorate the gym. Sarah had picked them up after she closed the store and they'd arrived home in time to enjoy Jonathan's homemade spaghetti and meatballs, served with a big tossed salad and a loaf of garlic bread. There was a lot to be said for a man who knew his way around a kitchen.

After dinner, he had returned to the school and she stayed to clean up his kitchen while the girls fussed with hair and makeup and changed outfits several times before each was satisfied with her appearance. Kate's preening didn't surprise her one bit, but this was completely new for Casey. Sarah had to admit she was more than a little intrigued.

"Look what we did with the tables," Casey said. "The centerpieces were Kate's idea."

"They're beautiful."

On Wednesday afternoon, Sarah had left the store in Juliet's very capable hands so she could drive the girls down to Sechelt to shop for decorations. At Kate's insistence, they had chosen small disco ball ornaments in several sizes, battery-operated LED candles because open flames in the school gym were strictly forbidden, and spools of silver ribbon. At the time Sarah had known the girl would come up with something amazing, and she certainly had.

Strings of tiny white lights had been used

to disguise gym fixtures, and between those and the disco ball and the faux candlelight reflecting off the table ornaments, the room was filled with sparkle and bling.

"Great job," Sarah said. "Very classy." She would make sure Kate's dad knew his daughter was the mastermind behind the stunning decor.

Speaking of Jonathan…

She scanned the room and found him on the opposite side near the DJ booth angled into a corner. Even from this distance, she knew his smile and nod were for her. The hands of the clock flew in reverse, the pages of the calendar flipped back in time, and for a few heartbeats she was at her very own first high school dance, wondering if the boy she liked might ask her to dance. Back then, he hadn't. Tonight, he might.

Were chaperones allowed to dance? As if she cared! For once in her life she was open to breaking a few rules.

She turned her attention back to the girls, watching them rush to join their friends. Casey was wearing her powder-pink cap-sleeved top with a slim dark gray knee-length skirt that Kate had insisted she borrow and a pair of black ballet flats. She had refused to wear the heels Kate had wanted to lend her, saying she was already tall enough. Her long blond hair, freed from its usual ponytail, had been pulled away from her face, fastened at the back with a large rhinestone-encrusted clip and left to cascade down her back in a river of loose curls. And all the credit went to Kate. She had pulled off what Sarah had never been able to accomplish.

Now, as she watched her daughter, this amazing and exuberant kid who had suddenly blossomed into a confident young woman right before her eyes, she felt her chest tighten. She had anticipated this moment, so why did it feel as though it was happening too soon?

"Hi. You look nice tonight."

She hadn't seen Jonathan make his way across the gym, but she smiled up at him, happy for the distraction. He always looked good but tonight, in black jeans with a black turtleneck pullover under a charcoal jacket, he sort of took her breath away.

"So do you," she said.

"Trying to look like an authority figure. Is it working?"

He looked like a movie star. "I'm sure all these kids will take one look at you and be on their best behavior."

He laughed at that. "Then mission accomplished." She watched him search out his daughter. "How long did it take the girls to get ready?"

"The better part of an hour, and that included several trips between your place and mine to figure out what they were going to wear. Kate even convinced my daughter to lose the ponytail and experiment with a little makeup. They both look great, don't you think?"

She glanced up and watched Jonathan watching them. "They do," he said. "The boys seem to think so, too."

It hadn't escaped her that right after Casey and Kate met up with Alycia at one of the tables, three boys joined them. Henry she already knew, and she was still trying to adjust to how much he'd changed over the summer. Thanks to a major growth spurt, he was now as tall as Casey. Sarah was willing to guess the other boys were Brody and Dexter. From listening to Casey and Kate, she knew Alycia and Brody were already an item, and it was clear that Henry had a thing for Kate. That left Dexter and her daughter. He was only slightly taller than Casey, which might account for her daughter's reluctance to wear heels. He was a nice-looking boy, dressed in jeans and a leather jacket that were probably meant to make him look less clean-cut than he clearly was.

"I have a feeling the next few years won't be easy ones," Sarah said.

Jonathan sighed. "I did not need to hear that."

Sarah smiled. "They're smart girls. As long as they know we trust them, and as long we keep the lines of communication open—"

"Communication," he repeated. "I think I'm finally starting to get the hang of it."

"How have things been with you and Kate? The two of you seemed fine over dinner." Kate had jokingly suggested he needed an apron after he sampled the spaghetti sauce and dribbled some down the front of his T-shirt, and he had affectionately pointed out that she was on laundry duty this weekend.

"Considering how it started, it's been an okay week. She's already caught up on homework assignments, and she got a C-plus on an English essay she turned in yesterday. And she talks nonstop about helping out at your store, so thank you again for giving her that opportunity."

It was almost impossible to believe that less than a week ago he'd been so angry when he found out Kate had been coming to the store behind his back.

"No need to thank me. She's a big help around the store, great with customers. I'd like to talk to you about putting her on my payroll—fourteen-year-olds are allowed to have part-time jobs as long as they have a parent's permission, and there's a little paperwork that needs to be done—but I didn't want to mention it at dinner tonight in case you want to think it over." Or say no altogether, which was his prerogative although she hoped he wouldn't exercise it.

"I think it's a great idea."

She hadn't expected such a quick response. "Thank you. Would you like to tell her?"

"No, I think you should. It'll mean more if she hears it from you."

"All right, but I'm still going to insist that she ask for your permission."

"Thanks. I appreciate that."

In the flickering light, his eyes went from dark to blue and dark again, and for a second or two she almost forgot what they were talking about.

"Kate told me about the talk you had with her yesterday," he said. "About the education she'll need to work for a magazine."

"Landing a job with a big magazine will take hard work and commitment, not to mention a good education."

"And she took everything you said to heart. Over dinner last night she told me she's going to look into colleges that have a journalism program. I sure wasn't expecting that."

Sarah was pleasantly surprised, too.

The music cut out then while the student council president, a senior who Sarah recognized as one of her customers, took the microphone and welcomed the freshmen to Serenity Bay High and then went on to describe some of the prizes that would be given out that evening. "But," she said, "you have to be on the dance floor to have a chance of winning!"

The music was louder when it came back on, and conversation was no longer easy.

"Is there anything I need to know about being a chaperone?" She tried to speak loud enough to be heard without having to shout.

"A few things. Make sure no one sneaks in or out the side doors. Check the girls' washroom every ten minutes or so and make sure there are no shenanigans going on in there."

She laughed at that. "Shenanigans?" Now there was an interesting euphemism for the trouble kids could get themselves into. "What do I do if I catch someone?"

"Let me or one of the other teachers know. We'll deal with it."

That was a relief. She was happy to keep an eye on the comings and goings, but she didn't want to confront a group of kids who were involved in any kind of "shenanigans."

"I'd better go make the rounds. Talk to you later?"

She nodded her agreement, and she would look forward to it.

He gave her hand a light touch. "You really do look great tonight."

She couldn't take her eyes off him as she watched him walk away, and she was grateful the room was too dark for anyone to see the heat that rose up and warmed her face. She was coming very close to falling for this man, falling hard, and if she was right about the signals he was sending her way, the feeling was mutual. And to her surprise, these feelings weren't completely terrifying.

CASEY HAD BEEN freaking out about this dance, but it wasn't as weird as she'd expected it to be. Helping with the decorations had been a blast, and getting ready with Kate had been fun, too. She wouldn't have looked nearly this good if she'd had to figure out what to wear on her own, and she could tell from the way Dexter kept looking at her that he liked what he saw.

She'd worried that having her mom here as a chaperone would be, well, weird, but Kate had reminded her that having their parents spend time together was a good thing. Thanks to her mom, Kate's dad had already started to lighten up on his high expectations. Now she needed to get her mom on board with keeping Petey because the shelter was supposed to reopen by the middle of next week. Still, seeing her mom talking to Kate's dad and remembering seeing them kiss was kind of weird, too. And just now he had touched her hand for a few seconds and it got even weirder. But now they were on opposite sides of the gym, keeping an eye on everything that was going on, and Casey started to relax.

"Come on, you guys," Kate said. "If we hope to win any of those prizes, we need to get on the dance floor." She herded the group into the middle of the gym and picked up the rhythm of the music.

The six of them formed a loose circle and she found herself between Dexter and Henry. Alycia was an amazing dancer, thanks to years of ballet classes, and Kate was awesome, too, so Casey did her best to match her moves to theirs. A group dance was way less nerve-racking than if they'd been paired up, though, and she was glad Kate had started it. She would've wanted to die if she'd had to dance with just Dexter, and she definitely would've wanted to die if Brody asked Alycia and Henry asked Kate but Dexter didn't ask her.

So this was good.

Really good.

And when Dexter's shoulder bumped hers—maybe by accident, maybe not—it was the best.

The music stopped abruptly and Casey found herself and Dexter sharing the beam from a spotlight.

"Congratulations to our first winners!" the DJ crooned into the mike. "Come on up here, you two."

"Cool." Dex was grinning at her, and then he flung an arm across her shoulders and walked her out of the circle of light and across the floor to the DJ station.

The guy jabbed the mike toward Dex. "And who do we have here?"

"I'm Dexter."

"And what's your name, gorgeous?"

"Casey."

"Dexter and Casey, folks. Aren't they a cute couple?" He handed an envelope to Dex. "And for their next date, we're giving them a coupon for one extra-large pizza at Paolo's pizzeria. Let's hear it for them!"

Their next *date?* Oh. No. This was a total freaking disaster. Now everybody would think she was…that Dexter was…that they were…

Oh. No.

And then it got worse. Way worse.

No, no, no, no, no.

Her mom was here. Now her mom would think…

Oh no.

Dex didn't seem to mind, though. His arm was still slung across her shoulders, and he smelled like leather and another scent she could only identify as something that made her light-headed. Had she told him her mom was here? She couldn't remember. What was the matter with her? Why wasn't her brain working?

"You guys are so lucky," Alycia said when they rejoined the group.

Casey ducked out of Dex's embrace.

"Free pizza, man." Brody slapped him on the shoulder. "Nothing tastes as good as free pizza."

Henry gave them two thumbs up.

Then Kate chimed in. "Hey, I have an idea. After the dance, why don't we see if our parents will let us go to Paolo's? I bet my dad will drive us, or maybe Casey's mom. We can all chip in for sodas and a couple more pizzas."

"Sure," Dex said. "What do you think, Casey?"

She'd come to the dance with Kate, which meant being here with Dex wasn't a date, it was just hanging out. But if he asked her to go for pizza and she went, would that be a date? Was he asking her on a date?

Casey stole a quick look around the gym and caught sight of her mom. She was standing by the ticket table just inside the entrance and when their gazes met, her mom blew her a two-handed kiss. She should have known her mother would be cool.

"I'll ask my mom," Casey said. "She's one of the chaperones."

The music started again and Dexter took her hand and pulled her out of the group so they were dancing together, just the two of them. This night couldn't get any better, she decided, especially if her mom let her go for pizza with her friends. That would be totally great, but she wasn't ready to ask yet. What if her mom said no? If she was going to be disappointed, she'd rather wait till the dance was over.

AS THE EVENING drew to a close, Jon was wishing he'd brought earplugs. It wasn't the music he minded; most of it was easy enough to listen to and certainly danceable if the gyrating mass on the dance floor was anything to go by, but the decibel level was a little over the top.

When did you get so old? he asked himself. Kate would probably tell him he'd been born old.

He hadn't seen her in a while but he knew she was somewhere in the crowd and dancing up a storm with the boy who lived across the street. Sarah had known the kid most of his life and assured him that Henry was a nice boy and a serious student. That was somewhat reassuring, given the behavior of several other students tonight.

Two boys had sneaked outside and were caught smoking in the parking lot. One young couple had been found exchanging saliva in the hallway by their lockers. The worst, though, had been the young girl Sarah had found throwing up in the girls' washroom. She was obviously inebriated—the evidence had been found in a flask in her handbag—and she had been discreetly escorted outside after her parents were called to pick her up. He hoped she'd learned her lesson and there wouldn't be a repeat of that incident. The other option was too horrible to even consider. Either way, though, she'd be seeing the school counselor first thing Monday morning, followed by a trip to the vice principal's office to find out what her punishment would be. He suspected tomorrow's hangover might suffice, and he hoped the counselor would follow up with the parents, too, and have a little chat about keeping the liquor cabinet under lock and key.

Given all that, he counted his lucky stars that Kate and her friends were having the time of their lives without needing to get into trouble.

He spotted Sarah by the concession table and after she waved at him, he walked over to meet her. She looked really stunning tonight. Sometime between taking care of the cleanup after dinner and driving herself and the girls here for the dance, she had transformed herself into a woman who looked way too young and far too hip to be the mother of a fourteen-year-old. Her slim black slacks were tucked into high tan-colored boots, and her hip-length lime-green top was cinched at the waist with a wide leather belt that matched the boots. Long green-and-gold enamel earrings swung from her ears and as always her hair shone like polished bronze.

She was a smart woman and a caring mother, and he especially appreciated everything she had done for him and Kate. Who knows where they'd be right now if he hadn't been the beneficiary of Sarah's insight and sage advice? But the bottom line was that he enjoyed spending time with her and hoped to spend more.

"Quite a night," she shouted once he was within hearing range.

"Tell me about it. Now you know why we need so many chaperones."

She gestured at the crowded dance floor. "Compared to all these kids who are behaving themselves and having fun, a handful of troublemakers isn't a big deal."

Trust her to take all of this in stride. "I don't suppose you'd like to have a heart-to-heart with the girl you found in the bathroom."

"No, I'll pass on that. Either she's learned her lesson or she's going to need more help than I'm qualified to give."

He wasn't so sure about that.

The song ended and the DJ's voice pierced the air. "All right, freshmen. This is it. One more song and that's all she wrote."

The announcement was met with groans and jeering.

This is it, he told himself. *Now or never.*

"Would you like to dance?" He drew a breath, waiting.

"Yes, very much."

He motioned toward the dance floor. "After you."

Given the upbeat playlist the DJ had been playing all night, he hadn't expected this to be a slow dance, so he offered silent thanks to the man when Sarah moved into his arms, one hand in his, the other on his shoulder.

He was far from being a great dancer, but he knew the basics and she easily followed his lead. While kissing her had instantly jolted him to the core, dancing with her felt more intimate, his awareness of her more intense. The warmth of her hand, the lightness of her touch, the hint of floral wafting from her hair—perfection.

Their audience? Not so much. If there was ever a need to keep it PG-13, this was it. Unfortunately several of the young couples around them hadn't seen the memo. Sarah must have noticed them, too, because she smiled up at him and gave a light laugh.

"At least our kids are behaving appropriately," she said.

His self-consciousness dissipated as he scanned the crowd and spotted Kate and Henry, then Casey and Dexter. Both girls had looped their arms around the boys' necks and the boys had wrapped theirs around the girls' waists. Relieved to see some space between those young bodies, he also realized the locked gazes meant that neither girl had any interest in what her parent was doing.

"Do you think they'd still be 'appropriate' if we weren't here to keep an eye on them?" he asked.

"I believe they would. They have a lot of common sense and self-confidence, and those are the tools they need to make good decisions."

She was right. She always was. "So you never worry about Casey?"

"Are you kidding? I never stop worrying, but I've done and continue to do everything I can to prepare her for the world. I have to believe that's enough."

He was sure she had, just as he was sure he had a lot of catching up to do. She looked up at him then and smiled, and for the rest of the dance he wasn't a parent or a teacher or a role model, he was just a man falling in love with a very beautiful woman.

CHAPTER SIXTEEN

ENERGIZED, THAT'S WHAT she felt, Sarah decided. Revived, aware that she was more than a mom and a businesswoman. She was a woman, experiencing the jumble of emotions and physical sensations that went with being in a man's arms. Years ago she had shut herself down, and she had done it intentionally, but now she felt as though a switch had been flipped back on. These new feelings were beyond her control, and they both excited and terrified her.

Then the overhead lights snapped on and the school gym lost its otherworldliness. Out of the commotion of students leaving, the cleanup committee whisking away the decorations and the DJ packing up, Casey emerged from the crowd with Kate and Alycia on either side and the three boys trailing close behind.

"Did you have fun?" Sarah asked.

The light in her daughter's eyes said it all. "Tons! We won a free pizza," she said. "So did Kate and Henry. So we were thinking… wondering if we can go for pizza before we go home."

Jonathan joined them in time to hear the request.

"With Alycia and Brody. The six of us," Kate said, in case there was any doubt about them not wanting their parents tagging along. "It's only nine-thirty."

Sarah looked to Jonathan to get his reaction.

"What do you think?" he asked.

"Have all of you talked to your parents?" she asked.

Shaking heads indicated they had not.

"Then you'll need to call them," Jonathan said. "And we'll want to talk to them, to make sure we have their permission."

"And you can tell them we'll drive you there and then we'll pick you up and take you home," Sarah said.

"Everyone stays at the restaurant till we get back," Jonathan added. "Are we clear on that?"

Casey launched herself at Sarah, hugging her and making her laugh. "Thanks, Mom."

"You're welcome, sweetie. I already know Kate and Henry and Alycia, but are you going to introduce me to the rest of your friends?"

"Sure. This is Alycia's boyfriend, Brody." The reference to someone else's boyfriend rolled off her tongue with ease, then she was suddenly awkward. "And this is my friend Dexter," she said shyly. "His family moved to Serenity Bay last year."

"Hi, Dexter. Nice to meet you." She watched him closely, not altogether sure she cared for the outward display of cockiness.

"You, too, Mrs. Stewart." He extended his hand and Sarah accepted the tentative handshake, noticing how his gaze darted away an instant after they made eye contact.

Nice manners, a little unsure of himself in spite of what he'd like others to believe, and possibly even a little afraid of her. All good.

Following a flurry of phone calls, during which either Sarah or Jonathan spoke to the other four parents, everyone piled into the two cars for the drive downtown to the pizza shop. Sarah pulled in next to Jonathan and rolled down her window in time to hear him remind the group that they'd be back to pick them up and drive them home in an hour.

"One hour," he repeated.

All six kids disappeared inside, swept along in a stream of laughter and easygoing banter, leaving Sarah sitting in a puddle of mixed feelings. She had wanted this for her daughter, the friendships, the fun, even the flirtations. Now that it was happening, she wouldn't mind turning back the clock, just a little.

Jonathan's passenger window rolled down. "We could go back to my place for coffee."

"Let's make it my place. I need to let the dog out for a while." Petey was becoming a bigger part of their lives every day. She and Casey hadn't talked about the situation, aside from discussing the fact that the work at the animal shelter was still ongoing, but the writing was on the wall. Casey and the dog had a serious case of mutual infatuation, and Sarah was starting to believe it was contagious. Plus she still didn't know where this thing with her and Jonathan was going, but if they started spending more time together, it might be good for Casey to have the companionship of a four-legged friend.

Jonathan waited until she had pulled out of the parking lot and then followed her home. As she drove, she kept checking the rear-view, noting the headlights at a safe distance behind, thinking ahead to how they might spend the next hour. Coffee would be the appropriate thing, no question. She wasn't even close to being ready for anything more serious, even though they had already kissed, twice. They'd also shared details about their personal lives and talked about their kids, and they danced well together. What they hadn't done was simply be in each other's company, unencumbered by all that other stuff.

That's what she needed. Coffee and calm. She glanced again at the lights in the mirror. She hoped that would be enough for Jonathan, too. At least for now.

KATE SLID INTO the U-shaped booth, squeezed between Henry and Brody. Brody put his arm around Alycia right away and she leaned against him. Across the table, Dex's arm stretched along the back of the seat behind Casey. Henry kept his arms to himself, folded on the table in front of him. He was shyer than the other two boys, but she still hoped that making the first move wouldn't be up to her.

"Will two pizzas be enough?" Kate asked.

"No way," Brody said. "Better get three. I can eat one all by myself."

"Seriously?" Casey's laugh was laced with disbelief. "You can eat an entire extra-large pizza?"

"Trust me," Alycia said. "He can."

"Don't forget Kate's a vegetarian."

She was grateful to Casey for reminding everyone.

Dex and Brody groaned, but Henry smiled down at her. "I'm good with that," he said. "Bring on the veggies."

It wasn't the same as having his arm around her, but it was a start.

The server came and took their order and returned a few moments later with a round of soft drinks.

"*So...*" Alycia said with dramatic emphasis on the first word. "Did anyone else see Casey's mom have the last dance with Kate's dad tonight? That's got to be weird."

Kate and Casey quickly exchanged glances across the table. Their mutual plan to get their parents together was their secret, and they'd also sworn not to tell anyone about the kiss.

Kate shrugged. "I don't think it's weird. I mean, our families live next door to each other. Our parents are both single and they were both chaperoning tonight—" Which was also something she and Casey had instigated. The best part was that it seemed to be working. Casey would almost certainly get to keep the dog. Kate's dad had changed his mind about letting her go back to help at To the Nines, and she was sure Sarah had a lot to do with that. He let her come here tonight with her friends, something he almost certainly wouldn't have done a week ago. If she had to guess, she'd say their parents were together right now, and the more time they spent together, the easier her life was going to be.

Life would be even better if Henry would make the first move. Any move, aside from agreeing to share a vegetarian pizza with her.

The pies arrived, the three huge plates taking up most of the table, so Henry had to move his arms, and the other guys needed both hands to grab slices and break the long strings of melted cheese that pulled away with them.

As the pizzas disappeared and the soft drinks were refilled, she started to relax. During her first week at SBH she'd been homesick, missing her friends in the city like crazy. Now it was impossible to believe she'd been in Serenity Bay for less than a month, had made friends, even had an almost-boyfriend. Her dad was happier, too, and that made life easier for both of them.

After a second slice, she wiped her hands on a paper napkin, crumpled it on her plate and let her hands drop to the seat beside her.

"Had enough?" Henry asked.

"I'm stuffed. Couldn't eat another bite. Have the rest if you'd like."

"Thanks, but I'm done, too." He dropped his napkin and leaned back against the seat, his shoulder touching hers.

Alycia was snuggled under Brody's arm again. Dex's arm was on the back of the seat again, but the tips of his fingers had strayed to Casey's shoulder. Lucky girls.

She moved her hands to her lap but before she could lace her fingers together, Henry's hand was on hers, pulling it back onto the seat between them, covering it with his. Instead of the out-in-the-open, arm-around-the-shoulder displays by the other boys, Henry's under-the-table hand-holding was just between them. Something no else could see, which made it even more special.

She gave him a quick sideways glance and smiled. He responded with a gentle squeeze of her hand, a slightly crooked grin and a flash of perfect white teeth. Her heart or something in her chest actually fluttered.

Finally, she thought. *Lucky me.*

IN HER KITCHEN, Sarah brewed a pot of coffee—decaf, she decided, given the late hour—while Jonathan took the dog out to the backyard. She pulled a pair of red mugs from a cupboard, set them on the counter next to the coffeemaker, and took out cream and sugar. She hunted through cupboards for something to serve with the coffee but all she could find were half a box of soda crackers, a bag of pretzels and Casey's stash of microwave popcorn. She was ready to give up when she remembered the box of After Eight chocolates she'd tucked away somewhere… aha. There they were. She tossed a handful into a small bowl.

Jonathan and Petey returned via the deck doors and she closed and locked them while he unleashed the exuberant little mutt.

Jonathan dropped the leash into the basket next to the door. "He's quite a character."

"He's that, all right. And of course Casey is completely and madly in love with him."

"But you're not?" He leaned an elbow on the counter and angled his head as though wanting to see if her expression matched her reply.

She sighed. "I'm kind of smitten, too. Stay down," she scolded the dog when he tried to jump up on her pant leg. "Your paws are all wet from the grass."

"Do you have a towel for him? I can dry him off while we wait for the coffee to brew."

"Thanks. It should be in that basket under the leash."

She watched him carefully and gently wipe

the dog's paws. Petey, who seemed happy with any kind of attention anyone was willing to give him, tolerated that, then dashed through the house as soon as his feet were dry. He returned with a squeaker toy as Sarah poured coffee and handed a mug to Jonathan.

"Let's go sit in the living room."

"Sure."

She followed him with her coffee and the bowl of chocolates and waited while he sat at one end of the sofa and patted the seat next to him. Exactly what she'd hoped he would do. She set the bowl on the coffee table and settled next to him, liking that this felt so easy and so right.

He held his coffee with one hand, using the other to draw her even closer.

She fought a yawn and failed. "This has been a really long day."

"It sure has. I was up and out for a run by six this morning."

I know you were. She still watched for him, which made her completely pathetic on so many levels, but she simply couldn't resist.

Petey jumped onto the sofa and curled up next to her.

"Since you and your daughter are so fond of this little guy, have you decided what you'll do when the shelter reopens?"

Sarah sighed. "I'm pretty sure we're going to keep him."

"That's not a surprise. Have you told Casey?"

"Not yet. I thought I'd hold off as long as possible, in case she changes her mind."

Jonathan laughed. "You think there's a chance that might happen?"

"Not even a remote one. It's mostly me, wanting to postpone the commitment as long as possible."

"I see."

After that they sipped their coffee in silence and Sarah let herself relax against his solid warmth. At some point she was vaguely aware of him removing the mug from her hand and setting it on the end table. Coffee and calm, she thought. Exactly what she needed, except now it was just calm. Even better.

"Sarah?"

She jolted awake, instantly aware of him next to her, stroking her hair.

"Oh! Did I fall asleep?"

"Yes, you did."

She sat up, straightening her clothes as she did. "I'm so sorry. You should have woken me up."

He smiled down at her. "I just did."

"Oh. What time is it? How long was I asleep?"

"Maybe twenty minutes. Now it's time to pick up the kids."

"Right." She jumped up, feeling disoriented, a little wobbly even.

He stood, too, and held her steady. "Take it easy," he said. "We have plenty of time."

They did? Oh, yes they did, she thought, realizing he was going to kiss her. Falling asleep on his shoulder might have been what she needed, but this was what she wanted. His hands holding her face, his lips on hers, firm, warm, with a hint of coffee and mint.

"Thank you," he said when he released her.

"For what?"

"For tonight, the dance, the coffee…this." He kissed her again, lightly this time.

"Oh. You're welcome."

"We should go."

"We should."

But they didn't. She leaned against him instead and they wrapped their arms around each other and for a full minute, maybe more, she simply let herself be. If they continued like this, would he eventually expect more? Probably. Of course he would. They enjoyed each other's company and they definitely had chemistry, but for now that was enough for her and it would have to be enough for him, too.

She tipped her head up to look at him. "Thank *you*."

"For what?"

"For taking it slow, not being annoyed that I fell asleep on you, not pressuring me into something I'm not ready for."

"My pleasure." There was a good-humored sparkle in his eyes and in his smile. "And now we really should go."

They went through the foyer and put on the boots, shoes and jackets they'd shed when they came in. By the time she stepped out into the cool nighttime air, she was fully awake. They still needed both cars since neither could accommodate all six teens. Again, Jonathan let her go ahead, and again seeing his headlights behind her made her feel watched over, safe.

"Slow down," she said to her reflection. And she wasn't referring to the speed limit. In the past she'd made the mistake of rushing into something that had felt right but wasn't. This time she would do things her way, and at her own pace.

THE MORNING AFTER the school dance, Jonathan was up at his usual early hour. Sometime overnight the fog had rolled in. From the deck he could barely make out the rooftops of the houses one street below, and he already knew from experience that it was even denser by the water. He would postpone his run, he decided, and do some things around the house instead. There were still a few boxes in the garage that needed to be unpacked, bathrooms to clean—he and Kate took turns with those and he was on deck for that—and the kitchen floor wasn't going to mop itself.

He also needed to figure out what to make for dinner that night. Better question, should they invite Sarah and Casey to join them? Saturday night pizza was a tradition of theirs, but since the girls had pizza last night, maybe they'd prefer something else. They had eaten dinner before the dance here, though. Maybe two nights in a row was too much? Or…

He could fix something for the girls to have at home and take Sarah out for dinner. Most of the time they'd spent together had been with the girls or out looking for the girls. A real date sounded like a good idea. Not that he had any expectations.

Last night, her comment about not wanting to make a commitment to the dog had hit its mark, even though he was sure she hadn't intended it that way. But he was smart enough to know that if she wasn't ready to commit to a dog, she sure wasn't going to commit to him after just a few weeks. Then she'd settled next to him on the sofa and within minutes she had relaxed and fallen asleep. He would never forget the feeling of holding her, listening to the soft sound of her breathing, shallow and even. He could have stayed there forever, or at least until his arm fell asleep, and when it was time to pick up the girls and their friends, he had hated to wake her.

And then, after they'd kissed, when she'd leaned in for a hug before they'd left to pick up the kids, he knew. This was it. This time it was really real. She was the one. She had thanked him for taking it slow and he'd decided right then and there that she could have all the time she needed because this time, for her, he had all the time in the world.

He had cleaned the upstairs bathrooms and the downstairs powder room and was about to start on the kitchen floor when the doorbell rang. It was just after nine on a Saturday morning.

"Who could this be?" he wondered, making his way through the house. Kate was still asleep and he would hazard a guess that all of her friends were, too. Maybe it was Sarah?

He whipped the door open and was surprised to see a courier.

"I have a package for Jonathan Marshall."

"That's me."

"Sign here, sir."

He scrawled his signature on the handheld screen and returned the stylus to the driver, who handed over the envelope in exchange.

Puzzling over who would send him something by courier, he shut the door and studied the package on his way back to the kitchen. It was from a law firm in Vancouver.

The law firm that had represented Georgette during the divorce.

A sick feeling pooled in his gut.

CHAPTER SEVENTEEN

JONATHAN TOSSED THE envelope onto the kitchen island, poured himself a cup of coffee and sat sipping it while he studied the return address some more.

"Maybe it's not that bad."

Right. When had Georgette's lawyer ever delivered good news? That would be never. One thing was clear, though. He wouldn't know until he opened it.

"Like ripping off a bandage," he muttered to himself, as he tore the tab off the packet and pulled out a thin sheaf of documents. The top sheet was an application to change an existing court order. *In the case between Georgette Ogilvie and Jonathan Marshall...*

She had filed an application to the court, asking to have the existing custody agreement canceled—a copy of which was attached—and grant full custody to her. He slammed the pages onto the counter.

What was she thinking?

When she'd moved to Europe, she hadn't

wanted to have Kate with her. She and Xavier had a busy schedule, traveling from country to country. At the time she had agreed that her lifestyle didn't provide a stable environment for a young teen. So now…what? Had she had a change of heart? Was she punishing him? Trying to ruin Kate's life because the kid had made one stupid mistake?

And what had he been thinking that night?

He never should have called Georgette, plain and simple. He understood where Sarah had been coming from, but he should have gone with his gut. Sarah didn't know Georgette. He did.

He grabbed his phone and brought up Georgette's number. "We'll just see about this."

"Hello, Jon. Or should I say *buongiorno*. Is everything okay?" She'd put on her old news anchor voice, smooth as silk and sticky as a spider's web.

"I was going to ask you the same thing. I just received a package from your lawyer."

"Oh, you have it already. Good. I asked him if I should call you, let you know it was on its way, but he advised against that."

Of course he did. Much better for Jon to be completely blindsided.

He stood at the sliding doors, stared into

the distance without fully registering the fog-draped trees and rooftops below. “Why are you doing this?”

“Because you’re obviously not up to the task of raising a rebellious teenager.”

“She’s not rebellious. She’s fitting in well, she’s already made new friends, her grades are good.” What more could either of them ask?

“Jon, you’re not being reasonable. Just the other day she ran away and had to be picked up by the police. Can you imagine how I felt, knowing that *my* daughter was sitting in a jail cell?”

And here comes the drama. “*Our* daughter was not in a cell. Kate and her friend were sitting in an office drinking sodas when we arrived.”

“How wonderful for them. Sounds like a real party. The bottom line is that she’s obviously not getting the supervision she needs. So we—Xavier and I—talked it over and decided the best thing for everyone is for Kate to come over here to go to school.”

He nearly dropped the phone on the floor, which was right about where his jaw was. “Last weekend you said you were in London.” Judging by the way she’d answered his call, this week it was Milan. “Where are you this week? Italy? How's she supposed to attend school on that kind of schedule?"

"She won't be traveling with us, except on holidays. There are lots of excellent English-speaking boarding schools over here. Italy, France, Switzerland, they all have them. She'll meet interesting people, learn new languages. She'll be better prepared for a successful career and she'll certainly see more of the world than if she stays in some poky little west coast town no one's ever heard of."

Boarding school? *Boarding* school? Now he wanted to throw the phone against the wall.

"There's nothing wrong with Serenity Bay. And lots of kids raised in small towns go on to have *successful* careers." He stopped himself before he pointed out that she was one of them.

"At least this way I'll be able to see her once in a while since she's stopped taking my calls."

That was news to him. Kate habitually checked her phone to see if her mother had called or sent a text message. Although now that he thought about it, he hadn't noticed so much of that this week.

"When did you call? Maybe she was in class."

"I'm perfectly well aware of the time difference and I can figure out when she's at school. I've called three or four times—mornings and evenings—and she never picks up."

Huh. Kate hadn't mentioned that, but after their heart-to-heart on Monday evening, he had a better understanding of how she felt about her relationship with her mother.

"I wish you had called me. I would have talked to her."

"Really? It seemed pretty obvious that you were behind this."

She knew very well he'd never done anything of the sort, and now she was trying to use this against him? Heaven help him keep his cool.

"I have never done that, Georgette. I've always encouraged you to call anytime you like, and there've been times—" No. He wouldn't say it. There had been times when Kate had waited to hear from her mother and he had gone out of his way to reassure her. Georgette had a lot of nerve trying to turn the tables on this, but that didn't mean he needed to lower himself to her level.

"Well, whatever," she said. "We shouldn't be talking about this anyway. My lawyer told me to let him handle it."

"We're her parents. Of course we need to

talk about this, and we should talk to Kate, too. Find out what she wants." And they should be able to discuss this like rational human beings instead of paying lawyers money that could be better spent. Like on Kate's college tuition.

"These are adult decisions. Kate is too young to be dragged into this."

Seriously? Right now Kate seemed more like an adult than her mother. "You don't think a judge will want to talk to her?"

Judges did do that, didn't they? It hadn't been an issue the first time because Georgette had willingly signed over full custody to him.

"I believe any judge will think I have the best solution to this problem. I can easily afford the best boarding school where she'll be monitored twenty-four/seven instead of being left unsupervised and getting into trouble with the law."

Now he was angry. Really, *really* angry. "Kate is *not* in trouble with the law. We had a misunderstanding, she was upset and she made a mistake. Why can't you—"

"Jon, I really have to go. We're on our way to a dinner party and I don't want to keep Xavier waiting."

His phone went dead. He stood there a few seconds longer, pressing his forehead against the cool glass. How on earth was he going to explain this to Kate?

"Who thinks I'm in trouble with law?"

He swung around to find her standing at the island…where he'd left the court documents.

"What's all this?" she asked.

"I didn't expect you to be up this early."

"The doorbell woke me up. What's all this?" she asked again. "Was that Mom? What's going on?"

After he had just told his ex-wife that Kate needed a chance to express her opinion on this, he couldn't very well keep her in the dark.

"Have a seat. I'll make breakfast and fill you in."

SARAH FASTENED THE week's worth of invoices with a paper clip and set them aside. Next up were yesterday's credit card receipts, which she hadn't had time to enter online yesterday because she'd had to pick up Casey and Kate at the school so they could have dinner and get ready for the dance. But first she needed a break from her Saturday morning paperwork.

"And another cup of coffee," she decided.

Downstairs in the kitchen she filled her mug, rinsed the carafe, stirred cream and sugar into her coffee, and sipped some on her way back to her office. "Ahhh. Perfect."

This would see her through the rest of the morning until it was time to get ready for work. She was halfway up the stairs when the doorbell rang. Likely someone here to see Casey, but she was out walking the dog so Sarah turned around and went down to answer it.

"Jonathan, hi. How are—" She cut herself off as soon as she saw the look on his face. "What's wrong?"

He jabbed his fingers through his hair and left them there while he shook his head. "I hate to bother you…I know you're busy… but I was wondering if you could spare a few minutes."

"Of course. Come in, come in. Coffee?" She held up the mug cradled in her hands. "I just drained the pot but I can make more. Come on into the kitchen."

"I don't want you to go to any trouble."

"It's just coffee. No trouble at all."

She led the way and offered him a seat at the island. That's when she noticed the envelope in his hand. He didn't say anything as she poured water into the coffeemaker and scooped coffee into the basket. He really wasn't himself and she assumed his concern was due to whatever was inside that package.

She left her mug on the counter next to the coffeemaker and took another out of the cupboard, then she sat across from him. "Okay, what's up? I'm guessing it's not good."

"It isn't. In fact I can't think of anything worse."

For a man whose daughter had run away less than a week ago, that was really saying something. She reached out, put her hand on the back of his, and waited for him to speak.

"Is Casey here?" he asked.

"She's walking the dog."

"Ah."

"Why?"

"I was wondering if maybe Kate had already talked to her." He turned his hand and wrapped his fingers around hers, as though he needed something to hold on to.

"I don't know. What's in the envelope?"

"Court documents."

She felt her eyebrows go up. "This doesn't have anything to do with the girls' little escapade the other day, does it?" Surely she would have heard something, too, if it did.

"Yes. No. Not directly."

Whatever it was, she could see this was

hard for him. Rather than keep pressing, she had to let him get the story out his way.

He pulled some official-looking documents out of the envelope. "These are from Georgette's lawyer. She's applying for full custody of Kate."

Sarah opened her mouth. No, there were no words, so she snapped it shut.

"She wants to take her to Europe and enroll her in boarding school."

Sarah was off her chair in a flash, dragging her hand out of Jonathan's in the process. "You can't be serious. Boarding school? What did Kate say when you told her?"

Or maybe Kate wanted to go and that's what had Jonathan all tied up in knots?

"She said no way. She says we're ruining her life, that she hates her mother, and that she'll run away again if we make her go."

"The poor kid. I don't believe for a minute that she'll run away again, but I'll be happy to talk to her, if you like."

"That would be great. I know she respects what you have to say."

Obviously the same couldn't be said about the girl's mother right now. "Thank you. That means a lot."

The coffee was ready so she poured a cup

and passed it to him, then returned to her seat with hers.

"Have you talked to your lawyer?" she asked.

He looked defeated. "No. I called and left a message so he'll probably call on Monday."

Sarah was willing to bet Georgette and her lawyer had purposely timed it so these papers arrived when Jonathan's lawyer wasn't available, leaving him to stew about this all weekend. What a hateful thing to do.

"I'm sure you have nothing to worry about," she said. Which was a big fat lie and they both knew it, but she pressed on with it anyway. "You're a great dad and Kate belongs here with you, not locked away in some hoity-toity boarding school. Besides, that must cost a fortune."

"For Georgette, money isn't an issue." He gulped a mouthful of coffee. "And because there's a lot more money in her bank account than there is in mine, she believes the court will rule in her favor."

"Money isn't everything. Kids need a family, not a fortune. They need parents to be there when they need them, setting an example for them. You're not just Kate's father, you're the role model who shows her how to live her life. Who's going to fill that role at a boarding school?"

Jonathan shook his head. "I don't know anything about boarding schools."

"Neither do I." But she knew that the kids who went there wouldn't get to spend much time with their families. "Has Kate talked to her mother about this and told her how she feels?"

"No, not yet. And as it turns out, that's part of the problem. Georgette called her several times this week and Kate never answered. Now, along with being convinced I'm an irresponsible parent who doesn't supervise his kid, she thinks I've turned Kate against her."

"Oh, for heaven's sake. That's ridiculous."

"To you and me, yes, but not to Georgette." He drained his mug and set it on the counter.

"Would you like more? I made lots."

"No thanks." He stood and stuffed the pages back into the envelope. "I've taken up enough of your time, and I know you have to go to work this afternoon."

She walked with him to the front door. "If you and Casey don't have plans tonight, you're welcome to join us again for dinner."

"Oh, thank you. That would be great but Liz Jacobson, the veterinarian who looks after the animals at the shelter, is having a barbecue for the volunteers who work there. She invited me to go with Casey. Petey's going, too."

"Sounds like fun." Poor guy. He definitely wasn't having any.

She reached up, placed her hands on either side of his face and trained her gaze on those very sad but oh-so-blue eyes. "If there's anything I can do, I want you to call, okay? That goes for Kate, too."

He leaned in and touched his forehead to hers. "Thank you. That means a lot."

"I'm serious about that. Anything."

KATE GRABBED HER phone when it rang, then hit cancel when her mother's picture flashed on the screen.

"Ugh! I hate you. Go away."

She pulled a pillow over her head and snuggled a purring Princess a little closer. She'd hated it when her parents split up, but she finally got used to living with just her dad. She'd hated it when they'd moved to Serenity Bay, but she already liked it here. She'd made new friends who turned out to be way cooler than she'd thought they'd be, and now she practically had a boyfriend. Last night he'd held her hand in the restaurant and again in the backseat of her dad's car on the drive home. He might even have kissed her if her dad hadn't been hanging around, waiting for her to come inside and for Henry to go across the street. Still, she'd gone to bed squee-ing over the hand-holding, then woken up this morning and squee-ed some more. And then her mom had to go and ruin everything…*everything*…with this stupid plan to send her to boarding school.

She pulled the pillow even tighter over her ears when her dad knocked on her bedroom door.

"Go away. Please."

The door opened. "It's me. Casey. Your dad said it was okay for me to come up."

She flipped the pillow onto the floor and sat up. "You heard what happened?"

Casey nodded. "My mom told me."

"Come in and close the door. I'm glad you're here. I need to figure out what I'm going to do."

Casey toed off her shoes and sat cross-legged on the end of the bed. "My mom said nothing's been decided yet, not until you go to court or something."

"You don't know my mom. If she wants something, she gets it. When she first went to Europe, she didn't want me there so she left me with my dad. Now she's mad at him because she thinks it's his fault I ran away, so she wants to stick me in a boarding school."

Her friend made an I-told-you-so face.

"I know, I know. It was a dumb thing to do but nothing bad happened. At least not till *this*."

"We'll figure something out," Casey said.

"Like what?"

She shrugged. "I don't know. We'll come up with a plan."

"I'll tell my mom that I'll run away again if she sends me away to school."

"Right," Casey said, and she was actually laughing. "'Cause that worked so well last time."

Princess stretched and then nudged Kate's hand. "So what sort of plan do you have in mind?"

Casey gave her a sly little smile.

"What? Have you thought of something?"

"Well, maybe. Remember that first night you came to my house and you said that if our parents…you know, got together…then my mom would let me have a dog and your dad would get off your case?"

"Yeah, I remember. And then we got them to take Petey for a walk and saw them making out."

"Ew. They were just kissing."

Kate laughed. “You’re so naive. Has Dex kissed you yet?”

Casey’s eyes went wide. “No!”

“The two of you were pretty hot on the dance floor last night, and he had his arm around you the whole time we were at the restaurant.”

Casey blushed like crazy. “What about you and Henry? Holding hands under the table, as if no one could tell.”

“You could?” Rats. She’d liked believing it was something only she and Henry knew about it.

“Has he kissed you?”

“No. My dad wouldn’t let us out of his sight last night.”

Her friend grinned at her. “Parents, huh? But I’m still having a hard time imagining Henry kissing anyone.”

“Um…why?”

“Because. He’s Henry. I’ve known him since we were little kids and it’s weird to think of him that way.”

“Well, I just met him and I can tell you it is so not weird.”

Casey pulled her ponytail out of its elastic, smoothed her hair back and refastened it. “Enough about kissing boys. We’re talking about the problem with your mom.”

Thinking about Henry was a very nice distraction, but she was right. "Okay, we'll save the boy talk for later. What were you saying about your mom and my dad?"

"Just that I think you might have been right. I think they do kind of have a thing for each other, and I'm pretty sure my mom's almost ready to let me keep Petey, and you said yourself that your dad has eased up on all the rules."

"I guess." Kate rolled Princess onto her back and scratched her belly. "But what does that have to do with me being shipped off to boarding school?"

"Well, if the judge knew your dad was seeing someone—"

"Someone like your mom."

"Yes, and if the judge knew that the person your dad was seeing was practically like a mother to you, maybe the judge would let you stay here."

Kate slid off the bed and grabbed a comb and hairbrush off her dressing table. "I'm going to fix your hair. That ponytail has got to go," she said. "I'm not sure about our parents, though. I was watching them last night and they hardly talked to each other."

"They danced together."

Kate brushed out her friend's hair, then

reached for a magazine she'd been reading and flipped it open to a page of celebrity hairstyles she'd noticed. "I'm going to try this one."

Casey glanced at it. "I can't wear my hair like that. Why don't you do yours that way?"

"Yes, you can. And it's easier to try new styles on someone else first. Now hold still." She swept Casey's long blond hair to one side and pinned it. "Anyway, like I was saying, our parents just had one dance. Otherwise they seemed to ignore each other."

"They were chaperones," Casey pointed out. "And they weren't exactly ignoring each other this morning when I came back from walking the dog."

"Really?" Maybe this was a possibility. "What were they doing?"

"I came up the back stairs onto the deck so I could wipe off Petey's paws before I let him in the house. I could see down the hallway to the front door, and they were standing there with their arms around each other."

"Making out?"

"Would you stop saying that? It's gross. And no, they weren't. They were just standing there holding on to each other."

Interesting. "I'll bet my dad wanted to talk to her about the papers my mom sent."

"Maybe. Anyway, I think they like each other and it might not take much, you know, to convince a judge."

Kate slid another pin into Casey's hair and finger-combed the waves into a cascade over one shoulder. "There. You look just like Carrie Underwood."

"Let me see." She hopped up and looked at herself in the mirror over Kate's dressing table. "Okay, yes, it's nice, but I can't wear my hair like this when I'm at soccer practice or working at the animal shelter."

"Sure, but you can when you're on a date with Dexter."

Kate laughed when Casey's face turned pink. She was tempted to tease her some more, but decided against it. "So, about our parents. This might work, but we'll have to figure out how we're going to pull it off."

"I'll think on it," Casey said. "Now can I have my ponytail back?"

"Sure." Kate plucked the pins out of Casey's hair and redid the classic ponytail. She was glad her friend had come over. She'd needed the distraction. "We should call Alycia and see if she wants to hang out this afternoon."

"Sure. My mom's at work so she won't mind."

And here's hoping Alycia mentioned it to Brody and that he would tell Henry and Dex to join them.

"Just don't say anything to anyone about my mom or the whole boarding school thing, okay?"

"Not a word."

"Thanks. Besides, if our plan works, it'll be just like the whole mess never happened."

"It has to work," Casey said.

And they sealed the deal with a high five.

CHAPTER EIGHTEEN

JONATHAN DIDN'T CONNECT with his lawyer until school was dismissed on Monday afternoon. After ten minutes on the phone with the man, he felt as though he'd been lashed to a railroad track in front of a locomotive on full throttle. Being awarded initial custody of Kate had been a straightforward matter.

Now things had changed. Georgette still traveled a great deal, but she did have a permanent residence. Her income was substantially higher than Jon's and she had a wealthy new husband. And then there was the not-so-insignificant matter of Kate recently being a runaway. Judges always based decisions on the best interests of the child, and under ordinary circumstances they most often ruled in favor of the mother. In this case, it was almost certain. The only positive thing he'd heard was that the judge would want to meet privately with Kate to find out how she felt about the current and proposed situations.

Kate wanted to stay in Serenity Bay. More

likely because of her friends than her father, but he'd take it. Her grades had improved, and she was genuinely sorry that her impulsive decision to take off had precipitated Georgette's change of heart. Now the most he could hope for was that the court would see he was a responsible father who was making a good home for his daughter. And he hoped Kate would show the judge that she was a kid who made a mistake and was now trying to make up for it.

His lawyer said the hearing would be scheduled in a couple weeks, so they had time to prepare. And then he'd asked something entirely unexpected. If there a woman in Jon's life, and therefore potentially in Kate's, that might tip the balance in his favor.

He'd had to be honest and say no. Sarah was technically in his life but she wasn't *in* his life, not in the sense the lawyer was talking about. Still, she had offered to help.

If there's anything I can do, I want you to call. Okay? I'm serious about that. Anything.

She hadn't really meant *anything.* That's just what people said when they felt bad for someone and didn't know what else to say. And he couldn't ask her to get involved in this.

No, that wasn't quite correct. He'd like

more than anything to have this amazing woman in his life, but this was not the sort of thing a man asked a woman to do as a favor.

Not even when he was desperate. Really, really desperate.

BY DINNERTIME ON TUESDAY, it was obvious to Sarah that something was afoot. For the past several days Casey had been moping around the house, very uncharacteristically, bemoaning the fact that her best friend was leaving in a few weeks and she would never see her again, and it seemed no amount of reassuring was going to change her mind.

"Kate says if her dad had a new wife or maybe even a girlfriend, you know, so they looked more like a normal family, then the judge would let her stay," she'd said over breakfast that morning.

The same thing had crossed her mind but with the hearing just a few short weeks away, there was no way that would happen. The possibility of him losing his daughter made her heart ache, but so did the idea of him having another woman in his life.

"I'm sure the judge will take everything into consideration before making a decision," she'd said, but Casey remained unconvinced and inconsolable.

Kate, understandably, had been even more distraught when she came to the store after school. This was her life, she'd insisted. And while attending a posh European boarding school wasn't exactly the end of the world, she saw it as the end of hers.

"I told my dad he should try online dating," she'd said after not so subtly bringing up the topic of her father's lack of female companionship.

Sarah had caught herself before she laughed out loud. Aside from that being one of the most preposterous things she'd ever heard, that sort of activity could spell disaster if Georgette's lawyer or the judge caught wind of it.

She had distracted the girl by offering her the part-time job she had discussed with Jonathan. Just a few hours a week, she'd warned, and contingent on her maintaining good grades. An ecstatic Kate had accepted, then tempered it by saying she would love to work at the store until her mother hauled her off to boarding school.

Now, as Sarah cleared away the dinner dishes and tidied up the kitchen, pondering the girls' fixation on finding a woman for Kate's father, Casey came in and dumped an armload of schoolbooks on the counter.

"Is it okay if I go over to Kate's to do homework? We have a big science report due tomorrow and it's worth ten percent of our final grade."

"What about Petey? He hasn't been walked yet."

"Right. I forgot." Then she cast a questioning glance at Sarah. "Unless, would you mind taking him out tonight? Just this once? This is a really big report."

She had a feeling "just this once" could become a semi-frequent occurrence. Which wasn't a bad thing, as it forced her to get out of the house and get a little exercise.

"All right, I'll take him, but only because it stopped raining."

"Thanks, Mom." Casey hugged her, grabbed her books and dashed for the front door.

Sarah hoped they'd spend at least as much time on homework as they would on their scheme to find Kate's father a fiancée.

AT THE SOUND of the front doorbell, Kate dashed down the stairs, narrowly beating her dad to the foyer.

"It's Casey," she said, flinging open the front door. "We're going to work on a science report."

Casey nodded in agreement, shrugging out of her jacket and tossing it on a hook in the closet. “It’s worth ten percent of our final grade.”

“And it’s due tomorrow.”

“Are you going upstairs or do you want to use the kitchen?” her dad asked.

“We’ll work upstairs. Have you already walked your dog?” Kate asked.

“No, my mom said she would take him since I have all this homework that’s due tomorrow.”

“That was nice of her.”

Right on cue, Casey smiled, totally sweet and innocent. “She asked me to tell you, Coach, that she’d be happy to have some company if you want to go with her.”

Her father gave them back-and-forth glances. Was he buying it?

“Sure. I could use the exercise. Is she going right now?”

“She was getting ready to leave when I came over here.”

Timing was everything, Kate thought, and they had timed this perfectly. They waited while her dad laced his sneakers and pulled on a hooded sweatshirt, watched him sprint down the porch steps at the same time Sarah and Petey were going down their front walk.

Kate closed the door and slapped hands with Casey. "Are we good or what?"

"We are awesome."

SARAH WAVED AT him as he crossed the lawn.

"Nice evening. You look like you could use some company." Judging from the girls' cryptic comments, he had a hunch this was a setup. If Sarah had really wanted company, she would have asked him herself. Now that he was with her, he realized he could use the company, too. He just wouldn't have asked.

They matched their steps and kept pace with the little dog trotting ahead of them.

"Did Kate tell you we talked this afternoon and I offered her a part-time position at the store?"

"It's all she could talk about over dinner." That and online dating, of all things. "Thank you again for doing this for her."

"She seems really excited about it, and I know she'll be great."

He decided to take the plunge. "She's worried about the custody hearing, though. We both are."

Sarah took a pair of gloves from her jacket pocket and pulled them on. "I'm sorry this is happening to you. I feel awful about encouraging you to call Kate's mom."

Terrible enough to make it up to him? "This is not your fault," he said. "I've gone around and around with this, and making that call was something that needed to be done. If anything like that happened while Kate was with her mother, I'd want to know right away." And he was just as certain that Georgette would have kept him in the dark.

"Have you spoken to your lawyer?" she asked. "Do you know if they've set a date for the hearing?"

"Yes, and yes. Talked to him yesterday. He called again today but I was with a class so he left a message. The hearing is in a couple of weeks."

"That soon?" she asked. "That's…wow… that's sooner than I expected."

"Me, too. On the one hand, it doesn't give us much time. On the other, I guess it's just as well to have it over and done."

They walked in silence for a bit. There wasn't much else he could say to her on this subject, at least nothing appropriate, and he couldn't clear his mind enough to come up with another topic of conversation.

"Have you noticed that the girls' behavior has been a bit strange the past couple of days?" she asked.

So, she'd picked up on it, too. "I thought it might be my imagination."

"It's definitely not. They seem to think that finding you a girlfriend, or better yet a wife, will convince the judge to let Kate stay with you."

He couldn't very well tell her it wasn't just the girls who were thinking along those lines. His lawyer had sent Jon's thoughts in the same direction. "Kate asked if I had considered online dating."

Sarah laughter was unexpected. "Casey mentioned that, too. But I think what they think is that you and I might…or that if we did…you know…"

Where was she going with this? "Are you saying you think that they think that the judge will think we're a family if you and I were…" *Okay, you can shut up now,* he told himself.

"That's a lot of thinking." She laughed again. "But yes, I'd say they've turned into a pair of matchmakers."

"I think you're right."

"We'll have to talk to them, explain that this isn't the solution to this particular problem."

"Unless—" he blurted, then immediately wished he hadn't. This was the wrong time to stop thinking.

"Unless what?" She stopped, reining in the dog, turning to face him.

"It's not the worst idea." It was infinitely better than trolling for a wife online.

"It's a terrible idea! We hardly know each other. You really don't know me at all if you believe I would go into court and lie to a judge."

Lie? That hadn't crossed his mind. "What if it was the truth?"

"Oh, please. We just met a few weeks ago. You can't honestly expect me to believe that you think you're in—" She stopped herself.

In love with her? He knew he was, and it was stab-a-knife-in-his-heart apparent that the feeling wasn't even close to being mutual.

"We'd be teaching our daughters that if they want something badly enough, it's okay to do whatever it takes to get it. What kind of example is that?"

A terrible one, and if she believed that about him, then she didn't know him very well, either. He wouldn't lie to a judge any more than she would, but neither did he plan to wear his heart on his sleeve. Whatever feelings she might have for him, he had completely misread them.

"I'm sorry," he said. "We should go back."

The walk home was brisk and made in stony silence.

"I guess I'll see you," he said.

"Good night." She picked up Petey, carried him inside and closed the door on what he had seen as his last hope.

SARAH CLIMBED OUT of bed the next morning with an aching head and a sick heart. Had she overreacted? Maybe, but to what? The idea that they pose as a couple? Or had he implied something else?

What if it was the truth?

Yes, she had feelings for him and there was no denying them, but not the let's-tell-a-judge-we're-heading-to-the-altar kind of feelings. Yes, after falling asleep on his shoulder a few nights ago, she could safely say they were more than friends, but it was too soon to know how much more. She knew too well that rushing into a relationship ended in disaster, and now there was even more at stake. It wasn't just the two of them who needed to be sure. Their daughters had to want it, too, and not just so they could continue to be best friends who lived next door to each other. They had to want to be a family.

She avoided her office, determined not to let herself check to see if Jonathan went running that morning, and went straight down to the kitchen instead. By the time her daughter straggled in, she had brewed a pot of coffee, taken Petey out to the backyard—they would have to have the yard fenced if he stayed—poured glasses of orange juice, and had waffles standing in the toaster and waiting to be heated.

Casey, ponytail swinging and already dressed for school in her usual jeans and high-tops, plunked her books on the counter next to the plate and cutlery Sarah had set out for her. Instead of a T-shirt she was wearing a soft blue V-neck sweater that Sarah had bought for her last spring but that had not yet been worn, and her lashes looked a little darker than usual.

Interesting.

"Did you finish your science report last night?"

"Uh, yes, we did."

"Good for you. Can I have a look at it?"

Casey had a sudden and intense interest in the empty plate in front of her. "I left it at Kate's. We're going to hand it in together."

"I see." She knew she had to say something about last night, and about the girls' apparent expectation that their parents would pair up and win the day in court. The direct approach had always worked for her, and this was no different.

"I know you want Kate to stay here with her dad. I want that, too—we all do—but you have to accept that it's up to the judge to decide."

"But that's so not fair. Kate should be the one to decide, not some stodgy old man who doesn't even know her."

Sarah didn't altogether disagree. "Not all judges are old and stodgy," she said instead, attempting to inject some levity into the conversation.

Casey was not amused. "You know what I mean."

"Of course I do, and I also need you to know that it's not up to me to fix this."

"What do you mean?" Casey asked, attempting to appear innocent.

Nice try. "I mean that Kate's dad and I know what the two of you are trying to do and I have to tell you, it's not going to work. Jonathan and I just met and we haven't had time to get to know each other."

Disappointment flooded her daughter's eyes, and Sarah shared her frustration. Maybe, if they'd had more time, this thing between her and Jonathan might have turned into something real. But she'd seen the hurt in his eyes last night. *I guess I'll see you.* She didn't expect him to forgive her anytime soon.

"I'm sorry, sweetie. I really am." And no one was sorrier than she was.

JON DECIDED TO forgo his run that morning. He'd stayed up too late, slept too little, and what sleep he did get had been troubled and his waking thoughts plagued with what-ifs.

In the kitchen he brewed coffee before taking a loaf out of the bread maker and setting it on a rack to cool. Last night his thoughts had been fully occupied, but he'd needed something to fill the time since he couldn't sleep, so he had started the bread, washed and dried two loads of soccer uniforms, and straightened up the books, papers and DVDs scattered around the living room.

Kate clattered into the room in black knee-length boots with impossibly high heels. The bottoms of her black leggings were tucked into the boots and the top part was covered up by a hip-length sweater with horizontal stripes in black and purple. She had swapped the huge black-and-white bag for a smaller fuchsia-colored one that was still big enough to accommodate her schoolbooks.

"How did the homework session go last night?"

"Good."

"Did you girls finish your report?"

She helped herself to a glass of juice. "Yes, we did."

"I'd be interested to see what you've been working on."

"Oh. Um, Casey took it home with her so she could fix one of the, um, diagrams. She'll take it to school with her and we'll hand it in together."

"I see." *Science report, my foot.* He'd bet anything that Sarah was getting the same song and dance from her daughter.

"How was your walk with Sarah?" she asked, just as smooth and sweet as the butter and honey she was spreading on a slice of bread.

"Not that great."

She looked up then, eyes filled with concern. "What happened?"

"She feels that you and Casey have come up with the idea that if she and I were…"

"Dating?"

Are we really having this conversation? Did he have a choice? Not according to Sarah. *We'll have to talk to them, explain that this isn't the solution to this particular problem.*

"Yes," he said. "That if we were 'dating,' then the custody hearing might go our way. But we're not, and we won't be."

"But Casey and I saw you. You kissed, you danced—"

No way was he prepared to talk about kissing Sarah, especially not with his daughter. "Sarah and I are friends," he said. "We just met and she feels…we *both* feel it's too soon for our friendship to be any more than that."

She didn't have to acknowledge that she and Casey were trying their hand at matchmaking. Her disappointment said it all.

He could relate to that, he really could. He hadn't entirely given up hope, either, and he intended to do whatever he could to turn the situation around, but that wasn't going to happen in time for the hearing. For that, they were on their own.

CHAPTER NINETEEN

Two days later at lunchtime, Kate waited for Casey by the entrance to the school's central atrium, then they sat with their lunches on a bench in the corner where no one could hear them.

"How's your dad?" Casey asked.

"He's being a grump."

Casey tore open a package of cheese and crackers. "My mom seems kind of sad, and I don't think she's sleeping very well, either."

Kate unwrapped her sandwich. "Neither's my dad. He's been doing crazy stuff like washing clothes in the middle of the night."

"Parents can be so weird."

"Tell me about it. Would you like half of my sandwich?"

"Sure. Thanks."

"My dad might be ready to give up on this but I'm not. My mom doesn't want me to live with her and there's no way I'm going to boarding school."

"You can't go," Casey said. "We need to

come up with a plan. I think my mom really likes your dad, but she says she's not rushing into anything because she just met him."

"My dad is saying pretty much the same thing. I can tell he's not happy, though."

"And have you noticed how they've been avoiding each other? My mom waits till after he leaves in the morning before she goes to work."

"Same thing when they come home." Kate lowered her voice when a group of their classmates came in and clustered on the next bench. "I don't think there's much we can do about it."

"I've been thinking about it," Casey said. "I think I know how we can get them together, or at least talking."

"Really? How?"

"Do you think you'd be able to get your hands on your dad's cell phone?"

"That's not a problem. He leaves it lying around all the time, and then when it does ring, he has to hunt for it."

Casey grinned. "My mom keeps hers in her briefcase. It'll be easy to find."

"What are we going to do, send fake text messages?"

"That's what I was thinking. But first I'll

talk to your dad after school and you'll need to go to the store and talk to my mom."

"About what?"

Two more kids came into the atrium and joined the group at the next bench. Not wanting anyone to hear what they were up to, Kate leaned in so Casey could whisper the rest of the plan into her ear.

"What do you think?"

"It's brilliant," she said. "That's definitely a high five!"

AFTER WORK THAT AFTERNOON, Sarah set her briefcase and car keys on the counter while she unpacked a bag of groceries, stowing frozen dinners in the freezer and assorted packages in the pantry. She never felt like cooking, but lately she didn't much feel like eating out, either.

Casey came in and lounged against the island. "What's for dinner?"

"I picked up some things we can heat up in the microwave. I hope that's okay."

"Sure. Do you mind if I use your phone to look up something? I just remembered that everyone wants to see a movie on Friday. I'd like to see what's on."

"Help yourself." Once she'd put everything away, she folded the reusable grocery bag and stuffed it into a drawer. "Would you like to have dinner now?"

Casey put her phone back on the counter. "Maybe later. I need to talk to Henry about having him take some photographs for the yearbook. Come on, Petey. Let's go."

Just as well. She could feel another headache coming on. Kate had come to the store that afternoon to tell her that her father had said no to the part-time job because he wanted her to spend her time on schoolwork. Talk about a flimsy excuse. Kate was keeping up with all of her assignments now, he'd told her that himself. This was about him and Sarah. She never would have pegged him as the vindictive type, but why else would he make his daughter stay away from her?

There was nothing she could do about it, though, and right now she needed a Tylenol.

Her phone buzzed as was she leaving the kitchen.

Casey came to see me about the soccer team. Very upset. Can we talk?

Paolo's at 7? Jon

Why would Casey be upset about the soccer team? And if she was, why hadn't she said anything ?

Sarah called Casey and heard her phone ringing inside her backpack. That wasn't going to work, so she called Henry's house. His mother told her they'd taken the dog for a walk.

If she didn't know better, she might think her daughter was trying to avoid her. She checked her watch. Six-thirty. She'd better go meet Jonathan, she decided. This could be something really important. She scribbled a note and left it on the counter where Casey would see it when she came home.

JON DIDN'T THINK he had ever been so disappointed with anyone. Casey had stopped by his office after school, on the verge of tears, and told him that her mom wanted her to drop the soccer team because she had too many other commitments. He'd met a lot of kids throughout his career and few were as capable as that girl was. Plus, she was one of his best players and the assistant captain. He was actually a little disgusted to think Sarah would use her kid to get back at him.

He was pretty sure Kate didn't know about this. She surely would have said something to him if she did.

"Dad?" she called from the foyer. "Casey

and I are taking her dog for a walk. I'll see you in a while, okay?"

"Okay." He still needed to make dinner, but this let him off the hook for a bit. He picked up the TV remote, thinking maybe the news in the rest of the world was even worse than it was in his, when he heard his phone beeping. Hoping it wasn't even more bad news, he followed the sound and found it where he'd left it on the counter by the coffeemaker.

Kate came to the store today. Very upset about her job. Can we talk?
Paolo's at 7? Sarah

Why would Kate be upset about her job? The way she talked about it, it was the best thing in her life right now. And if she was upset, why hadn't she said anything to him about it? He called Kate's phone and heard it ringing in her bag in the foyer. It was now six thirty-five. If he wanted to get to the bottom of this, he'd better go meet Sarah. It's not as though he had any other options.

JONATHAN WAS ALREADY at Paolo's, sitting at a small table tucked away in a corner of the restaurant when Sarah arrived.

He stood and waited until she was seated

before he sat back down again. He looked tense.

"Hi."

"Hi," he said. "I got your text message."

"I didn't send you a text message. I got yours, though, asking me to meet you here."

"I didn't send one, either."

He leaned back in his chair and she could see the light come on for him at the same time it did for her.

"Kate," he said.

"And Casey. Those two little monsters."

"Casey came to see me in my office this afternoon," he said.

"Kate came to see me at the store, too."

Maria scurried over to take their order.

"Coffee, please," Jonathan said.

"I'll have the same, please."

Maria nodded and headed back to the kitchen.

"The text message you didn't send said she went to your store today, and then something about her being upset about the job."

"She did come to see me. She said you had changed your mind about the job and weren't going to let her take it after all."

He gave his head an exasperated shake. "Let me guess. You received a message that said Casey came to see me about the soccer team."

Sarah nodded.

"She said you were making her drop the team because she had too many commitments."

She stared at him in stunned surprise, and then she started to laugh. He joined her.

"I would never pull her off the team."

"And I'm as excited as Kate is to have her working for you. She's applying herself at school, being more responsible...well, except for this."

Sarah laughed again. "I wonder whose idea this was? Casey's or Kate's?"

"I suspect what one doesn't think of, the other one does."

That was true. The coffee arrived and Sarah busied herself with the cream and sugar, suddenly feeling self-conscious because she knew he was watching her.

"I like it sweet."

"I can see that."

She took a few sips, inhaled the rich scent of the dark Italian roast, then set her cup down. "So, how do we handle this?"

"I'm guessing we shouldn't ground them."

She was glad he could still make her laugh.

"Oh, I think we can be more creative than that."

He held up his cup and she tapped hers to it. "While we think about that, I want to say I'm really sorry about the other night. You've already been a big help with Kate and I had no business trying to pressure you into doing something that made you uncomfortable. I was way out of line."

"I'm sorry, too. I'll admit I was surprised, but I completely overreacted." And she had been more surprised by his feelings for her than the proposition. "The thing is, I rushed into a marriage once before and it was a total disaster, almost from the beginning. I promised myself I would never do anything like that again."

Jonathan appeared to be searching for words. "You thought I was asking you to—" He gulped some coffee, sputtering a little before he continued. "To marry me?"

"Well, no, not exactly. I thought…I don't know what I thought. I didn't know exactly what you wanted from me, and I panicked."

He leaned on his forearms. "There's no way you could have known what I wanted. I didn't know myself. But I've had a couple of sleepless nights to mull it over."

That made a couple of sleepless nights times

two. "And did you figure it out?" She held her breath while she waited for his answer.

"I want you in my life. I want you and your daughter in mine and Kate's."

She started breathing again. "I'd like that, too. For me and Casey."

She reached across the table and he took her hand. "If there's even a remote possibility that you'd be with us in court that day…and I'm not saying I need you there, but I would like to have you there. If you'll agree to come with us, it'll be a privilege to introduce you as my friend and Kate's mentor."

She felt herself tearing up. "Of course I'll go. I wouldn't miss it. And if there's anything else…"

He shook his head. "No, that's it. The rest is up to me and Kate, and a whole lot of luck."

For several minutes they drank their coffee in silence and she realized it was the most comfortable she'd been a long time. He knew how to let her be. No one else had ever done that for her.

"So what are we going to do about those girls?" she asked.

"What do you have in mind? I'm not very creative when it comes to this kind of thing."

Sarah grinned. "I am. I was thinking a little dose of their own medicine."

He chuckled at that. "I was thinking we should thank them for setting us up, but I like your plan better." He took her hand again, ran his thumb across her palm. "What are you suggesting?"

She pulled her phone out of her bag. "I say we send our daughters a text message and say we've agreed that a time-out for both of them will be the best thing for everyone."

"Oh, now you're thinking like a teenager." Jonathan took his phone out of his jacket pocket.

They tapped out messages to their girls, reading them out loud, making each other laugh before they sent them.

"You two lovebirds, you are wanting to order some food?" Maria stood beside their table, beaming.

Jonathan leaned back in his chair and smiled at her. "Hungry?"

"Starving."

"What about the girls?"

"If you ask me, we should let them stew for a while."

"I like the way you think."

Maria set menus on the table, went away and came back with a lit candle. "Very romantic, yes?"

It was romantic, and even better than that, it felt real.

KATE KEPT AN eye on the driveway from her bedroom window and she could see Casey doing the same. Their parents had been out for more than two hours, and after she and Casey had received those text messages, they were both trying to figure out if that was a good thing or a not-so-good thing.

Finally two pairs of headlights pulled into the yard, first Sarah's and then her dad's. He stepped out first, jogged around Sarah's car and opened the door for her.

Kate's phone buzzed to signal an incoming text. It was from Casey, who was watching from her room next door.

They're here! Wonder what took so long.

Don't know. Do U really think R plan backfired?

Hope not. L

Me 2

She saw Sarah take her dad's hand, watched him help her out of the car.

They don't look mad.

She hoped Casey was right. Sarah closed her car door and then they stood there, probably talking. It was too dark to tell, but they looked the opposite of mad.

Can't see much.

Me either.

She and Casey had been stunned by the messages from their parents. Hadn't they figured out that this had been a trap? Or were they messing with them? Did they think it was funny, or were they mad at them?

Sarah looked up then, first at Casey's bedroom window and then at Kate's. She said something to her dad, and then he held out his arms and Sarah stepped into them and… Ha! She fired off another message.

Do U C what I C?

Yes! High 5!

And they each slapped a palm to the glass.

CHAPTER TWENTY

ON THE DAY of the custody hearing, Jon and Sarah and Kate and Casey made the trip by car and ferry to Vancouver. He'd never been to court before and had no idea what to expect. He'd felt somewhat reassured, though, when his lawyer told him the courtroom would be closed. Child custody cases were closed to the public, so it would be the four of them, plus his lawyer and Georgette's lawyer.

Finding out his ex-wife hadn't been able to make the trip here had been no surprise and a huge relief. He couldn't tell if Kate shared the sentiment, and he sure wasn't going to ask.

After they arrived, Kate had spent nearly an hour in the judge's chambers. She'd seemed quietly confident when she emerged and disinclined to discuss what she and the judge had talked about.

Finally, half an hour later, they were ushered into a small courtroom and shown where to sit.

A clerk stood and faced them. "Madame

Justice Constance Burgess presiding. All rise."

Everyone stood as a small woman with wiry brown curls entered, black robe swishing around her, and took a seat behind the large desk at the front of the room.

They all sat again, and Sarah placed a reassuring hand over his.

Finding out that a female judge would hear the case had unnerved him. Would a woman be more inclined to think a child should be in her mother's care?

Judge Burgess perched a pair of reading glasses on the end of her nose and opened a folder on the desk.

"In the case of Georgette Ogilvie and Jonathan Marshall…" She peered over the top of her glasses at Georgette's lawyer and speared him with a sharp gaze. "Where is Ms. Ogilvie?"

He stood. "My client is unable to attend today, Your Honor. She resides in Europe and she had prior commitments. She's asked that I speak on her behalf."

Sarah squeezed Jon's hand and glanced at him. What he saw was his own resentment mirrored in her eyes. All this, and Georgette couldn't be bothered to show up?

"She resides in *Europe*?" the judge asked. "Europe is a big place."

"In the south of France, Your Honor, but she and her husband travel extensively. You may recall she used to be—"

"I know who she is," the judge said. "Thank you."

The man sat.

The judge turned a few pages, some quickly; others she scanned more slowly. She took off the glasses as she looked up and set them squarely on the stack of papers.

"Mr. Marshall, your daughter and I had a very nice chat. She's a charming girl. Bright, too, but I'm sure you know that."

"Thank you, yes." He pushed off the seat but she waved him down. "No need for all that up and down. We're having a conversation here."

Good to know.

"Kate, is this your friend Casey?"

"Yes, ma'am."

"Nice to meet you, too, young lady. Kate tells me you're a soccer player."

"That's right. Kate's dad is my coach."

"Good for you. I kicked a few balls in my day."

Surely she meant soccer.

"And you are Sarah Stewart, Casey's mother."

"I am."

"Kate says you own a clothing store and that she works for you."

"That's right."

The judge considered that for a moment. "She's a little young to have a job. What does she do for you?"

"She only works a few hours a week, contingent on keeping up at school, mostly doing window displays and helping customers. She also set up and maintains a Facebook page for the store."

"I see." Her honor turned her attention back to Kate, smiled and softened her tone. "You're an enterprising young woman. I meet a lot of teenagers who would love to be paid for spending time on social media."

Kate and Casey put their heads together and giggled. Regardless of what her decision was going to be, Jonathan liked the woman's droll sense of humor and appreciated how she immediately put the girls at ease.

"Mr. Marshall. I've read your statement. It's was very thorough."

"Thank you." Should he be thankful? He wished he knew. This woman would be a fierce opponent at a poker table.

"Is there anything you would like to add?"

If there was, it had leaked out of him the minute this woman stepped into the room. Besides, he had poured everything he could think of into that statement, slaved over it for hours. Then Sarah had read it and said it was so touching, it made her cry.

"No, Your Honor. But thank you."

She picked up her glasses, put them back on and straightened the stack of pages in the folder. "All right then. I've reached a decision and I see no point in prolonging this."

Georgette's lawyer cleared his throat. "Your Honor, if I may."

She paused. "No, you may not. I read Ms. Ogilvie's statement as well. I assume that if she had more to add, she would be here in person."

Sarah's grip on his hand tightened. She was a lifesaver, and he was hanging on for dear life.

"But she's—"

"I have a dim view of parents who file for custody and then can't be bothered to appear in my courtroom. But you can tell her that had she been here, my decision would be the same. Kate Marshall will remain in her father's care and custody."

The girls let out a whoop and flung their

arms around each other, then Kate whirled around and hugged him. Really hugged him. "Thanks, Dad. Now we can be a family," she whispered. "All of us."

Outside the courtroom, he thanked his lawyer, at least he thought he did, but he was mostly focused on the three women in his life. Kate, his amazing daughter. Sarah, the beautiful woman he'd fallen in love-at-first-sight with. And Casey, his daughter's best friend and, he hoped, her soon-to-be someday sister.

He knew Sarah wasn't ready to make a commitment, but she'd get there. He was sure of it. And now that his family was staying intact, she could take all the time she needed because now he had all the time in the world.

EPILOGUE

Ten months later

SARAH PEEKED BETWEEN the curtains of the cabana that had been set up on the lawn of the Serenity Bay Resort.

"Is everyone here?" Casey asked. "Are they ready for us?"

"Should be any minute now."

"Can you see my dad?" Kate asked.

Jonathan, heart-joltingly handsome in an off-white summer tux, waited in the late afternoon sunshine near the water's edge. "Yes, I see him."

"I hope he didn't see you," Kate said. "It's bad luck."

Sarah let the curtain fall back into place and turned to face her daughter and her soon-to-be daughter. "No, he didn't see me. Now come here," she said, pulling them both in for a hug, feeling like the luckiest woman alive.

And then the music started and the curtains were drawn aside. Casey and Kate, arm in arm, made their way down the flower-lined walkway to the beach. They looked adorably sweet and so grown up in identical yellow off-the-shoulder dresses, each with a bright orange sash at the waist. Kate had vigorously lobbied for heels but Casey's preference won out so they wore white ballerina flats instead. Their bouquets, smaller versions of hers, consisted of yellow and orange roses, dahlias and ranunculus—her favorite flowers in her favorite colors and absolutely perfect for summer. These two amazing young women, best of friends in spite of their different interests, were about to become sisters.

And then it was her turn to follow the path that led to her future, their future. The girls insisted on taking credit for all of this—Casey for coming up with the plan that brought their parents together and Kate for convincing the judge to let her stay with her father. Sarah and Jonathan were happy to let them take the credit because they were…happy.

Now as she walked past a cluster of family and friends seated on white folding chairs, she only had eyes for him. She was grateful he had come into her life and so very thankful that the man who had become her best friend in the world was about to become her husband. As she approached, he extended his hand and she readily put hers into it. This was where she belonged, side by side with him.

"I love you."

"I love you, too," he whispered.

"Dearly beloved…"

THE SUN WAS setting when Jon led his wife onto the dancing platform that had been set up just above the high tide line. She was a vision in an ivory cocktail-length dress—and yes, thanks to her and his daughter, he was completely conversant in all things fashion. He also had a deep appreciation for Sarah's ability to organize a wedding while running a business, working out a study schedule that put both girls on the honor roll, and planning a honeymoon. She only half-jokingly said she would be unstoppable now that she no longer had to shop for fast food and pick up takeout, and that made him love her even more.

"Happy?" he asked as he swung her into his arms to hold her close.

The music mingled with the rustle of the yellow, orange and white bunting she and the girls had strung around the makeshift dance floor, strings of white lights twinkled in the deepening dusk.

"The happiest." She laid her head on his shoulder and he pressed his cheek to her hair, loving that he could do this for the rest of this life, loving the scent of floral on the sea breeze, loving her.

"Happier than you'll be tomorrow when our flight lands in Paris?"

"That'll be a different kind of happy," she said. "That'll be magic."

She was right. It would be magic. Ten days to themselves to explore the city she'd always dreamed of visiting. Meanwhile the girls would visit Kate's mother. After losing the custody suit, Georgette had really stepped up, and now her wedding gift to the girls was a tour of Italy. Any city they wanted to see. Casey was excited about going to Naples and Pompeii, Kate was desperate to see the fashion houses in Milan, and the two of them couldn't wait to sail the canals of Venice in a gondola. Then their daughters would join them for a week in London before they came home to Serenity Bay.

His household had been packed up, in labeled boxes this time, and he and Kate would move next door with Sarah and Casey when they returned. Everyone was excited about the move except Princess, who grudgingly tolerated Petey.

"Our girls look happy, too," he said.

Kate danced with Henry and Casey with

Dexter, and after all these months he was only now getting used to the idea of his daughters actually dating. Sarah had been right about them, though, as she was right about everything else. They were good kids, making good decisions, and as Sarah liked to remind him, living by example.

"They do look happy, don't they?"

"And beautiful. You chose exactly the right dresses for them."

"Aren't they perfect? They're happy yellow dresses."

"That's a good description."

She lifted her head and smiled up at him. "It's not just a description. Happy Yellow Dress is the designer's label. Kate loves her stuff."

Of course she did. There was a time when talk of labels and designers had made him apoplectic but now, thanks to Sarah's influence, those things weren't about trying to impress. They were simply about finding enjoyment in beautiful things.

And he knew all about enjoying beauty, he thought, pulling her close again, guiding her around and between their guests.

"Can you believe those girls will be sophomores in the fall?" he asked. "That they'll be away at college in a few years?"

"Slow down," she whispered. "I still haven't wrapped my head around spending the next ten days without them."

Her earnestness always touched him. "Ah, but Paris will be magic, remember?" Long walks along the Seine, sipping cafe au lait at a sidewalk cafe, and starry, starry nights. "I love those girls with all my heart, but Paris will always be ours."

She leaned into the dance, rested her head on his shoulder again. "Paris will be ours," she said. "Always and forever."

* * * * *